SEARCH THE BELOVED

SEARCH THE BELOVED

Catherine Colette

Book Guild Publishing
Sussex, England

First published in Great Britain in 2005 by
The Book Guild Ltd
25 High Street
Lewes, East Sussex
BN7 2LU

Copyright © Catherine Colette 2005

The right of Catherine Colette to be identified as the author of this work has been asserted by her in accordance with the Copyright, Designs and Patents Act 1988.

All rights reserved. No part of this publication may be reproduced, transmitted, or stored in a retrieval system, in any form or by any means, without permission in writing from the publishers, nor be otherwise circulated in any form of binding or cover other than that in which it is published and without a similar condition being imposed on the subsequent purchaser.

All characters in this publication are fictitious and any resemblance to real people, alive or dead, is purely coincidental.

Typesetting in Baskerville by
SetSystems Ltd, Saffron Walden, Essex

Printed in Great Britain by
Antony Rowe Ltd, Chippenham, Wiltshire

A catalogue record for this book is
available from the British Library

ISBN 1 85776 938 4

DEDICATION

This story is dedicated to everyone everywhere who sets out in search of The Beloved.

ACKNOWLEDGEMENTS

Warmest thanks to: The Book Guild team for their patience, Lillian Obligado for her lovely artwork on the cover, Viesia Wroblewski who taught me to use the computer without which this story would never have left my head, Nadina Redeva-Girod for her knowledge of ancient Greece, Susan Tiberghien, for her expertise in the art of writing, Vivienne Barned, for her encouragement and suggestions.

And for their loyal friendship throughout: Maisie Malarbre, Margaret Millet, Angelica Collis and David Walters.

INTRODUCTION

THE BELOVED has two distinct meanings; the first is obvious, the second less known.

When a seeker of truth experiences the Divine within him or herself, the rapture of it has been likened to a meeting with 'The Beloved.' The experience, is universal and not restriced to any particular religion or faith. But mystics have trouble explaining it, which is why descriptions come in different ways, such as, Mystic Marriage, Self Realization, Enlightenment, Moksha and many others. It is said to be the greatest ecstasy of which a human being is capable, and the goal that, consciously or unconsciously, we all seek on our voyage through life.

Kahil Gibran, in his inspired work *THE PROPHET* speaks more eloquently of love to seekers of The Beloved, than any one I know, so let his words illumine the story you are about to read.

> Then said Almitra, Speak to us of Love.
> And he raised his head and looked upon the people, and there fell stillness upon them. And with a great voice he said:
> When love beckons to you follow him, Though the ways be hard and steep.
> And when the wings enfold you yield to him,
> though the sward hidden among his pinions may wound you.

And when he speaks to you believe in him,
though the voice may shatter your dreams as the north wind lays waste the garden.
For even as love crowns you so shall he crucify you. Even as he is for your growth so is he for your pruning.
Even as he ascends to your height and caresses your tenderest branches that quiver in the sun,
So shall we descend to your roots and shake them in their clinging to the earth.
Like sheaves of corn he gathers you unto himself.
He threshes you to make you naked.
He lifts you free from your husks.
He grinds you to whiteness.
He kneads you until you are pliant;
And then assigns you to his sacred fire, that you may become sacred bread for God's sacred feast.
All these things shall love do unto you that you may know the secrets of your heart, and that knowledge become a fragment of Life's heart.

But if in your fear you would seek only love's peace and love's pleasure,
Then it is better for you that you cover your nakedness and pass out of love's threshing-floor.
Into the seasonless world where you shall laugh, but not all your laughter, and weep, but not all of your tears.

Chapter One

If the truth were known, everybody's story would arise from the mists of antiquity, but Anna Edwards had to find this out for herself.

Born to a traditional middle-class English family in twentieth century Cambridgeshire, all Anna ever wanted was a husband and a home. Her easy-going nature, charm and good looks, should have made this modest ambition easy as e-mail, and yet it did not. When disappointment brought her to question the happenings in her life, the message that popped onto her screen came in a single word – *search*! And when she searched, amazing things happened.

But let us go back to the beginning; one hundred years before the birth of Christ, when Athens was a province of the mighty Roman Empire, and Anna was known as Anthia.

An open horse-wagon laboured uphill, its heavy wheels grinding and crackling upon the gravelly road. A vivacious pair of newlyweds, journeying from Athens to consult the Oracle in Delphi, sat on the cushioned bench behind the reins. The young man, Peteos, was tall, well-built and had an abundance of dark curls held back from the brow with a gold band. Members of his family always consulted the Pythoness in the Temple of Apollo at the start of a marriage, and there was no question that their only son should break with this tradition. His bride, Larentia, was of a fairer complexion and observed the passing countryside through sparkling hazel eyes. They were exuberantly happy.

Peteos pointed to an encampment on the high ground. 'The Roman garrison,' he said. 'They have a controlling view of the land and sea from up there.'

'How long must we bear with these Romans?' she asked disconsolately.

'Until we throw 'em out!' Peteos replied, kissing Larentia on the back of her neck.

One week later Delphi was behind them, and the wagon rolling back towards Athens. The couple sat close, their lighthearted expressions now shadowed with perplexity over what the Pythoness had said. They repeated her words: *Love and joy be yours, but union at a price. Children three. One a choice must make to rise or fall before the purifying flame.*

'What could possibly be the price of our union? Are we not properly wed?' Larentia questioned.

'Of course we are. I really don't know why we follow this archaic tradition. Neither my father nor grandfather understood a single word of the oracle's mutterings, and their lives were none the worse for it.'

'Ah, but tradition is everything to you Athenians,' she teased. 'We from the north prefer actions to words!'

Peteos's arm slid round his wife's waist to draw her closer, but she jumped away, laughing. 'Not *those* actions. Not right now, anyway.'

'Well, only old Cronos will reveal what we are to know. In the meantime, what about those three children impatient to be born?'

'Perhaps I'll invite one into my womb tonight,' she replied impishly.

'Mm, by starlight then. Tomorrow we'll be home!'

The wooded slopes on the outskirts of the capital rose before them late the following afternoon. Soon the wagon turned off the sweltering road to trundle along a dusty track, and finally up a smooth pine-shaded avenue leading to Peteos's family home. The imposing old villa had been the gift from Athens to Peteos's father Thestius, as a reward for his proficiency in resolving conflict before blood flowed; a skill that had earned him the title of 'Arbitrator'. Even the Romans respected him.

When their destination was reached, the wagon was not halted before the sober Dorian pillars of the gracious front entrance, but driven round to the stables and water troughs at the back. With the clatter of wheels on the paved yard, dogs barked, geese cackled and doves rose into the air with a melodious flurry of wings. A cat arched its back as it peered down from an old stone wall. Sparrows flew from the granary and servants bustled into the house to tell their mistress, that the long-awaited day had come.

'Refreshments. Refreshments,' Myrrha called excitedly to her maid, as she hurried out to greet her son and daughter-in-law.

'I thought you'd never get here!' she exclaimed, first hugging Larentia and then her son, who kissed her affectionately on the cheek. She then led them through to the courtyard; a wide square open to the sky and surrounded on all four sides by a covered cloister where long marble tables and cushioned benches made it the family's favourite meeting place. In the centre stood a circular lily pool perpetually replenished from the mouths of white dolphins; their fine marble bodies now glowing pink in the lingering light of the evening sun. Terracotta amphoras brimming with flowers or climbing plants, filled every niche and corner with colour and perfume.

As they wandered out, Myrrha nodded to the maid carrying a platter of refreshment and, having indicated the table where they were to be placed, linked arms with her son and daughter-in-law and drew them affectionately to the cushioned seats.

'It's wonderful to be home,' Peteos said, kissing his mother's cheek again, a gesture Myrrha feigned to take for granted though an undeniable glow of pleasure brought colour and life to her still beautiful features

'I want to know simply *everything*, darling,' Myrrha urged, even before they were seated. 'Now what did the oracle portend?'

'Really, Mother,' he chaffed. 'You know very well that telling brings bad luck.'

'Nonsense!' she responded. 'You don't still believe all that, do you?'

'Even if I don't, why take chances?'

Larentia laughed. 'To be honest, we didn't understand a single word.'

Looking sympathetically at her daughter-in-law, Myrrha had to admit that neither she, nor her husband, had much to remember of their marriage oracle either. 'Couldn't make head nor tail of it,' she said.

'But where is Father?' Peteos questioned, looking round.

'I was about to tell you. He's resolving a dispute in Corinth. Nothing much this time, apparently. He's taken Elcyon with him. You know, the one who is to replace him in the Assembly when his term of office ends next year.'

'Corinth?' Peteos looked concerned.

'I know, darling. I tried to stop him. Elcyon is perfectly capable of managing on his own. But alas – you know your father.'

They chatted on, catching up on the doings of the household, until the sky turned indigo and a chill descended. The maid reappeared with shawls, but Myrrha waved them aside and rose to her feet.

'Thank you Phyllis, but we will dine inside tonight, so get Abas to light the fires.' Then turning to Peteos, 'Show your bride the house while there is still some light. I doubt if she remembers much from the day after her wedding.'

'I remember every bit of it,' Larentia protested. 'And loved it, immediately.'

'Like me?' Peteos chaffed.

'Well, this is to be your home now,' Myrrha said, 'and we are going to have a little ceremony of blessing and welcome when Thestius returns.'

Thestius took longer to return than expected; weeks dragged by and the ceremony was held without him. It was irksome, of course, but Myrrha refused to worry; she had become accustomed to Thestius's delays during the 30-odd years of their marriage. She knew that her husband never left arbitration until every detail had been satisfactorily addressed.

Three months passed and Myrrha, chortling with delight, began to gather friends and relations for another ceremony; that could not wait for her husband's return. Larentia had indeed conceived under the stars on the eve of the couple's return home, and in order, that the conception remain secure, offerings to Ilithyia and Hestia had to be made in the family shrine.

Larentia's pregnancy was well into its sixth month when the quarrel in Corinth was over, and a horseman clattering into the courtyard brought word that Thestius would soon be home. Such joyous news threw the household into a frenzy of preparation for the feast of welcome. Moreover Myrrha could now add relief to her joy; this would be the last mission her husband could be called upon to make on behalf of the Greek council. Next year he was planning to devote himself entirely to his lands, and he would be all hers.

It was soon after the beast to be sacrificed for the celebration had been selected, and arrangements for its butchering made, that delight turned to shock. Thestius was dead! The messenger explained how, on the very eve of his departure from Corinth, Thestius had felt excessively tired and gone early to bed. The strain of those long taxing months had taken a heavier toll on the old man than anyone realized, and the servant, sent next morning to awaken him, found that he had died in his sleep.

Veils of mourning now swathed Myrrha's ashen face, and subdued servants went about their duties in total silence. Even the dogs didn't bark in the stableyard where a harnessed stallion waited while Peteos took leave of his family.

First he embraced his mother, hugging her tightly. 'I shall see that Father is buried with all the honour and dignity that is his due,' he said.

Choking back her tears, Myrrha slipped a protective amulet around her son's neck and intoned the blessing of Athena, but did not wait to watch him go. With solemn eyes Peteos then turned to Larentia. She too slipped a protective amulet around his neck and made to hold him close but, wanting to imprint her image upon his memory, he held her back a little.

'Your love will be my amulet,' he murmured, and then embraced her for a long moment before promising to be home well before the birth in three moons time.

After the funeral in Corinth, Elcyon, now in charge of the arbitration, did not give Peteos permission to leave. The dispute Thestius had gone to resolve had flared up more dangerously than ever. To avoid outright war, negotiations had to be reopened, and Elcyon deemed it essential, to keep the old 'Arbitrator's' son at his side.

Three moons dragged by. Anxiety replaced the sparkle in Larentia's hazel eyes. Her delivery was now imminent, and she was still without word of Peteos's return. Then, early one morning, hammering hooves in the stable yard heralded a messenger. Thinking it must be Peteos, Larentia struggled to her feet and reached for her peplos.* But before she

---

* A Peplos is the loose tunic-like robe worn by the women of Ancient Greece.

could put it on, her maid entered with a scroll. Trembling, Larentia took it and started to read, colour draining from her cheeks with every line. The worried maid hurried away to fetch Myrrha who rushed into the bridal bedroom still in her night attire.

'What is it? What is it?' she exclaimed.

'He's been accidentally wounded,' Larentia replied, staring at the message incredulously before handing it to Myrrha. 'His life is in danger. It was a spear in his lung.'

For the sake of the one to be born, Myrrha subdued her own feelings and played down the news. 'They reported my husband dead once,' she said. 'Yet within a moon he was home, fit as a fiddle. They sometimes make mistakes, child.'

She put her arms around Larentia and cradled her daughter-in-law as though she were a child, but Larentia was too shocked to weep or to speak.

Pierides, the family physician, was sent for. He arrived within the hour bringing a sleeping potion which they spooned into Larentia's mouth as though she were a stricken animal. It had the desired effect however, and as Larentia slipped into slumber, she was aware of Myrrha's soft chanting. 'Life and death the Gods so say, while loving mortals wait and pray.' Myrrha's own married life had been so pocked with her husband's absences, that these words had become her favourite homily.

The potion kept Larentia sleeping throughout the day and into the next dawn. On waking, she felt stronger than ever in her life and knew exactly what she must do. Her mother-in-law might 'wait and pray', but she would act, and quickly.

At the arched portico of the Smaller Sanctuary of the Temple of Athena a gaunt woman with tangled gray hair waited. She wore the robes of a priestess, and a knowing smile parted her lips as the horse-drawn litter stopped at the foot of the Sanctuary's nine steps. She watched immobile as a fair young woman, heavy with child, laboured up towards her carrying an alabaster vase – her offering for the Deity.

'What brings you to this sacred place?' asked the Priestess.

'I am greatly in need of your blessings and those of Athena,' Larentia replied.

'What blessings do you seek?'

'My husband is wounded and not expected to live. I will offer anything you wish that he return home to us, healed.'

Without a word the Priestess took the precious vase, circled it three times before the statue of the goddess, and placed it upon the altar. She then turned to gaze intently upon the young woman. It seemed an eternity before she spoke.

'Your husband is indeed dying,' she said at last. 'But his life *can* be spared.'

Fire rose in Larentia's waxen cheeks. 'His life can be spared,' she echoed.

'Yes, his life can be spared.' The old Priestess repeated. 'But only in exchange for your most prized possession.'

Frantically, Larentia envisioned her few valuables. The heavy gold necklace Peteos had given her on their wedding night. Jewels inherited from her mother. Her life-long maid, and even Penelos, her adored dog. What else? What else?

The old Priestess shook her head. 'Such things are valueless in the eyes of Athena.'

'But I have nothing more!' Larentia protested.

'Nothing?' questioned the Ancient One, directing her gaze towards Larentia's womb.

Horrified, the girl's hands cupped her belly.

The Priestess nodded indulgently. 'Is *this* not the most prized of your possessions?'

Tears of wrath sprang to Larentia's eyes. 'You cannot take my child!'

'Take? No!' The Priestess rebuked quietly. 'The Goddess is not a thief.'

'Never will I give the Goddess our first-born. Never!'

The Priestess waited for a moment before inclining her head in acquiescence, 'So be it,' she murmured.

Larentia, too, bowed her adieu, a trail of teardrops darkening the flagstones behind her as she left. With mind and heart in turmoil, she carefully descended the Temple steps and walked pensively across to where her maid waited in the litter. Giving her infant to the Temple of Athena is a mother's greatest sacrifice for the child, whether it be male or female, must leave home for ever at the tender age of six. It is a lot to ask. Too much! But what were the chances of ever seeing her beloved Peteos again?

The horse moved forward. 'Wait!' Larentia cried, struggling to alight.

'But Madam,' her maid protested, 'this is no time to go climbing up and down steps. Think! The child might be born tomorrow . . . or even today!'

Larentia *had* thought. And before her resolve weakened, she hurried back to where the old Priestess seemed almost to be waiting for her.

Without the usual ceremony Larentia approached, and with ill-concealed rage said, 'Athena shall have this child!' She did not wait for a response, but turned and left.

The very next day a daughter was born, and within two moons Peteos returned, weak but alive. For the homecoming and the birth, a double celebration stirred the tranquil dwelling among the pines. They named the child Anthia. Peteos was so delighted to see the rosy little bundle that he half forgot his regret that his first-born was not male.

At the conclusion of the week-long festivities, Larentia intended to tell her husband about the dreaded bargain. But the task was too difficult and she decided it could wait until Peteos was a little stronger. When Peteos's strength returned, Larentia faltered still. But by this time there was movement in her womb and again she decided to wait a little longer. It was only after her son, Thestius, was born that she delivered herself of the weighty secret. Peteos remained silent for days, but what could he say? He had his life, his wife, and now a son.

A child given to the Goddess is prepared for the consecrated life almost from babyhood. Frequent visits to the Temple School are necessary for a subtle vibratory familiarization to take place, and to avoid homesickness at the time of separation. These children were also honoured above their playmates, so as to instill an awareness of their sacred status. Parents, on the other hand, enjoyed no such solicitude. And as the spring festivities in Anthia's sixth year approached, the stone in Larentia's heart grew heavier. For at the completion of these festivities, her little daughter was to be dedicated to the Goddess and must then leave home forever.

The painful chasm left in the family's hearts and home after Anthia's departure, was greatly alleviated when, two months later, Larentia bore her third child, Lavinia. Before Lavinia was fully weaned, however, another diversion intervened. Peteos was appointed overseer to the important trading post of Thessalonica, and the family moved to the north. These two events distracted Larentia from her grief. But whenever she looked wistfully across the sea towards Athens, Myrrha would comfort her with the famous saying, 'Athena's children never weep.'

Chapter Two

Thanks to a scrupulous preparation, young Anthia adapted well to the structured life of the Acropolis school. At first she enjoyed the company of the future priests and priestesses for they learned and played together. But when they reached the age of nine, it was in different quadrangles that they slept and worked. The girls then began the sacred task of weaving the Deity's robe, and the boys, an equally sacred task, constructing the throne on which Athena's flower-bedecked statue rests when she is paraded through the streets of her city.

The young ones' schooling was meticulous, rhythmic and relentless. The day began with exercises in breathing, conscious walking, conscious thinking and silent no-thought. Then there were lessons in music, dance, poetry, nature study and herb-culture. As they grew older, the future wise ones learned astrology, alchemy, healing and the psychic sciences. Then, three months before they turned 15, they were prepared for their first initiation into the Sacred Mysteries.

Every movement was monitored, every thought and attitude studied and corrected. When revolt began to rise in Anthia's heart, reddening her cheeks and stiffening her body, she was unswervingly reminded that the disciplined life was but the exalted choice of her own soul, that service to the Goddess was the highest honour Athens could bestow, and advancing through the Way of the Mysteries the noblest undertaking possible for any mortal.

On the night of the first full moon after Anthia's fifteenth birthday, the sound of singing could be heard in the little garden behind the Great Temple where the children of the lower school had gathered to burn Anthia's child-frock, and celebrate the ending of her childhood years. If this occasion marked a solemn transition, it was a joyous one too. With whoops of delight, Anthia's companions hurled her old garment into the flames and as it burned away, danced around the fire singing a farewell hymn. Anthia then stood before her guardian, the Old Priestess who helped her don a long white robe that tied in a simple knot at the left shoulder. This apparel was worn exclusively in the Sanctuary where Anthia was about to receive her first initiation and pronounce sacred vows. She would then emerge as a neophyte, live in another part of the temple precincts, and only connect with her former companions when the whole community gathered for the libations of dawn and dusk.

The procedure had been rehearsed many times. Anthia knew exactly what she had to do, and say in the Sanctuary. Outwardly she appeared confident, but inwardly she trembled. There had been a choice, but a meagre one. She could have rejected the higher calling and entered the Path of Dedication, a slower way, a gentler discipline and a life of mundane tasks; but there was no question of that. If Anthia trembled as she was robed in white, it was because she knew she was entering a path of no return.

Rarely did the Old Priestess smile, but, as she knotted the white garment at Anthia's left shoulder, she beamed with something akin to motherly pride. Over the years an unspoken bond had arisen between Anthia and her guardian, though Anthia was never told that it was the Old Priestess who had heard the call from the babe in Larentia's womb pleading for another chance to complete her earthly initiations on the Acropolis. It was because of this, that Anthia's tender years had been entrusted to the aged seer, but now that task was done.

Anthia hugged her childhood companions, whose time for initiation was not yet ripe, and followed the Priestess across the patch of green towards columned portico of the Parthenon. Once inside, they walked to the far end of the echoing oratory, where gentle pressure on a part of the stone wall opened a hidden door. Anthia stood back that her guardian might enter first, but the Ancient One shook her head. 'No, Anthia, now and forever you must go alone.'

They looked at each other for a brief moment, embraced warmly and then Anthia stepped through the opening in the wall and the old Priestess quickly closed the door behind her.

Once through the secret door, Anthia found herself in a short torch-lit passage, leading to a flight of steps that spiralled down through solid rock. At the bottom, an Initiate of the Mysteries waited. It was Phyleus, her teacher of history and numbers, leaning on his oaken staff. He was a man whose head and torso seemed to have been chiselled by the gods, but a birth defect of his pelvis and legs made walking difficult.

'Welcome, Anthia, daughter of Peteos,' he said in ritualistic tones. 'We are entering the Sacred Sanctuary of the Mysteries where Astraeus, our High Priest, will speak with you. He will search your heart for love and sincerity, and test your knowledge. If he finds you worthy, we will witness your vows.'

Having said this, they moved along the corridor towards a rectangular chamber excavated under the Great Temple. At the entrance, Phyleus edged back, for once again, Anthia had to move forward alone.

A little fearful, the future neophyte advanced into the sanctuary where flaming torches attached to the rock-hewn walls shed a mellow light, and a copper brazier diffused smoky emanations of rosemary and thyme. In the middle of the chamber stood Astraeus, the High Priest, flanked by eight initiates, four male and four female. At the far end, glowing in the light of a single flame, a metal spiral, wider at the base than at the summit, towered from floor to ceiling with grace and majesty. Ceremony demanded that the neophyte-to-be pause and study it before turning to face the High Priest who would question her on its meaning.

Before her, the massive cord-like structure rose in three harmonious yet diminishing spirals. A leaden base, resembling the massive body of a serpent-headed reptile, weighed the structure to the ground while three coils spiralled upwards, the scales gradually turning from lead to luminous silver and finally pure dazzling gold. The light of a long motionless flame, rising from a lamp set on the floor in the centre of the spirals, lent a lifelike quality to the scaly coils.

Anthia bowed in the way she had been taught, and turned towards the High Priest and the eight white clad initiates.

'Have you imbibed its meaning, daughter of Peteos?' Astraeus asked softly.

'Yes,' Anthia replied. 'It tells of our progression from matter to the infinite.'

'Correct.'

Anthia looked up at the oval face and dark eyes of the High Priest. He was short and round – his physique not imposing, and yet he radiated a majesty that left no one in doubt as to who he was. Rumour had it that he was past his seventieth year, yet his appearance betrayed no more than 40 summers. He smiled encouragingly.

'And the flame?'

'Universal love,' Anthia blundered impulsively. Then quickly corrected herself, 'No! Universal energy.'

Astraeus did not reply at once. He seemed not even to have heard as he looked silently at the neophyte whose youth and beauty were to serve the purpose of her soul in this incarnation.

'Anthia,' he said at last, 'in our school, as you already know, there are four progressions.' He turned and pointed to the arch directly behind the symbol. 'Beyond that arch is another chamber with yet another symbol, and beyond that, a third chamber and third symbol. Finally, we have the fourth and ultimate chamber which is not truly of this realm; it is totally empty. To integrate the knowledge of the third chamber and the third symbol is not within the reach of all in a single lifetime, and even those who succeed, may have to wait many incarnations before attaining to the mystical fourth.' He paused. The assembly wondered what all this had to do with the meaning of the Flame.

'So, daughter of Peteos,' he resumed, a smile curling the corners of his lips, 'when you *really* understand energy to be one with love, you will have skipped the second and the third chambers, and find yourself directly in the emptiness of the fourth!'

Sympathetic murmuring rose from the initiates while the tense young neophyte waited. Astraeus continued. 'The flame that is here, and in the other chambers also, represents the truth of spirit in relationship with matter – that same truth which, one way or another, consciously or unconsciously, all men seek between birth and death. To serve the Flame, is first to experience the light dwelling within yourself. Having achieved this, you will automatically perceive that same light dwelling in all humankind; service to them then becomes effortless. Getting to this point however, takes much time and great effort.'

Astraeus turned to Phyleus. 'Phyleus, you are given the charge of guiding this daughter of Athena through the first progression. Tell her now why the The Flame is ever a symbol of truth.'

Phyleus cleared his throat. 'Fire purifies,' he began. 'It

destroys the dross of our lower nature to expose the pure eternal light dwelling within. A flame represents the eternal destruction and emergence that is the way of creation. A flame is Helios, without which this planet would be barren. A flame is therefore life, and – '

Astraeus raised his hand. Phyleus fell silent. 'We have reached the point where borrowed knowledge poisons,' Astraeus interrupted. 'If Anthia does not discover life for herself, she will have learned nothing while thinking she knows all. This leads to the next question.' This was one for which Anthia was not prepared. 'Now why do you suppose that in this holy place, on this solemn occasion, we wear not our ceremonial robes hemmed in gold as for the public ceremonies, but the simplest of apparel with no distinction between male and female?'

Anthia's mouth trembled, but she remembered the answer. 'To impress upon our minds that man is, in essence, spirit clothed in flesh and not merely a body to hide or enhance with garments. There is no distinction between the robes of male and female on this occasion, because the principle of essence is undivided energy.'

'A good answer,' the High Priest responded. 'Though the implications may, in fact, mean little to you right now. This is not your first sojourn on the Acropolis, as I believe you have been told. You were tested before and moved mightily forward along the way. Now, like a swallow returning to its nest of many seasons, you have chosen to come again, for greater testing and deeper knowing. Never confuse knowing with knowledge; one is alive, the other dead. And remember that the tests to which you will be subjected become more searching as the way progresses, but the recompense is immeasurable. Is it still your desire to follow this exalted way?'

'It is,' Anthia replied.

Astraeus closed his eyes, and with a gesture of supplication spoke in a voice that seemed to come from afar. 'You are here, Anthia, to sanctify the choice of your soul with a vow of perpetual virginity and lifelong service to Athena.'

'That is so.' The formal response.

'Who will be your mentor and protector?'

As previously arranged, Phyleus staggered forward on his stick to stand at Anthia's side, where he promised to guide, protect, teach and examine the young Neophyte.

Astraeus then raised his hand over Anthia's head as she knelt to repeat the age-old pledge. Three times she vowed never to divulge the secret knowledge of the Mysteries, and three times offered herself in virginity and service to Athena. Finally she pronounced the solemn recognition that no other alliance was ever to supersede her vow – on pain of death.

Chapter Three

For as long as Caesar received his tribute, the Athenians' cherished traditions remained relatively undefiled by Roman rule, and citizens went about their lives in peace. If they tolerated the disciplined intruders who had dared declare their ancient territory a Roman province, it was because they had no choice. But for all that, neither the Roman regime nor the Athenian political council ventured any confrontation with the religious affairs of the Acropolis. Goddess Athena reigned supreme. She embodied the sacred heritage and unique identity of Athens. She assured victory, protection and prosperity. Anyone who meddled with her sacred cult must expect the ugliest of consequences.

Unlike the famed rites of the Eleusian Mysteries, those of the Acropolis remained purposely obscure. This was because the High Priest and celebrants of the public cult of Athena were also neophytes and initiates of the Mystery School, but to preserve the Mysteries from profane interference, the distinction between the two functions was kept deliberately vague.

Every Mystery School has its own distinctive methods for bringing souls to spiritual enlightenment. In many such schools aspirants are fiercely guarded from all the corrupting energies of the outside world, but in this respect the Acropolis school differed.

The Order of Athena considered it important that the neophytes' natural curiosity concerning life lived by ordinary people should be satisfied, and thereby eliminated. When the young ones know the world for the mountain of suffering that it really is, and put all worldly thoughts behind them, their minds are freed for the more refined awareness of the second initiation. It was therefore stipulated that each neophyte pass a three-month phase known as 'The World', where they serve and observe in the different workshops administered by the Temple School, in and around Athens. Neophytes were carefully matched with the milieu chosen for them, and appropriately prepared for this phase of their schooling. 'Move through earth's playground as oil moves through water', they were told, and they would be told it again, for wherever their assignment might be, an initiate was there to guide them.

When she turned 18, Anthia's period of service in The World fell due. Phyleus announced that she would be going to the Pilgrims Temple situated on the road half-way between Athens and Delphi; it was also an age-honoured watering place for pilgrims and travellers on their way to the Sanctuary of Apollo and the Oracle of Delphi. She was assigned to the watchful eye of Jocastra, a Priestess dedicated to medicine and ministering.

It was Phyleus's duty to accompany his charge to her new abode, and they started out at daybreak in a horse-drawn wagon. Anthia appeared at the meeting place just as a stable hand was hoisting her beloved mentor onto the horseman's bench behind the reins. Never could she fathom why the omnipotent Creator endowed this man with a head and torso of such harmony, while mangling his pelvis and legs so that he could hardly walk. And yet, despite this appalling disability, never once had she noticed anger or impatience flash from Phyleus's steady brown eyes. When he was seated, Anthia picked up his oaken walking stick, handed it up, and then climbed aboard to sit on the cushioned bench beside him.

With the eastern horizon already aglow, they joined a line of other wagons slowly descending the Sacred Way. Anthia glanced happily across at her mentor who was fingering the reins reflectively. For a long while they did not speak. Anthia felt extraordinarily adult, and even a little cocky because her studies had passed so easily, while others spent long hours in 'services' to atone for repeated mistakes. The concept of punishment was unheard of in the Temple School, all error was absolved by 'services to fellow men'; such acts were made to purify the spirit, and refine sensitivity. Even death for an unfaithful virgin was not deemed a punishment; that too was necessary for the soul's eternal journey.

But how would she fare now? Neophytes were always warned that The World would be one of the most deceptive experiences they were likely to encounter.

'Observing *sounds* easy,' Phyleus often said, 'but it calls for greater balance than you can imagine.'

However, as they rolled down the Sacred Way bathed in the wonderful crisp morning air, Anthia couldn't imagine how her devotion to the Goddess Athena, Astraeus, Phyleus and her fellow neophytes could ever falter, let alone be superseded by other fascinations. The Acropolis was home. The Acropolis was all. What in The World could be more fulfilling than that?

As the first rays of morning sun began to warm their shoulder blades, they reached even ground and turned onto the Delphi road.

'Daughter of Athena,' Phyleus said, pulling gently on the reins. Anthia stopped daydreaming and sat up. This manner of address usually meant that something was amiss. She turned apprehensively to face her mentor.

'I will tell you a little story,' he said mischievously.

'I'm listening,' responded his pupil with some relief.

'Once upon a time, centuries ago, there lived a wealthy merchant who lived with his family near Olympia. As was the custom, all of his daughters were married to the sons of other rich merchants, and all of his sons furthered their father's trade. All, that is to say, except one, whose name was Theras. Endowed by the gods with a handsome face, a powerful body and a competitive nature, Theras trained as an athlete and soon became a famous runner. As you can imagine, with such an abundance of gifts he drew to himself all that he desired – women in particular. Girls of his own social standing were not available; for them it was a matter of marriage or disgrace.

'For a time therefore, he helped himself harmlessly to the prostitutes of the town. A problem arose, however, when he became infatuated with a lady of the forbidden category who ardently returned his affection. The affair had to be kept secret, of course. But happiness was theirs till the day her womb began to fill with his child. Well, the shock of father-hood so overpowered the poor fellow that his love for the lady vanished, and instead of honourably marrying the girl, he simply abandoned her to her fate.'

'What fate was that?' Anthia enquired.

'She was automatically disowned by her family, and survived out in the hills fed by a shepherd in return for watching his sheep. But she died alone in a shepherd's hut after giving birth to a still-born baby. At the enquiry, Theras denied all knowledge of the affair. And because he was a celebrated athlete nobody pursued the matter . . . except the gods.'

Silence followed this baleful tale. 'Any questions?' Phyleus asked.

'Well,' Anthia said thoughtfully, 'wasn't it obvious what kind of a man Theras was? I mean, to take the courtship so far without any promise of marriage?'

'Of course,' Phyleus replied, laughing. 'Obvious as the

nose on your face. But Eros is blind you know – always has been, always will be. The desire we are speaking of is difficult to understand without having experienced it. Even then,' he added, turning to look at the young neophyte, 'it isn't really understood because passion is not of the mind – you see?'

His listener blushed, returning her gaze to the horse's tail as it switched about his shining chestnut flanks. She imagined she knew more about desire than she dared admit; none of the neophytes spoke of such things and she presumed her fiery feelings on hot summer nights to be a little abnormal. Perhaps Phyleus had guessed as much, and was counselling her with his usual tact and understanding.

'Great strength is required to withdraw in the heat of desire, Anthia,' he continued. 'And the inevitable emptiness that follows that kind of denial is painful.'

'Are you saying that Theras couldn't help it?' Anthia asked, hoping the conversation wouldn't flutter too near to herself.

'Partly.'

'You mean, it wasn't entirely his fault?'

'No. He was responsible and so was she. But in matters of physical attraction, there is always a clear fleeting moment, when yes or no is decided, and withdrawal, though excruciatingly difficult, *is* possible – you see?

'I see,' Anthia replied mechanically, for with the exclusion of such a dilemma ever entering her own life, she wasn't going to be sidetracked from the rest of the story. 'Go on,' she urged. 'You said that the gods punished him.'

'No, Anthia. I said that nobody pursued the matter except the gods. And, as you should know by now, they never punish – only teach.' Phyleus paused, remembering the agonizing years before he himself understood this truth, and how much lighter his life became when he experienced his deformity as a lesson, rather than a punishment.

'*Do* go on,' Anthia insisted.

'Well, I was born to an unmarried woman in the poorest, roughest, dirtiest district of Athens.'

'No. The athlete I mean.'

'Same story,' Phyleus said seriously.

'*You* were Theras?' she gasped. 'I can hardly believe it!'

'When my mother saw that I had a lifelong infirmity she wanted to be rid of me. She tried several times, but as you might have noticed, the gods had other plans.'

'And I thank them for that,' Anthia interjected.

'I was only a few weeks old when, on a cold night, I was left high on the hillside to die. But the next morning a shepherd discovered me, warm and contentedly suckled by one of his ewes. From my clothing he guessed from where I had come, and walked through the streets of that district until my mother was found. Poor and ignorant, she really was not capable of managing a child in my condition, so her next attempt was to drown me in the sea. This time it was fishermen who saved me, and threatened to report the incident if my mother tried again. Attempts on my life were stalled after that, but I grew up neglected and rejected, pulling myself around on my hands, begging for food. By the time I was about seven, and still unable to walk, prostitution became my mother's way of survival and my continued presence became a threat to her livelihood. Something had to be done. Another plan was launched, and this time, I'm happy to say, she succeeded.'

Anthia's eyes bulged. 'How?' she asked.

'Well, she dreamed that I should be taken to the Acropolis and simply pushed over the rock.'

'Like an unfaithful virgin,' Anthia giggled; for no particular reason this tragedy seemed irrepressibly funny. Phyleus continued.

'She put me on a wheeled board, dragged me up to the gatehouse, made the usual offerings and, in spite of her dubious appearance, was granted entry. She'd not gone far, still dragging me along behind her, when a neophyte doing "services" for some negligence and wishing to add to his merit, offered to care for me while Mother entered the temple to make her supplications – Entreaties, no doubt, for the successful relief of her burden undetected. However, when she emerged ready to execute her plan, there was I, sitting on the neophyte's knee. At that moment the High Priest chanced to come by, and offered my mother money if she would donate her child to the Temple School. I'll never forget the look on the neophyte's face when the High Priest proposed this. But as you can see, she did not refuse. Now, Anthia, you take the reins while I give my back a rest.'

Phyleus and Anthia changed places on the driver's bench. With the reins in her hand and the chestnut stallion making good progress, another question arose in Anthia's mind. 'Phyleus,' she said. 'Does this mean that all birth deformities have karmic implications?'

'Not in the strict sense of that word, child. But it is a good question,' Phyleus answered. 'As you already know, when souls descend into flesh they do so to learn through experience – rather like a child going to school. Some learn fast, others more slowly. The precise lessons needed, and how best to learn them in earth's school, are chosen in the world beyond where all the determining factors are clear. If, at a certain point in its evolution, the soul sees that progression would be furthered, or accelerated, by difficulties of a physical nature, it may bravely choose this way. Do you see?'

'Yes. I vaguely remember you saying that before.'

'I don't want you to chew on this complicated subject now. If memory is shaded when we return to earth it is for a reason, and you will know more at the proper time.'

With the sun rising to its zenith, their destination appeared in the distance. Phyleus was about to point to the circular stone Temple surrounded by wooden vendors' kiosks, when a roar on the road behind made him snatch the reins from Anthia's hands and manoeuvre horse and wagon off the road. Within seconds the roar became the sound of pounding hoofs and clashing metal wheels as three Roman war chariots hurtled past in a cloud of dust, forcing foot-travellers to jump for their lives.

'What was that?' Anthia asked as the noise died down.

'There's a sizeable Roman garrison on the high ground between here and Delphi,' Phyleus replied. 'But we needn't worry, they have their own deities and doctors, and orders from the Governor not to interfere with us.'

When the dust had settled they moved on, and half an hour later drew level with a wide square opening out to the right of the road. At the far end stood the circular stone Temple of Athena with two straight rows of wooden vendors' kiosks running down to the road on either side. In the centre a tall sycamore cast dappled shade over a wide stone well. Contrasting with the tranquillity of the countryside, the Temple Square hummed like a beehive. Pilgrims and priests, beggars and merchants, came and went to the strains of vociferous vendors plying their trades in everything imaginable. Pulling up under a cluster of pines, Phyleus wiped the sweat and dust from his brow with his forearm, and turned to scrutinize the vibrant melee for the face he knew.

'There she is,' he exclaimed, and reaching for his stick, brandished it in the direction of the well. 'Jocastra!' he shouted.

A pleasant-looking woman in her rounded middle years, wearing a light blue peplos with the silver emblem of Athena on her left shoulder, looked up. She'd been drawing water from the well, and brushed a wisp of silvery gray hair from her face before peering round for the voice that had called her. On seeing Phyleus she smiled broadly, left her jar, and beckoned to a saddle-maker in a nearby kiosk before walking over to the road.

'Phyleus!' she greeted smiling broadly. 'You've brought me a visitor, I see.'

'More than a visitor,' Phyleus responded with his usual geniality. 'I've brought young Anthia to savour The World in the Place of Potions. It's a while since you had an assistant. I'm sure you could use one.'

While they spoke the saddle-maker, obviously familiar with his task, climbed aboard the wagon, grasped Phyleus under the arms, and lowered him gently to the ground. Anthia handed him down his stick and then jumped to the ground.

Jocastra's eyes appraised the young neophyte as she offered a welcoming smile and then, taking Phyleus's arm, helped him across the square to a long, low building up near the Temple. Anthia followed behind. They entered a wide portal, over which the insignia of Athena and 'The Place of Potions' was carved in bold letters. The one rectangular room, built entirely of wood, was not partitioned; one half was furnished with benches and straw mattresses for sick pilgrims, the other rigged with shelves and a table for the concoction of pomades and potions. Hanging from the rafters, a profusion of drying herbs swayed in a draft from the open door, diffusing a sweet and peaceful aroma.

Jocastra showed them round and, for the benefit of her new assistant, described some of the problems brought for her care; she scrutinized Anthia from time to time as she spoke. The child seemed keen, but very young. And did she have to be quite so pretty? She'd be wearing the big silver emblem of Athena, a protection no Athenian would dare desecrate – but the others?

The next day Phyleus was lifted back onto the wagon; a pilgrim returning to Athens departed with him. It was not a lengthy farewell, for he would be returning from time to time to see how his charge was progressing. As Anthia reached up with his stick, he unexpectedly leaned down towards her. 'Give of your fruits not your roots, Anthia,' he whispered.

Anthia nodded obediently but was annoyed; he'd said that twice already. Didn't he realize that the Acropolis meant more to her than life itself?

The moment Phyleus had gone, there was work to do. Anthia's long white peplos had to be exchanged for a shorter pale blue one, and Athena's disc attached to her left shoulder.

'Blue is more practical than white,' Jocastra explained. We get all the dust from the road here, and often care for pilgrims who haven't washed in weeks.'

For two months Jocastra taught while Anthia observed, learned and was examined. She noticed how competently Jocastra questioned to establish the cause of pain before preparing a concoction, and how gently she dressed the wounds and sores. Though always busy, she was never hurried, and would lend an ear to many a long litany of woe. Her humour and common sense earned her the respect of all who needed her; the vendors would do anything for her, and so would Anthia.

It was only when the intensive training of the first two months had ended, that Jocastra left Anthia to work alone while she rested, or spent a day herb-gathering in the hills. Anthia relished these challenges, and was beginning to feel she could handle anything, when early one morning, three Romans in battle dress entered the square and marched purposefully toward the Place of Potions.

Confident though she was, Anthia was not prepared for this! She had never seen a Roman close-to before; much less spoken with one. Their language had been taught, but she'd learned it badly, and it so happened that Jocastra had just departed for a day in the hills.

The party advanced. It consisted of two bodyguards and

their commanding officer; a tall, clean-shaven man with light brown hair, blue eyes, and wearing the uniform of a Centurion. Anthia's first instinct was to hide before they spotted her through the open door, but when she saw blood spurting from the Centurion's hand, she grabbed a thick fold of linen and ran out towards them. The foot soldiers nudged each other with lascivious grins as the linen was wrapped firmly around the wound and pressure applied. Without a word, the Centurion was then drawn into the Place of Potions and made to sit on a low bench with his hand held high above his head to slow the bleeding. Nevertheless the bleeding continued and several changes of linen were needed before the deep slash from wrist to thumb could be inspected.

'How did you do this?' Anthia asked in faltering Latin, causing the guards to smirk again.

'I was attacked on the road by a woman with a knife,' he replied candidly. Anthia nodded innocently as she sponged away the clots, and then applied a stinging solution that usually evoked a wince, if not a yell. The Centurion did neither. He merely gazed admiringly into Anthia's face and, with imperfect Greek but undeniable charm, thanked her for coming to his rescue.

Anthia was just beginning to think that Romans weren't *all* dictatorial barbarians, when she noticed the two foot-soldiers nosing inquisitively around Jocastra's pots and jars. The Centurion's glance followed hers, and a ferocious growl brought the men to instant attention.

'Out!' he ordered. Then, returning his appreciative gaze on Anthia, added, 'They shall be punished for their impertinence.'

'But they've done no harm.'

'Not yet,' he conceded. 'But they'll be taught a lesson just the same.'

'Please don't,' Anthia insisted.

The Centurion's mouth softened, and he looked at her with a tenderness she didn't immediately understand. There had been no opportunity to inform him of her sacred status, and this was the first time a man had regarded her as anything other than a ministering neophyte. Her cheeks flared and she bowed her head even lower over the cleansing of his wound hoping he'd not notice. She wondered too, if the fearful beating of her heart was as audible to him as it was to her.

With the bandage hastily completed and a vial of the stinging solution placed firmly in the Centurion's uninjured hand, Anthia told him to have it applied twice a day and moved briskly towards the door. Instead of leaving, however, he hovered on the threshold spinning out time with aimless remarks. Finally he asked if he might return the following day.

'I believe you have a surgeon in the garrison,' Anthia replied.

'He died yesterday, and his replacement will be a while coming.'

'Is there nobody else?'

'Nobody who could do it as well as you,' he replied suavely.

Anthia had never experienced this kind of insistence before, but knowing Jocastra to be back at dusk, she nodded and with contrived nonchalance said, 'Oh, very well.'

When Jocastra reappeared that evening, Anthia lost no time in telling her about the Centurion. 'If he comes tomorrow, your Latin being more fluent than mine, I was hoping that you would like to dress his wound?'

'Attacked by a woman?' Jocastra laughed. 'More likely the other way round!'

'Oh no,' came the rather too speedy retort. 'He seemed

something of an aristocrat. Very respectful and a deal more grateful than any Greek. He only came here because the Roman surgeon has just died.'

Jocastra poured water into an earthenware basin and began to wash her hands. 'Romans!' she muttered. 'Even the most civilized are not to be trusted.'

'If he comes tomorrow, I'm sure you will change your mind,' Anthia countered.

But Jocastra turned, angrily wagging a wet finger, 'Never trust a Roman, Anthia. Never!'

Next morning the Centurion came, his bandage in tatters. While the bodyguards were ordered outside, Anthia scanned the square for Jocastra's silvery head – but in vain. She turned towards the Centurion, pointed to the wooden bench, and sped away to fetch Jocastra.

First she ran to the Temple, but Jocastra wasn't there. She then enquired up the lines of kiosks, but without success. Across the road where the mules were tethered, the guardian hadn't seen Jocastra either. In her plight she even questioned strangers on the road, but vacant looks and shaking heads was all she got. Tears of frustration blurred her vision as she retraced her steps, hoping against hope that Jocastra might be there when she got back – but she was not.

The Centurion's face broke into a warm smile as Anthia re-entered heart racing from her fruitless exertions. Nodding perfunctorily she unraveled the dirty bandage and found the wound suppurating badly.

'Why didn't you get someone to apply the solution I gave you and cover the wound with clean linen?' she asked.

The Centurion looked boldly back, and with an enchanting smile repeated what he had said the night before. 'Because, fair lady, nobody could do it quite as well as you.'

Anthia was embarrassed. Nobody had addressed her in

those terms before. But rather than let him think it mattered, she scolded him instead. 'Well, it's a lot more swollen than yesterday, and you are going to have an ugly scar.' She placed her cool hand fleetingly on his hot forehead. 'What is more, you have started a fever!'

Her voice remained steady, but she was not at ease because the Centurion still looked at her in that disconcerting way. To make matters worse, she could see the necessity of his returning once, if not twice a day, to cleanse the wound. Oh where, in the name of all the Gods, had Jocastra gone?

With the wound neatly dressed and a fever-chasing potion given, they walked to the door where the Centurion again bemoaned the absence of his surgeon. He gave a handful of coins to his bodyguard, who dropped them noisily in the offering jar. 'It would be expedient if I came tomorrow too, wouldn't it?' he said, leaving Anthia with the realization that she'd never really learned how to say no.

She wanted to shake her head, but found herself nodding and silently vowing not to let Jocastra out of her sight until the Centurion had come and gone. She was about to ask that he arrive before noon, when the unexpected sight of Phyleus lumbering across the square distracted her attention. The Centurion noticed too and, supposing Phyleus to be another patient, left quickly. Anthia rushed towards the visitor.

'Oh Phyleus! It's so good to see you. Have you come to stay for a while? Or is it time to take me back?' Anthia had served in the Pilgrims' Temple for almost three moons now; her experience of The World was drawing to a close.

'No, child. I'm afraid not,' he replied, heaving himself up the step and into the cool, sweet-smelling place. 'Where is Jocastra?'

'I wish I knew,' Anthia replied. 'She's not in the Temple

or the square, so I suppose she's been called to the pilgrims' encampment up the road.' Just then, Jocastra appeared in the doorway.

'Phyleus!' she hailed. 'What a wonderful surprise, and to what do we owe the honour of this visit?'

An uneasy silence followed, then Anthia was sent to the cookhouse for refreshments. When she returned with honey-cake and pomegranate juice, Jocastra broke the news.

'Phyleus has just asked me if you are capable and trustworthy enough to be left on your own for the next ten days. You see, Astraeus wants me back at the Great Temple for the autumn celebrations. I believe you could manage alone for that short time – couldn't you?'

Anthia nodded and smiled. This was a challenge she'd normally have enjoyed, and yet a wave of consternation swept over her. It wasn't the added work she dreaded, but something else. Something that had only just happened, and something she simply couldn't bring herself to mention in front of Phyleus. However, there'd be plenty of time to draw Jocastra aside and ask what to do about the Centurion, and in the meantime, she had better prepare Phyleus's bed.

'Where would you like your mattress placed this time?' she asked – he often preferred to sleep under the stars.

Phyleus shook his head. 'I'm sorry, Anthia, I had planned to stay a day or two, but old Pylos died yesterday and must be buried tomorrow, so we have to leave at once.'

Delighted to be spending a few days on the Acropolis, Jocastra hurried to the temple to gather some belongings and sent Anthia to the cookhouse to buy provisions for their journey. Back from the cookhouse, Anthia was determined to talk to Jocastra alone, but with Phyleus seated immovably on the patient's bench, and Jocastra hurriedly tidying away her morning's work at the far end of the room, privacy was impossible.

'Jocastra?' Anthia said nodding her head pointedly

towards the door. 'There is something I must show you before you go.'

'Oh? What is it?' Jocastra asked, without looking up.

'It's the water-drain on the roof.'

'Oh that! Don't worry. The nail-maker is mending it tomorrow. Now, if we don't depart at once, we'll not reach Athens before nightfall.'

Ten minutes later, the distressed neophyte found herself standing alone on the dusty road in the hot sun, waving goodbye to the only person in the world who could advise in the matter that troubled her so.

Chapter Four

Just before dusk, the shadow of a tall man darkened the open doorway of the Place of Potions. Anthia looked up, to see the Centurion without a bodyguard, and dressed in the simple robe of an Athenian; he smiled with the confidence of an old friend. Acknowledging his presence Anthia smiled back, but told him she would have to hurry for the daylight was fading fast.

This time the wound showed signs of progress, but the Centurion's quiet charm was more insistent than before. Dressing the wound in silence, Anthia's cheeks reddened again. Yes, she knew perfectly well what these stirrings were about.

'Transmute,' they taught in the sacred school. 'If you can watch the emotion with total detachment and remain perfectly centred, it will dissolve like a cloud before the wind.' But the sensations Anthia experienced now, were more overwhelming than anything she had ever had to deal with before.

'If I were to come twice a day, we would have the wound healed in no time, would we not?' said the Centurion with another of his enchanting smiles. But the non-committal murmur given in reply, failed to register.

'You would not refuse me that, would you?' he pursued.

Confused, Anthia retreated into silence. But when the

unanswered question could be borne no longer, she replied, 'Oh, very well; on condition that you come in daylight.'

'Have I not always come in daylight?'

'We are sparing with lamp oil here.' A weak excuse, but the first that entered the neophyte's head.

The Centurion left as discreetly as he had come, showing the usual courtesy and respect. For a moment Anthia wondered if he really *was* the threat she had imagined. As for those feelings – well, she would just have to disregard them. Jocastra had said 'never trust a Roman', but this one seemed harmless as a puppy and every bit as endearing.

The following morning he was there again, and for the sake of the injury, Anthia agreed that he should come morning and evening for the next seven days. He addressed her by her name, saying that she should call him Othila. When Anthia told him of her sacred status, he nodded reverently and said she had nothing to fear from him. He was, however, perfectly aware and rather flattered, by the evident effect his presence was having on the maiden; it amused him to watch her learn the feminine art of evasion.

During the course of his visits, Anthia lost some of her shyness and Othila enjoyed amusing her with tales of Rome and the Empire. He claimed to be the commander of the nearby garrison, and indeed had been inspecting the Roman force when he first appeared at the Place of Potions, but neglected to mention that he was also the Governor of Athens and the province.

By the time the wound was healed, their association had developed into one of relaxed cordiality. The troubling arousal Anthia experienced with each of his visits, she dismissed as merely a temporary challenge to her feminine nature; soon she'd be saying a definite, if diplomatic, adieu.

On the morning of Othila's last visit to the Place of Potions, a leaden sky hung heavily over the Temple Square. Not a breath of air stirred the sycamore leaves, for the storm rumbling over Delphi would soon be overhead. The animals sensed its overture too; dogs howled, horses and mules tugged at their tethers, and braying donkeys grated on everybody's nerves. Kiosk vendors drew in their wares and everyone waited for the relief of rain. Just before midday Othila appeared, unaccompanied, and wearing a plain Athenian tunic.

Having inspected the healed laceration, Anthia launched into her carefully prepared adieu. 'Well, I'm happy to say that your hand is now sufficiently healed for your valet to . . .' A resounding clap of thunder drowned the rest of her sentence. The building shook: the earth reverberated beneath their feet, and a sudden gust of wind caught the oaken door slamming it shut with a momentous bang. First they jumped, and then they laughed. But laughter was brief. All at once the potion-laden shelves began to shake: pots and jars clinked against each other before crashing tumultuously to the floor.

'Earthquake!' Othila exclaimed, and gripping Anthia's arm, pulled her after him to the door. It was jammed. He threw his weight against it repeatedly but it wouldn't budge, so he strode over to grapple with the wooden bars of the window. It was then that a second quake struck, making the whole room sway to the sound of groaning beams and splintering wood. The Centurion looked up sharply to see a writhing rafter tilted towards the floor where the petrified neophyte stood, and leapt to snatch her away.

'Just a little quake,' he said comfortingly as he held her protectively to himself. Anthia closed her eyes and felt his lips brush the top of her head.

When the shaking stopped, they knew they were hopelessly trapped. Nothing stirred outside. The square was in shock. A sudden coldness filled the air and Othila's arms tightened around Anthia as he braced himself for another tremor. But all that came was the roar of rain, resonating wildly upon the damaged roof.

How long they stood thus entwined was time unmeasured, but time enough for Anthia to feel cared for, protected, and something more. Her feelings for the Centurion were now less trivial than she had imagined.

When the rain ceased, there came a hammering on the oaken door and anxious faces peered in through the tenaciously barred windows; it was the kiosk men fearing for the safety of their Priestess. Several together tried to unhinge the massive portal, shouting reassurances until they levered it free enough to produce an opening wide enough for Anthia's patient to slip outside and this he did, furtively, without so much as a backward glance.

'Very gallant,' the kiosk owners commented. 'Are you hurt, Anthia?'

'No, not at all.'

The following morning, a perplexed and shaken aspirant of the Sacred Mysteries set about restoring what order she could to the damaged Place of Potions. Chaos was everywhere, and yet the outer confusion was nothing compared with the turmoil in Anthia's heart. She may not have drained the world's enchanting cup, but the sweetness of that small sip still lingered on her tongue. She wanted to believe her testing over, for testing it surely was, but Othila had aroused the woman in her and she had found it pleasurable.

During the day, with Jocastra absent, extra work kept Anthia too busy to dwell on her difficulty. But when she entered the Temple to sleep, the marvels of Rome that Othila had loved describing flooded her dreams, the Emperor's banqueting halls echoing with music as the handsome Othila escorted her to a privileged place. By perfumed pools he sat with her, and they drank together from fountains of wine.

Virgin and neophyte Anthia still was, but the thought of Othila forever gone, caused a stifled sigh and an aching throat. She scolded herself for this and her dreaming, but Jocastra would soon return to give her something else to think about. And, as her term in The World was virtually over, Phileus would come any day now, to take her back to the Temple School, out of temptation's way.

With an angry scar on his hand and a strangely unsatisfied heart, the Roman Governor returned to Athens and his airy villa by the sea. He hadn't intended such a long absence, and now there was a lot to catch up with. He was greeted by his scribe, Tullus, who lost no time in presenting the recent missives in their order of importance.

The first referred to the Governor's successor. The honorable senators had at last made up their mind, naming Atacus, the supposed amateur of Athenian art and culture, to replace him. Closing his eyes, Othilarius brought to mind the good-natured, slightly obese, middle-aged nobleman whom he considered to be the greatest ditherer of all time. 'It'll take more than a dilettante interest in culture and customs to keep order here,' he said aloud. 'On the other hand,' he thought with a wave of satisfaction, 'to be replaced is one thing, surpassed quite another, and with Atacus at the helm, there is little chance of that. Good, good,' he murmured, placing the scroll to one side and holding up his hand for the next.

Ah! His own position. He'd waited moons for that. He read it once, and then studied the scroll a second time. Tullus hovered, grinning discreetly, and waiting his master's reaction to the news that his forthcoming appointment was to be discussed *personally* with no lesser a person than great Caesar himself!

Othilarious's life-long ambition was about to be realized, and he paused to savour the news. He had come a long way since, as a beardless youth, he had left his father's Tuscan farm to join the mighty Roman Army. He might have started as a mere standard-bearer, but it hadn't taken long to elbow himself into officer's uniform. The Gods had been good, he conceded, they had gifted him with a handsome face, innate authority and a natural ability to manipulate truth. And then of course, there was Julia. As a junior officer he had courted and conquered Julia, the less than lovely daughter of Rome's foremost senator. When he'd made marriage to the girl a necessity, promotion swiftly followed. He'd had to pay tribute to a loveless marriage, perhaps, but he'd not be where he was now, without it.

'Yes, yes, Tullus,' he said, somewhat impatiently. 'What's next?' But the remaining scrolls were of trifling importance. In truth, they escaped his concentration altogether; his anticipating mind already marched through the solemn arches of the Roman Senate to peerless power and matchless glory.

After Tullus had left, Othilarius called for a flagon of wine and had his goblet filled to the brim. 'I'll drink to my future,' he thought, taking a generous draft. And then, conjuring up his meeting with Caesar, padded thoughtfully towards his favoured place at the balustrade overlooking the sea. As he reached the centre of the columned hall he paused to look down, and then stepped back to contemplate a circular mosaic he'd hardly noticed before. Bending for a closer look, his gaze met the ferocious eyes of a magnificent Neptune, face aglow, hair, beard and purple cloak flying behind him in the wind. One hand brandished a silver trident over a gray-green sea, the other held taut the golden reins of his sea-chariot drawn by laughing white dolphins. Othila was stupefied. How could a work of such power have escaped his notice all these years? Perhaps it was his coming triumph that had made him aware of it, or perhaps it was the wine.

He peered into his goblet; it seemed unusually heady that afternoon. Ah, foxy Sinis! He might have known. If that Greek bitch of a housekeeper had managed to hold sway over the domestic affairs of the Governor's villa since time immemorial, it was because of her unswerving ability to humour her masters at the crucial moment, and a change of masters was indeed crucial for her. If she were not warmly recommended to the incoming Governor, her future might look very bleak. But for all her perspicacity, Othilarius did not like her. No, not at all. She smiled too rarely, moved too silently and spoke too smoothly. She had served the two governors before him, but it was said that she hated them both.

Leaning against the balustrade and staring out to sea, the master of the house waited for the midday meal. He'd be eating alone for once, and was glad; it would give him time to savour the good news and indulge in a little reverie. He imagined the tall fine beauty of the young neophyte as he presented her to Caesar. How jealous all those lascivious, potbellied senators would be. Virgin of Athena indeed. What a waste! He was 20 years her senior perhaps, but what of it? Divorcing Julia, who had refused to leave Rome when his duty took him to Athens, should be a painless procedure; she'd not seen his 'essentials' in years! He must find an excuse to return to the Temple of the Pilgrims – to thank her perhaps. Yes, he must thank Anthia again and to make a more substantial offering. He'd take it slowly, though. What was it his father used to say? 'A good wine should always be tasted timidly before it is drunk.'

Somewhere behind the pillars the dining bell jingled. A breeze ruffled his hair and filled his lungs with its salty splendour. Before turning to go in, he raised his goblet to the sea and the city that lay beyond – the only one worth dying for – Rome! Ah, the wine was superb – strong and velvety, as she would be if he were to touch her. His goblet drained, he strode across the hall, but stopped by the mosaic to salute the lord of the waves; it evoked something of his own invincible strength. He threw back his head and laughed; the echoing hall laughed with him. 'By Jupiter. And thou, O noble Neptune,' he said, raising his empty goblet. 'I'll drink to thee, and to the laurel crown.'

Chapter Five

Help from Athens was prompt. Carpenters and materials soon arrived at the Pilgrim's Temple to repair the earthquake's damage. A fresh supply of medical provisions and a letter from Jocastra arrived with them. Anthia read the missive, hearing Jocastra's caring, humorous voice in every line. She was writing to say she'd be back ten days later than expected.

Jocastra's words resonated a sense of normality, but as Anthia needed time to come to terms with recent feelings and events, the delayed return came as a relief. 'Take heart,' the letter said. 'When Phyleus brings me back, he'll take you home with him. Now, precious sister, the herbs and concoctions I am sending are the last of the Acropolis reserve stock, so guard them with your life.' The letter ended with thanks for Anthia's patience, without which Jocastra might not enjoy additional days in the sublime presence of Astraeus.

With the Place of Potions made sound again and a new stock of medicines on the shelves, life should have returned to normal – but it did not. A veil of anxiety hung over the ministering neophyte. If dreams of Rome ceased, it was because her conscience now kept her awake. What she initially dismissed as unimportant suddenly swelled into an awful question. Should she lose the trust of Phyleus or Jocastra by telling them about the incident? After years of learning how to distance herself from the power of emotions, what excuse could she offer? Astraeus had never denied human emotions, he had accepted them as 'natural and unavoidable', but had always said they 'should be treated as poisonous snakes . . . a fascination to be observed – not played with'. And Anthia had played. She had imagined the unspeakable, and desired the forbidden.

Now that Othila was gone forever, Anthia tried to rein in her feelings and let her mind obliterate all that had happened. But, no matter how hard she pulled on the reins, her desires rampaged with all the vigour of a bolting horse. Guilt encroached with nightfall, prodding the young neophyte as she lay on her mattress, reasoning and re-reasoning. Unlike the vials and jars, her vows had remained technically intact, so what had she to confess? If, on the other hand, she admitted her feelings for the Centurion, she might well endure years and years of 'services'. Was that really necessary? Memory and desire would fade before long, so let the matter drop! But the matter refused to drop; it hung about her like a damp cloak.

After three sleepless nights and as many arduous days, Anthia's resistance weakened, and the truth she'd been suppressing rose effortlessly to the surface like a bubble in a pond. 'I'm in love. I can neither help, nor hide it,' she said aloud. 'And I will tell Jocastra the moment she returns.' The Temple echoed her words and the bubble burst. Relief came, and with relief, strength to face whatever lay ahead. Sleep descended after that – the deepest in days.

The fire that had started in the cookhouse overnight and spread to the kiosks on either side, was raging by dawn. Alarmed shrieks from man and beast and the smell of smoke, brought Anthia running sleepy-eyed to the Temple door. Travellers trotted their frightened mules to safety, women ran with crying babies, and kiosk owners darted hither and thither salvaging their wares. A soft breeze encouraged the flames. The Place of Potions had started to burn also. Chains of able-bodied men passed water jars up and down the line which stretched from the well to the conflagration, but the water only hissed contemptuously as the inferno raged on. A purplish spark falling on Anthia's bare foot brought her to her senses. If she didn't move fast, not only would the Place of Potions be gone, but all the medicines with it, and she had enough bad news for Jocastra already.

Nobody noticed Anthia slip into the Place of Potions, where voracious flames licked their way towards the shelves at the far end of the room. Having gathered the hem of her garment into a pouch, she swept as many jars and vials as possible into it, and then picked her way back through the debris to deposit them on the stony safety of the Temple floor. With each return, the fire had ravaged further, but, determined to have them all, she kept going until one last run would finish the job.

In the meantime, the exhausted men on the water chain had dropped their jars and abandoned the square without noticing the slender neophyte still running back and forth. They must have assumed that she too had given up, for only a fool would approach the Place of Potions now. A smouldering beam obstructed the entrance and the roof looked far from sound.

No matter how dangerous this last run might be, Anthia would not fail Jocastra whose approval she needed more than ever now. She must jump the beam and grab those last jars even if it meant getting burned.

So back she went, hitched up her peplos and was about to jump, when the roof collapsed right in front of her. Gasping in surprise, Anthia leapt back inhaling a lungful of ash and smoke as she reeled away. Her throat was aflame. She could hardly breathe.

Death felt very near to the frightened neophyte as she staggered towards Athena's cool abode, but on reaching the

Temple steps, her vision blurred, her legs crumpled, and then – oblivion.

'Well, Tullus,' Othilarius remarked cheerily, as his valet helped him on with the Centurion leathers. 'This'll be my last inspection of the garrison. I shall miss them when I get to Rome.'

Of late, the Governor's household had seen a remarkable upswing in their master's mood as he sipped his evening wine by the balustrade. They noticed how impatiently he stared up at the moon; in just four days, its full face would look down on him, and then the *Juno*, that had sailed his successor into Piraeus with pomp, would be taking him back to Rome. But now that his success was certain, the waiting had become irksome.

Reflecting on his term of office, Othilarius could not help but congratulate himself. He had made an excellent job of Athens, kept the testy Greeks out of revolt, not a breath of scandal marred his name and now the time for his rightful reward had come.

'And tomorrow, Tullus,' he continued, slipping a silver band up his brawny arm, 'I'm taking Atacus on an inspection of the shipyards, so we will need the usual entourage again. Where is Atacus? It's time we left.'

'Atacus sends his excuses, my lord. He has lumbago.'

'Lumbago! On a beautiful morning like this?'

'He is sending his aide-de-camp, Otus, to the garrison instead, sir.'

'Very well,' Othilarius snapped tersely, as he moved briskly through the hall and out to the forecourt where two military chariots and a party of outriders waited. Having taken his place beside Otus in the larger of the two chariots, he gave the order to proceed but remained in hunched rumination.

'Atacus is not a soldier but a soft-seated aristocrat,' he

groused to himself. 'He'll have to do better than this if he expects to hold Athens in abeyance. Huh, the military will soon play him up if he fails to inspect them personally *and* regularly. But there again, he's not a soldier, so how could he know? And I'm not an aristocrat, so what can I say without him telling me he already knows?'

Cocks began to crow in the fresh morning air as they rattled through the villages, and the warmth of a rising sun dispersed the mists of Othilarius's grouchy mind. He looked across at young Otus sitting silently waiting to be spoken to.

'Well, Otus, how are you finding your new post? And what think you of Athens?' he questioned somewhat pompously as the party turned onto the Delphi road.

'Easily the most beautiful capital I have ever seen, sir.'

'More wondrous than Rome?' Othilarius grinned, for the question held a barb of loyalty for the young man.

'Totally different, sir.'

'What would you say was the difference?' Othilarius pursued.

'Athens is a place of grace and beauty, yes, even magic,' Otus replied. 'But Rome . . . Rome has all that, and infinitely more.'

Othilarius looked across at his companion encouragingly. 'More?' he echoed.

'When Rome roars, the world trembles,' Otus answered arrogantly. 'Power lives in every stone, every arch, every tower.'

The Governor liked that answer. He would memorize it. In his younger years the intelligentsia had scoffed at his lack of culture; they'd have derided him openly were it not for his influential father-in-law. Otus's reflections on his own lips would sound good in the Senate where an eloquent turn of phrase was always applauded.

'Ah, so you think Greece relinquishes power to elegance?'

he pursued, hoping for more, and watching with amusement as the aide-de-camp's face lit with enthusiasm.

'Elegance has a power of its own, sir,' the apprentice diplomat replied. 'It conquers – differently.' Otus would have liked to discuss the subtle power of grace and beauty as opposed to brute force and ignorance, but he didn't think this successful commander, whose brute force had always won the day, would appreciate such things. In any case, Uncle Julius Atacus had warned him not to be too clever. 'Let us just say,' Otus concluded quickly, 'as power is to Rome, so grace is to Athens.'

'He's done it again!' Othilarius thought, but made no comment because the cavalcade had broken into a brisk trot and the clamour of hoofs on the road trampled their conversation too. The two men therefore sank into personal reveries that the fragrant, dew-soaked fields and mellow mists of morning, could but enhance.

Relaxing in the serenity of the countryside, the departing Governor wondered why it was that he invariably found a foreign land at its most beguiling only when he was about to leave it. He recalled the the flower-swept hills of Palestine. Of course they had bloomed every spring, yet he'd only noticed them as his boat pulled away from the port on the day of his departure.

A respectful nudge from Otus brought Othilarius out of his musings. An outrider had levelled with their chariot and was pointing to a column of smoke in the distance. Othilarius shrugged. Just a local rout; a barn fire perhaps. There'd been no rain for weeks. But, to avoid appearing ineffective in the eyes of his cultured companion, he ordered four of his guard ahead to investigate.

'Expecting conflict, sir?' Otus asked.

'Gracious no! The people travelling this road are mostly pilgrims headed for Delphi.'

'Ah yes. The fabled Sanctuary of Apollo . . .' Otus begun.

But his sentence faded in astonishment, as the Governor leapt to his feet and began pummelling the charioteer's shoulder as though it were a punching bag, shouting, 'Gallop! Gallop!'

But as there was nothing in their surroundings to give cause for alarm, Otus assumed that the frustrated general was simply indulging in a bout of battle fever.

Soon the chariots halted before the charred and abandoned square. The only structure left intact was the circular stone temple. Othilarius's face hardened and his jaw muscles twitched. A member of the advance party approached and saluted. 'Anything to report?' the Governor asked.

'Just one corpse, sir.'

'Only one! Where is he?'

'It's a she, sir.'

Without ceremony Othilarius jumped to the ground and hastened across the smouldering square. He stopped at the foot of the Temple steps where Anthia lay, her peplos torn and pocked with holes from falling sparks. The soldier was about to turn her over with his foot, when the Governor sank to his knees and gathered the limp form into his arms.

'Who is the fool that can't tell living from dead?' he growled.

Otus stood up and looked around. Why should a local fire trouble the Governor so? The sight of Othilarius walking back to his chariot, a woman in his arms gave a clue, yet managed to make him feel painfully inadequate. 'Had I known, sir,' he stammered feebly, stepping down from the chariot, 'I'd have . . .'

Ignoring Otus's mutterings, Othilarius turned to one of the outriders. 'Get back to my villa by the short route and warn Sinis of a casualty. Tell her it's a woman, and get her to send for my personal physician.' Then, holding Anthia more securely, he mounted the smaller and swifter of the two chariots, and turned to the perplexed aide-de-camp. 'I have an important job for you, too, Otus. You are to take the party up to the garrison and make my excuses to the commanding officer whose name is Gallus. If you are requested to inspect the troops, inspect 'em!'

Otus's jaw dropped. He had no practical experience as an aide-de-camp, or anything else. Uncle Julius had only recently accepted to train him – and the training had not yet begun. 'What the devil do I say to the troops?' he stammered. But his lordship neither heard nor cared – his chariot had spun dizzily towards Athens, and was racing away in a cloud of dust.

The fresh air brought Anthia to dazed consciousness. First she was aware of speeding wheels on an unpaved road, and then felt her head jogging against something hard; a burnished breastplate. Through her half-closed eyes she saw a broad leather strap under the Centurion's handsome chin. Nausea rose in the pit of her stomach, and supposing the perception to have been another of those treacherous dreams, she reeled off into blackness again.

Othilarius looked down from time to time, stroked the matted hair and searched the smoky countenance for signs of recovery. Why he should feel so tenderly he couldn't say. He desired her, of course. Forbidden fruit she most certainly was . . . and with the bloom still on it! Still, Priestess or no Priestess, he could probably have her, and, remembering her blushes, the pleasure might be had without so much as a skirmish.

As they approached the villa, a breeze from the sea brought Anthia to herself. She opened her eyes but quickly shut them again, for the chariot pivoted slowly into the forecourt of a wealthy residence where a barking dog and the twitter of servant's voices met her ears. The fainting spell had passed, though a lump throbbed on the back of her head and cloudy thoughts drifting through her mind made no sense at all. She was aware of being transferred into the arms of a slave whose bare feet moved soundlessly across the tiled floor, while Othilarius's sandalled stride echoed in the hall behind them.

The slave was about to lay Anthia's cinder-besmeared, smoke-smelling body on an immaculate reclining couch when a woman's voice snapped, 'Stop!' The arms that held her hardened; Anthia now knew that this was no dream

'I can stand,' she whispered, but the frightened slave tightened his steely grip until a protective cloth covered the couch where she was to lie. She opened her eyes, and the owner of the voice came into focus. It belonged to a tall, angular woman dressed in black with grey-streaked hair pulled back from a sallow, cadaverous face. Her eyes, dark and small as Corinthian grapes, looked derisively down upon the charred Peplos as she stood over Anthia like a bird of prey.

'Do you remember me?' It was the Centurion, taking Anthia's dirty hand in his and regarding her with concern. Anthia nodded. She remembered the fire, but couldn't make out where the Centurion had come into it. 'I've brought you to my villa,' he continued. 'My physician is here, and the servants will care for you until you are fully recovered.'

'I think I'm all right now. I'm not hurt, just dirty,' Anthia replied.

Relief smoothed Othilarius's brow. 'Even so, you are shocked,' he declared softly. And, turning to the hawk-like housekeeper he ordered her to care for Anthia's needs until he returned later in the day.

As he spoke, Sinis's expression slid with serpentine smoothness from thorny sharp to rippling velvet. 'Of course, my lord. A perfumed bath is this moment being filled, and Midea knows where to find attire befitting a maiden of

Athena.' Those watchful eyes had not overlooked the silver emblem still attached to what remained of Anthia's peplos.

The thought of being cared for by this dark creature was dreadfully distressing, but the state of Anthia's clothing barred all thought of escape; for the next hours at least. Weariness and weakness waved over her again; the Centurion had been right – she was more shocked than she realized.

Towards evening, Anthia awoke to find Othilarius looking silently down at her. She had been bathed and massaged and dressed in a gown more suited to a princess than a priestess. She had slept deeply, and felt restored. Again taking her hand in his, he related how he had found her, and she listened without interrupting. She was wondering what Phyleus would say if he could see her now? And how he would respond if he knew to what extent the Centurion's charm was flooding over her again?

'I must get back to the Acropolis before dark, or search parties will be sent,' Anthia said anxiously. But, like a child with a butterfly, Othilarius was not quite ready to let her go.

'You must dine with us first,' he said firmly. 'Sinis has ordered a special meal for you. Afterwards my litter will take you up to the Acropolis.'

Feeling it ungracious to leave her rescuer so abruptly, and with the assurance that he would not try to retain her, Anthia accepted to stay till after the meal. The effects of shock had completely dissipated, but she drank the honeyed wine ordered by the physician to impart strength. It was the luxurious surroundings and the Centurion's attentiveness that troubled her most, and no medicine on earth could remedy that.

Tullus joined them for the evening meal; dinner in the company of a virgin of the Acropolis was a unique event.

The girl was certainly shy, but with a little encouragement she spoke quite well. Othilarius watched guardedly as the neophyte's grave expression and manner, quietly succumbed to the thoughts and gestures of a budding woman. She was obviously quite unaware how perfectly, if not delightfully, visible her feminity shone up from beneath the surface. He wanted her more than ever now. He would tell her who he was, protect her, and take her to Rome. Yes, he'd smuggle her onto the *Juno*; only four short days remained before she sailed.

With the meal over, Tullus thanked his host and stood to leave.

'Tullus,' Othilarius called after him. 'Tell Sinis to have the litter prepared on your way out. Our priestess must reach the Acropolis before moon-shine.'

Tullus obeyed, his voice echoing in the hall. 'My Lord Governor requests that you have his litter harnessed right away, Sinis.'

They rose from the table and drifted over to the balustrade to contemplate the sea. 'Why did Tullus refer to you as "My Lord Governor" just now?' Anthia asked.

'Because that is who I am, or I should say, *was*,' Othila replied, with commendable modesty.

Anthia looked at him disbelievingly. She had taken the Centurion to have less than 40 summers; too young for a Governor, surely? Besides, the Athenians had dubbed him 'iron fist', and anything less 'iron' she could hardly imagine.

'You see the moon,' he continued, sliding a fatherly arm about her shoulder and pointing to the diaphanous orb in a paling sky. 'Well, in four days' time it will be full, and round, and bright.' Anthia felt his eyes looking down at her in that disturbing way again. Something undeniable began to stir in her belly, but she fixed her eyes rigidly on the moon. 'And then, a ship will sail me back to Rome.'

The unguarded pang of regret that surged into Anthia's

sentiments did not escape Othilarius's notice. Sinis had chosen a particularly heady wine that evening, and although Anthia had taken but a few sips, he yearned to fill her goblet and lead her to his sleeping couch forthwith. Nevertheless he had not ceased to be aware that she was a virgin; any precipitation would frighten her. He knew the dangers of forcing, and wanted her consent or the evening would be spoiled. She had not shaken free from the arm around her shoulder.

'Anthia,' he said casually. 'Why have you given your beautiful womanhood to an indifferent temple?'

'Our Temple is not at all indifferent, and virgins chosen to serve the Goddess are highly honoured in Athens. I have already told you that,' she replied earnestly. But instead of putting him off, her words, and above all her looks were having the opposite effect. She turned her back to the sea so that his arm fell from her shoulder. If she could just remain aloof until the litter was announced, leaving would be smooth and without regret. She wanted to step tactfully away, but the balustrade was at her back and a sideways movement might betray her fear. Her best option was to answer a serious question seriously and hope the litter would be announced before she'd finished.

Othilarius accepted the diversion, following Anthia's barricade of words with pretended attention. She was speaking of her childhood, the public ceremonies and the honour of being a virgin of Athena. Her voice accelerated nervously in an attempt to drown out the secret dialogue Othilarius's presence was holding with another part of herself. Her cheeks tingled and, having emptied her brain of words, the monologue ended incongruously, 'Where is the litter?'

'Hush,' Othilarius soothed as very gently he drew her tense form against his own, and held it there.

'It's almost dark. I have to go,' Anthia protested. But did not tear herself away.

'Yes, in just a moment. I want to hold you a little longer and then I'll take you back to the Acropolis.'

Again Anthia knew the delectable feeling of warmth and protection; it was the most powerful experience she had ever known. No man would hold her thus if he did not love her. But she had to go. 'Surely the litter is ready by now?' she said.

'What's the matter?' Othilarius whispered caressingly, and made this his moment to tell her of his desire to love and protect her – always. He confessed that he had wanted her from their very first meeting and had, even then, envisioned taking her to Rome and making her his wife. He would never force or hurt her. She was free to leave – immediately – if that was her wish . . . but was it?

'I have given promises and made solemn vows. To break them means death,' Anthia replied.

Again, instead of shaking him into seriousness, her words only strengthened her allure, and he made them an excuse to hold her even closer. 'Do you really suppose I'd let them destroy you?'

At that precise moment, Anthia did not think so. 'The litter?' she murmured, pulling away slightly, her words resembling the feeble cry of a drowning woman going down for the last time. This was the moment for which Othilarius had so patiently waited. Tenderness came with soft laughter as his hand slipped delicately to her breast, then his lips met firmly with hers. For a moment Anthia struggled, but then melted. Phyleus's words about the one clear moment rose in her memory, only to vanish for Othilarius's caresses had already aroused her beyond recall.

Neither of them noticed Sinis wafting silently behind the pillars like a puff of black smoke. She had a few last duties to perform before she could retire. After laying a clean white sheet on her master's sleeping couch and adding more cushions, she stole into his study, took a blank scroll from the shelf, and scratched a few words upon it. She then hurried out to the stableyard, where a slave had been waiting by the harnessed litter for more than an hour.

'I want this delivered to the Acropolis school an hour before dawn – not a moment before, or after. You understand?' she said, handing him the sealed scroll.

'And the litter?' he asked.

A smile of consummate satisfaction besmirched the bitter lips, and her voice softened. 'We'll not be needing that tonight.'

Chapter Six

When Anthia awoke, the ochre walls of the bedchamber glowed warmly in the rays of a rising sun. She was instantly aware of what she had done, and what she had allowed to transpire, but it had all seemed so natural and so right that she could find no place for guilt. And yet, the sadness and disappointment she would bring her beloved mentor, and the fact that she would never see his kind face again, made her want to weep. If only she could explain to him, to Astraeus, and to all, that she loved them truly but that her place was now in the world at Othila's side. Of this she was completely sure.

Turning under the rumpled sheet, Anthia stretched a languid arm across the bed, but Othila was already up, dressed in a toga and intent upon a scroll by the window. Tullus was heard moving boxes in the adjoining room, and every now and then, the shadow of an armed guard crossed the window as he paced the length of the balustrade. As she sat up, Othila turned to look at her. An abundance of dark hair swirling stormily about her face and shoulders heightened the translucence of her fine white skin; her lips, slightly grazed, had lost their innocence, and her eyes shone like stars. Leaving the scroll on the sill, he went over to the bed. Anthia's outstretched arms encircled his neck, and were he not taking Atacus to the shipyards that morning, he'd readily have yielded. Instead, he kissed her forehead and disengaged a little briskly.

'You slept well, I see,' he said. 'Are you hungry?'

'Starving!'

Othila got up and opened the door to an adjoining room. 'Breakfast for a starving lady, Tullus, please,' he called. But the remarkable Sinis was waiting behind the door. He did not like that woman.

'I have much to do before we leave, my sweet,' he said, returning to sit on the bed. 'I'm taking Atacus to inspect the shipyards today, but I'll be back before nightfall.'

Fear sprang into Anthia's eyes. 'Take me with you,' she pleaded. 'I cannot stay in this house alone.'

Othila laughed. 'Alone? Funny girl! This house is teeming with mortals, all ready to do your very least . . .' He broke off, just remembering that he'd given permission for his entire staff to attend the three-day Bacchanalia. 'Sinis will be here and so will Tullus,' he said.

'You don't understand!' Anthia protested. 'Any Athenian that knows who I am, and where I belong, would instantly return me to the Acropolis. That housekeeper woman of yours is Greek, and she knows exactly what to do with me. Have I not told you? My vows are now defiled. They'll throw me off the rock. I'm a fallen woman . . . can't you see?'

'Calm yourself, darling. Sinis would not dare betray you under my very nose.'

Anthia wasn't satisfied. Her thoughts raced desperately for a means to convince him of the dangers his Roman status had kept at sword's length. Inexperienced though she was, Anthia could see that Othilarius had become so accustomed to power, that he couldn't conceive of anyone, Greek or Roman, daring to lay hands on the woman he had claimed for his own.

'Be patient, my love,' he continued soothingly. 'In three short days we'll be far away.'

'And there's another thing,' Anthia went on, tears of anxiety toppling onto her cheeks. 'Any Athenian woman found to have slept in a Roman bed is deemed a traitor. Do you realize what that means?'

Knowing all too vividly the fate extended to Roman traitors, Othila stiffened and considered the matter more seriously. He was thinking how best to manage the situation when Tullus entered to announce the arrival of Atacus, followed by Sinis with a breakfast tray. Her movements were slow and precise as she placed the tray silently on the bed, her small sly eyes absorbing every detail. Before she reached the door, however, her master called her back. The tall dark figure froze as she turned to face him.

'Sinis,' he snarled. 'This lady is to be protected at all costs.' Sinis made no reply, but defiance glared across the ramparts of her silence. Othilarius stepped menacingly towards her. 'Nobody is to enter this house, and not the servant's quarters either. Am I understood?'

'Yes, my lord.'

But Othilarius didn't like the look in his servant's eye. 'Just remember, Sinis, if anything befalls this lady, *you will pay with your life.*' He hailed the guard whose shadow had just passed; the soldier retraced his steps and saluted at the window. 'I want an armed guard of forty to seal this house immediately,' he ordered. The soldier saluted again, and hastened away. With a derogatory gesture Sinis, too, was dismissed. As she left, Tullus re-entered to remind his master that Atacus waited.

In spite of all these dire warnings and protective measures, Anthia read the message in the Greek woman's eye and planned her own safety. She would exit by the window, cross the terrace, jump the balustrade, and drop onto the shore where she could hide among the rocks till sundown. Othila might be angry, but at least he'd find her alive.

Othila bent to kiss his new love. 'The sun is climbing fast, my sweet, and I must go. Anything you desire is yours. Nothing and nobody can harm you here.' He kissed her a second time, and then departed.

The moment he had gone, Anthia quickly dressed and knotted her hair at the nape of her neck. Her sandals were nowhere to be found; precious moments had to be spent looking for them, but the rocks could not be borne without them. She had to escape before the house guard arrived, or remain at the mercy of Sinis.

With the house-guard safely on its way, the Governors and their escort rode confidently out of the villa gates. But as the sound of their hoofs faded in the distance, a covered wagon rolled quietly into the forecourt. Two men jumped down. One held a sack, the other a rope. From a side door Sinis beckoned.

Anthia had reached the window when they burst in and grabbed her from behind. A muted scuffle ensued. One man pinned her arms to her side, the other deftly slipped a long narrow sack over her head and pulled it down to her ankles. She tried to scream, but a woman's hardened hand slammed across her mouth and she felt a cord lashing the sacking tightly to her body. In ominous silence Anthia was dragged squirming towards the door. Petrified and gasping for air, she was hoisted aboard the wagon and laid face down on the floor.

They kept her prone until the struggling ceased, but as the vehicle got under way, gentler hands behind her untied the rope and helped her sit. The familiar rhythmic churning of the wheels had a calming effect, and having salvaged her senses from the initial shock, she peered through the loosely woven sacking, and recognized two stable hands from the temple equerry behind the reins. Someone else was there too, behind her, but she was unable to turn her body or head. Shifting her position slightly she looked down and could just make out the tip of an oaken walking stick lying on the boards at her side. Tears rose. 'Phyleus!' she cried, trying unsuccessfully to turn, but there was no response. Instead, a woman cleared her throat. Had they sent a Priestess, too?

As they neared their destination, the woman cleared her throat again and a metallic accent cut in above the churning wheels. 'I wish to speak with Astraeus *personally*. You understand?'

Sinis! What had she come for? Wasn't betrayal enough? But of course! After Othila's threat she could never return to the villa, and must be coming to demand a substantial reward for her patriotism.

'You do not give the orders here.' It was the quiet power of Phyleus's voice that she knew so well.

Defiled by a broken vow, the fallen neophyte was carried unceremoniously through a back entrance and down innumerable steps. They dumped her in a narrow cell smelling of corn. The sack was jerked up over her head and the heavy door barred noisily behind her. The unused store-room was long and narrow. It was lit through a slanting aperture high in the wall, so that sunlight formed a dazzling pool on the smooth stone floor. Dazed and unbelieving, Anthia stood where they had left her. She didn't need to move to see all there was to see; a wide wooden bench serving as seat and bed, a horse-hair blanket, a water jar, a small earthenware basin resting on a shelf, and a covered bowl set on the floor in the corner. The rest of the cell was relentlessly bare. Having ascertained that no escape was possible, she went to the bench and sat staring vacantly at the wall opposite.

It was some time before she noticed a neatly folded square of rough black material, which she mistook for a meagre pillow. On closer inspection however, it unfolded into a simple garment with a horizontal opening at the neck and a cord-like belt. Revolted, she threw it on the floor. 'How long will it be before Othila comes to get me out of here?' she wondered. She knew he'd be inspecting the shipyards till sundown, so it looked as though she'd have to bear with it till first light next day.

Fear and emotional exhaustion led to a timeless sleep. But when Anthia opened her eyes again, the pool of sunlight was gone and an early-evening sky glowed feebly through the aperture. In an hour, darkness would bring Othilarius back to his empty villa. All the prisoner needed now, was patience. Tomorrow her beloved would be upon the rock demanding her release in no uncertain terms. She even pictured herself pleading with him not to take revenge.

The sound of bolts scraping back shocked Anthia out of her reverie and back into fear. Phyleus stood on the threshold, a bundle in his hand and an inscrutable expression on his face. The door was closed by unseen hands as her mentor limped heavily forward.

He did not speak at once but, having recovered his breath, proffered the bundle.' You must be hungry?' he said cheerfully.

'I don't think I can eat just yet.'

With an understanding nod, Phyleus placed the food next to the water jug, picked the black shift off the floor, then limped over to the bench and sat down beside her. 'You must put this on,' he said.

'What difference will *that* make?'

'Your sorrow is my sorrow,' Phyleus replied, looking straight into her eyes.

'What proof do you have of a transgression that I should wear black?' she demanded, hoping that without proof they would let her go.

'Even if we could not tell through the emanations of your aura,' he replied, 'the servant Sinis brought the nuptial bed sheet bearing your vibrations also!'

Anthia was momentarily stumped; denial would only add

to ignominy. 'Phyleus,' she pleaded after a moment's thought, 'I know I am no longer worthy of the Mysteries, but what is wrong with leading a simple human life with the man I love?' Even as she asked the question, she knew the answer – but she had to try.

Phyleus looked at her sadly, shaking his head.

'But this *has* to be possible,' she insisted, raising her voice. 'Othila will not leave me here to die. He promised to take me to Rome and make me his wife. Romans of his status keep their promises, you know.' Having unleashed some of her anger, Anthia looked into the sweetness of Phyleus's eyes, and found tears flooding uncontrollably out of her own.

The patient initiate, so acutely aware of the neophyte's emotions and the blindness they caused, shook his head again. He reminded her that after making solemn vows of chastity in the Order of Athena, the soul cannot progress through secular life without risking a loss of consciousness that could take many lives to recuperate. 'It is imperative that you assume your responsibility, Anthia, and forgive.'

'Forgive! Forgive whom?'

'Yourself, to start with. Go deep within as you have been taught. Get to the crux of the matter while your heart still throbs. Allow the mirror of events to show you the difference between flesh and spirit. For countless lives you have voyaged to this moment, but the journey goes on and will not end until you experience the ultimate truth of yourself. You can do it now. But if you do not, the same emotional situation will arise in a future life, to help you try again.'

'I know,' Anthia responded mechanically. What she was really grappling with, was how to get out of the corn store and into the arms of her beloved.

Phyleus continued patiently. 'If you make use of this seemingly tragic situation in the time that is left to you, higher understanding will come. Then much of the work will have been done, and you will find only gratitude towards the woman who betrayed you, and the man who seduced you for his own pleasure. Forgiveness frees the spirit as you well know, thus you will never need to repeat this anguish for the sake of learning the same lesson again.'

'But he *will* come!' Anthia raged. 'Do you really suppose that a Governor of Athens would leave me here to die? He'll be here – and you'd better not resist him!'

Ignoring this outburst, and knowing that for as long as Anthia believed in her rescue she would never make the monumental effort the circumstances offered, Phyleus explained and repeated that Othilarius could not come because the power of Athena prevented him. His voice was firm, but his eyes were pools of pain. And yet, for the first time in her life, Anthia could not believe him.

'When Othila gets here,' she insisted, 'there will be nothing to forgive.'

Phyleus stood to leave. From force of habit his stick was in Anthia's hand. 'Thank you,' he said, as he made ungainly steps towards the door. Having tapped upon it, he turned again to face the narrow cell. 'Remember, we all feel for you, Anthia. If we reside upon this planet it is because not one of us is truly pure. Astraeus will send for you soon. Do not distress yourself on account of his words. They will be in accordance with the enlightening spirit, that once meant so much to you, and the order of Athena.'

'The longing of my soul is for Othila, and he will soon be here!' Anthia shouted at the closing door – then burst into tears.

Through the opening high in the wall, a tiny sliver of sky turned from pale blue to pink to indigo. Anthia watched the changes and waited for the stars, wondering which constellation would visit her through the small aperture. Before the stars appeared, however, the bolt was drawn back and Anthia, daughter of Peteos, was summoned before Astraeus, High Priest of Athena, in solemn audience.

Every member of the Mystery School was present to witness judgment. The ritual was conducted with dignity and love, but anguish filled every heart. Anthia's infidelity to her vow of chastity was simply declared, and its consequences stated. She was to be cast from the Acropolis' eastern rampart on the eve of the full moon in three days' time. Astraeus urged Anthia to forgive as Phyleus had done.

The whole awesome procedure would have been unbearable were it not for Anthia's belief in Othila's love for her, and the conviction that he would soon be there to reclaim her. When Astraeus raised his hand in final blessing, she looked into his solemn face wondering how, with all his wisdom and light, he could pronounce such a sentence knowing full well that it would never be carried out.

Chapter Seven

Othilarius travelled back from the shipyards in a jovial mood, anticipating the welcome he was about to receive from the most delectable creature in all Athens. They would dine quietly that evening, but the feast he was planning for her in Rome was to celebrate a great lady; for that was what he intended to make her after he had claimed his seat in the Senate.

'Anything to report?' he asked the officer guarding the forecourt.

'Nothing, sir.'

'Very good. I'll keep a reinforced house-guard until I leave. I'm not expecting trouble, but you never know.'

The Governor's residence seemed uncannily silent. Lamps glowed, and yet an eerie emptiness pervaded. Without changing his dust-laden garments, Othilarius went from room to room looking for Anthia and calling for Sinis. Passing the scroll chamber he encountered Tullus, beside himself with apprehension.

'I must speak with you at once, my lord,' he said.

'Where is she?' his master shouted.

'Sinis and the lady left early this morning. That is to say, before the house guard arrived.'

'Left! What in the name of Jupiter is going on in this house?'

Putting his finger to his lips, Tullus backed into the scroll chamber. Othilarius followed. 'I cannot tell you exactly what happened, sir,' Tullus said. 'For after you drove out of the villa, I returned to my work here. Shortly afterwards, I heard the house-guard arrive and hurried to your quarters to check that the lady was there, but she was nowhere to be found. Sinis too seemed to have disappeared, and all her belongings with her. I realized then that she had taken the lady back to the Acropolis and would not be returning.'

'They couldn't have gone far,' Othilarius cut in angrily. 'Didn't you have the wit to order the guard to give chase?'

'That I did,' Tullus replied. 'A detachment sped towards Athens immediately. But the intruders must have made an early start; the officer in charge reported seeing a covered wagon enter the citadel just as his contingent arrived at the foot of the rock, and without the Governor's permission, the military could go no further.'

'A carefully planned abduction,' Othilarius growled. 'Did you question the staff?'

'The cook, you mean Sir? He was drunk – totally unconscious. The others have not yet returned from the Bacchanalia, and I imagine they too will be inebriated for a day or two after all the feasting.'

'Indeed.' Othilarius replied, breathing heavily. He was in shock. Not so much because he'd now have to retrieve his new love from the priests, but because he'd been monstrously outwitted by a mere housekeeper!

'I have tried to limit the damage to yourself and the lady, Sir.'

'Damage?'

'Well, yes, Sir. A virgin of Athena found under your roof risks a sentence of death; and there will be talk. If accusations point in your direction, Atacus will ask questions of your staff. The cook couldn't have seen anything, and I took the liberty of letting the house-guard believe it was the Lady Nerva that they were guarding as she would be travelling with you to Rome. I even persuaded the guard you called into the bedchamber, that the lady he saw there, *was* the Lady Nerva. The officer who went in pursuit of the covered wagon had orders to capture it and bring it back to the villa; there wasn't time to explain who or what it contained. On his return, however, he wanted to know what the chase was all about.'

'What did you tell him?'

'I said valuables from the house had been stolen.'

Othilarius nodded distractedly. His Roman scribe went on. 'And I hope you will not think it too much of an impertinence, sir, but I took the liberty of inviting the Lady Nerva to your dinner table "again" this evening so that she will be well and truly seen by our staff returning from their festivities.'

The Lady Nerva, a beautiful young Egyptian widow, had become the most frequent of the Governor's mistresses and was well known to the household. Othilarius, however, had grown a little tired of her.

'Do you think we need a decoy?' he questioned. 'After all, I can't deny having given succour to the Acropolis girl injured in a fire, but there is no proof that she slept in my bed. In the absence of my wife, I can sleep with whom I like, can I not? So in whose interests would it be to challenge me? I appreciate your loyalty, Tullus, but what would all the fuss be about?'

'There should be no fuss, sir, and soon you'll be gone. But according to custom, after three days the lady must die.'

'Yes, yes, Tullus, I know. Tradition demands she be thrown over the rock,' Othilarius said impatiently. 'But I hardly think you need worry on that score. I'll go up and fetch her. Considering all the tolerance we've shown the religious affairs of this city, the High Priest, what's-his-name, won't dare refuse me this little favour. As for Sinis, it's good riddance to bad rubbish!'

To accommodate Tullus's precautions, Othila took the Lady Nerva to his table as well as his bed that night, and for good measure allowed her to imagine she'd be joining him in Rome . . . at a later date.

If Tullus was to be believed, only two days remained before Anthia's execution. But for a man used to conquering cities – nay countries – retrieving a single lady from an undefended rock in a Roman province which until yesterday had been under his own command, seemed like child's play. However, if an unmarred reputation was to be upheld at this critical moment in his career, the usual display of force, threat or brutality, was not an option. Instructions from Rome made interference with the religious rites and customs of Athens a grave offence. His predecessor, Chilio, had been disgraced for just such an infraction. And although the business of freeing Anthia seemed simple initially, Othilarius gradually realized that if the general populace knew the facts, it might be enough to set the city in revolt and jeopardize his future prospects.

The alternative to force is always threat, diplomacy or gold, Othilarius conjectured. Certain lords of the Greek council were not above 'compensation', so why should the priests of the Temple be any different? However, if by some unfortunate chance the holy men lived up to their reputed integrity, the situation could turn nasty. Rather than risk his own good name, Othilarius needed an emissary to go in his stead – someone with a more spiritual turn of mind. He closed his eyes to conjure up a face that would fit the mission, but none appeared.

Calling for wine, Othilarius wandered into the scroll chamber to browse through the names on the Roman Register. Moonrise found him there still, his dinner uneaten and the quest for a trustworthy man unsatisfied. He thought he had friends, and certainly there were many who owed him a favour, but now, in the hour of his own need, not one could he find. As for a spiritual turn of mind – well, he must have been dreaming!

Left with the probability of having to rescue Anthia on his own, Othilarius surveyed the terrain with military precision. The Governor's baton could no longer be shaken for it was now in the hands of the last man on earth in whom he could confide. If he honoured the priests with a personal visit, it would point to a Roman culprit, and even after a hefty bribe these matters had a way of flying to the Rome faster than wind. If he dressed as a rich Phoenician or Judean merchant rattling coins in exchange for she whom they sought so wantonly to destroy, success was not assured and he risked finding himself under investigation, lock and key, or worse.

Confounded, Othilarius began to wonder just how much this pretty little priestess really meant to him. His wealth was scarcely enough for his seat in the Senate; were his reputation, his future *and* his fortune, worth endangering on Anthia's behalf? The faint hope of a solution came when he remembered Mynas.

Now and again during his governorship, disguised as a foreign ne'er-do-well that he'd named Mynas, Othilarius had wandered through the disreputable taverns of the city gleaning more facts in one evening than all his officers could provide in a month. If the Temple was needy, the priests greedy, or if a disgruntled populace murmured against their Deity, he would hear about it there. More effective than battering rams, such information might lever breaches in the enemy defences that a little gold would widen sufficiently to extract the prisoner.

It was late. Nothing stirred in the villa and nobody questioned the Governor leaving his villa for a breath of fresh air, nor suspect that the bundle under his arm was a stained tunic, a ragged wig and a false beard. As usual he took a horse from a nearby farm and rode to a coppice on the outskirts of town where he tethered his mount, and donned his disguise. A near-full moon lit his way.

'Mynas, you old scoundrel. We've not seen your scabrous carcass in months,' was the raucous greeting that welcomed him to the first tavern. 'Where've you been?'

'Business, dear friends, just business,' Othilarius replied with the inebriated smile and rolling drawl that he'd made his chief characteristics.

Soon he was chafing them on his own account. 'Morality!' he declaimed censoriously. 'How dare you Athenians speak to me of morality, when Athens allows her sacred virgins to dally with ordinary folk like you and me?' The statement fell on questioning looks; they'd heard nothing of that.

When he staggered, belching, into a third tavern, Othilarius bumbled into a group discussing the fate of a neophyte serving at Athena's Temple on the Delphi road. A pilgrim, they said, had deflowered the girl after the fire, and although she'd been taken advantage of in a moment of crisis, they weren't surprised to hear that she was to receive the traditional punishment the day before the full moon. Mynas burped loudly. It was a relief to know that fingers pointed away from the ex-Governor, but the integrity of the revered priests was never questioned.

Weary and disappointed, Othilarius made a bundle of his disguise, returned the horse, and shortly afterwards re-entered his villa by a side door he had been careful to leave unbarred.

Early the next day, having seen the last of his belongings aboard the *Juno*, Othilarius garbed himself as Mynas again and returned to the city. It would quell his impatience to leave, if nothing else. But as gossip flies faster than flames in Athens, by mid-morning the whole population was wise to the virgin's fate. The scandal had surfaced in all the taverns like flotsam from a wrecked ship – a ship named *Othilarius*.

'Not a pilgrim after the fire,' they said, 'but the Governor himself.'

'Atacus, you mean?' Mynas drawled.

'Ba! He couldn't fuck a goat! No, Othilarius, Iron Fist, the one that's leaving on the full moon.'

Mynas spun a convincing alternative tale. But the townsfolk preferred, nay relished, the story as it stood; it satisfied their insatiable appetite for drama. And what more dramatic than noble Greek defiled by Roman foul – and not just any Roman, either!

Greatly disturbed, Othilarius made for home. Having washed and changed, he glimpsed Atacus between the pillars of his hall striding furiously back and forth over Neptune as though some terrible catastrophe had shaken his world. Before making his presence known, therefore, he beckoned a servant and ordered the last of his Tuscany wine to be brought to the balustrade immediately. Whatever the crisis, Tuscany wine always minimized its effect; Sinis had taught him that.

'Ah! There you are.' Atacus hailed without ceremony, shaking with anger. 'I'm given some very disturbing news concerning your person, Othilarius.'

'Atacus, my lord,' Othilarius said, a suave smile blanketing a mountain of misgivings. 'What brings you to my house in such a frenzy?'

Conscious that his nerves were getting the better of him, Atacus cooled his tone and relayed the rumour that Othilarius had only just heard himself.

Othilarius laughed. 'My dear Atacus,' he said, astonished at the speed with which such information had reached the old man's ear. 'Is *that* all?'

'Do you realize what this means, sir?' Atacus spluttered. 'Have you not the slightest idea what Athena's cult is all about? Its importance to Athens and the Athenians? This kind of trouble could easily lead to an uprising, and that would cost me my position.'

'Calm yourself, my lord,' Othilarius cajoled and, nodding to the wine bearer, took the new Governor's arm and strolled with him out to the balustrade. Their goblets were filled, and by the time his irate compatriot had taken a draught or two, Othilarius had gathered his wits.

'Now, now,' he soothed. 'They're only pulling your tail. Any excuse is good enough to cause trouble when power moves from one Governor to another. Nothing to worry about – Athens is known for it! They're eager to test your leather. They need to know what sort of Governor they'll have to contend with – nothing more.'

'So what, in your view, am I supposed to do?' Atacus questioned softly, for the mellowing properties of Tusan's wine were beginning to take effect.

Shaking his head wisely, Othilarius said. 'We are not provoked, Atacus. The strong are never provoked – you know that.'

At a slight loss, Atacus remained silent for a moment, and then boldly faced his host. 'I take it you are innocent of the whole accusation? I mean, with all Athens at your feet you wouldn't be so ignorant as to desecrate a virgin of the Temple, would you?' He paused and with a wily glance said, connivingly, 'Or, will you be seeking a touch of diplomatic concealment?'

Othilarius was not deceived by this tactic and, laughing heartily at such an absurdity, replied. 'My dear Atacus, the girl we rescued after the fire may, or may not, have been a virgin but she was unconscious when we found her, and her peplos in a terrible state.'

'Yes, so Otus told me.' Atacus replied dryly. 'But what possessed you to bring her back to Athens yourself? After all, Otus was in attendance, and four out-riders there to assist you as well.' His anger was rising again. 'Well, weren't there? And what is more, Othilarius,' he shouted, 'how dare you treat my nephew in that outrageous manner?'

'I see you don't trust me – Sir,' Othilarius replied accusingly. 'But to answer your question. Had the out-riders that morning been tried and disciplined Roman soldiers, there'd have been no problem. But unfortunately they were barely recruited ruffians from Mesopotamia still chaffing in their new uniforms. I'd be sorely guilty if I were to leave any woman, let alone a priestess, to their unsupervised care. As for your nephew, my Lord, he almost fainted when he saw the alarming state the priestess was in. He is still very young, you know.'

'Yes, he's had a protected life, of course. But to leave him to do the inspection alone . . .?'

'Try and see my dilemma, Sir. You have just this minute told me that the religious and political affairs of the Acropolis are not to be despised. So would it have been wise to ignore a priestess in distress, particularly at this delicate juncture when power shifts from one Governor to the next?'

Atacus was silent but not satisfied. After a moment, and a long noisy sip of his wine, he re-launched the attack. 'Who would have known you passed by the burnt-out square?'

'Oh everyone! News travels fast around here.'

'Still, you had no right to throw Otus in the deep like that.'

'I only dared do it, Sir, because he was *your* nephew,' Othilarius said flatteringly. 'A noble, however young, is usually equipped to handle any situation. Gallus, the garrison commander is a most civilized man; and, in view of the circumstances, would have seen Otus through his first diplomatic mission like a father. Of course if you had been there it would have been entirely different. As it happened, however, all Otus had to do, was ride the ranks in the governor's chariot dispensing a farewell gesture from time to time, and let Gallus improvise my address. Did Otus report any difficulty?'

'No,' Atacus replied gruffly though failed to repress a smile. 'As a matter of fact he rather enjoyed it. And now I'll have to teach him that he is not yet a qualified diplomat!'

That smile, more welcome than the dawn to Othilarius's nerves, lifted the atmosphere to a more genial level. 'You don't suppose I'd seduce a priestess of the Acropolis with my mistress Nerva under my roof, do you?' he questioned,. 'Tullus was there too. Ask him, if you like? And, my lord Governor,' he added good-humouredly, 'do you seriously give credence to every piffling rumour that brushes your ear?'

Ignoring this last remark, Atacus continued. 'Tullus has already been questioned – a good fellow – you're taking him with you, I suppose?'

The departing Governor had not envisaged this, but in view of all that Tullus had done for him lately, he answered perspicaciously. 'Tullus is a free man. I'm leaving the choice to him.'

They stood with their thoughts for a while, watching the gulls rise and swoop over the gently undulating sea. Atacus's dewlaps had ceased quivering and lost their reddish tinge. The mellowing wine may have quelled the lion's roar, but Othilarius was far from tranquil. 'How do you find our wine?' he asked.

'You bathe in the blessings of Dionysus,' his guest replied approvingly.

'My reserve is all but consumed, unfortunately, but if you would honour me by sharing the midday meal, I'll tell you how it can be procured in the future.'

'With the greatest of pleasure, my dear fellow,' Atacus responded, warming to his host. Dionysus on an empty stomach tended to make him overly talkative and that would never do. However, in the beautiful residence, soon to be his, and with his host's self-assurance a balm to his nerves, even Athens seemed less daunting at that moment. 'I only hope,' he continued as they walked along the balustrade to the marble table set in a shady alcove, 'that I manage to keep this exquisite city as serene as you have.'

'Of course you will,' Othilarius assured, as more liquid diplomacy gurgled into Atacus's goblet. 'Moreover, with your knowledge of the country and its customs, even better!'

As the meal progressed Othilarius watched his guest; waiting for the right moment. Slight inebriation revealed the man but not to his advantage; the enraged Grecophile was not taking the neophyte incident lightly. 'We'll run the culprit to earth!' Atacus shouted, making the table reverberate under his fleshy fist. 'Even if he has fled to Rome, we'll find him' he spluttered, eyeing his host, decisive for once. 'Rome must be seen as just. Public disgrace and dismissal will be his lot.'

In an effort to diffuse the accusation in that look, Othilarius nodded understandingly and, with an air of detachment, seized his chance. 'I have learned that at sundown the lady must die. As you are so concerned, what might you say if a peaceful contingent were to present itself to the Acropolis with apologies, money, and a promise to see justice done if they would agree to reinstate the young victim or, perhaps, simply banish her? I would go myself if you thought it would help.' Atacus said nothing. Othilarius continued. 'Would that not demonstrate to your beloved Athenians that Rome is not only just, but compassionate also?'

Atacus reflected silently, took a sip of wine and again shot that penetrating look across the table into the face of his host. 'No,' he said. 'For one thing, the Athenian doesn't reason as we do. And for another, the Senate would certainly condemn such action as interference in the religious affairs of the country. And that, as you know, would be an irreparable blot on my reputation – and yours!'

'Not justified, you mean?' Othilarius said thoughtfully.

'A dangerous precedent, more like. But anyway, you yourself told me the penalty for such action, and this is not the time to incite trouble in Athens ... or Rome, for that matter.'

After this, insistence could only invite suspicion so Othilarius moved on to explaining the intricacies of bringing that special vintage of Tuscan wine to Athens.

With the meal over and more pleasantries exchanged, Othilarius led his guest towards the forecourt to bid him farewell. 'Don't be bothered by this little rumour,' he said casually. 'There may be a brief disturbance, but you'll get used to such things; they never lead anywhere. Do nothing, Atacus, and the episode will be forgotten within a moon or two. Investigate, and your baton plunges into a hornets' nest, and hornets here have stingers longer and more unpredictable than Damocles' sword.'

The new Governor's mouth formed a perfect 'O' as he looked gravely into his predecessor's eyes with a gaze that showed he had begun to doubt his own judgment. From across the forecourt, his litter approached. 'Thank you, dear fellow, for your most gracious hospitality,' he said and when seated turned to his host. 'We meet again after tomorrow, for I am to accompany you to Piraeus where the *Juno* awaits you. In the meantime, I'll give thought to your valuable counsel ... Regarding the wine, that is to say.'

Othilarius stood alone in the empty hall looking down at Neptune's mighty head. The dart of suspicion in Atacus's regard had troubled him. But Atacus, the gods be praised, was a ditherer so unlikely to follow through without proof, and Tullus had taken care of that. He'd never before permitted a pretty woman or anyone else, to come between him and his life-long ambition. And now, with all the bother this naïve, deluded, creature was causing, a tide of irritation swirled over the quicksands of attraction and desire, obliterating them completely. 'I certainly did not force her, nobody could accuse me of *that*,' he said to himself self-righteously. 'The litter was at her disposal all evening and had she asked for it *convincingly*, I'd have taken her up to the Acropolis myself. She knew the score, and took the risk. It's unfortunate that Rome forbids my interfering with the affairs of the Acropolis, but there's nothing I can do about that!' He paused to scan the situation for the umpteenth time, but without further inspiration. 'It's a pity,' he sighed, 'but yes, she knew the score and I cannot save her from the consequences of her action.'

Having thus shaken a little order into his conscience, Othilarius felt a lot better, almost normal in fact. He thanked the gods that he'd soon be safe in Rome and made a slow reverential bow to the Lord of the Sea. For a moment he thought the mosaic was answering him, for Neptune's head appeared to move – though whether it was up and down, or from side to side, he could not tell.

Chapter Eight

The prison bench was hard, and sleep fitful on Anthia's first night in captivity. Dry-eyed she heard the strident cockcrow of a chilly dawn, but warmed herself with thoughts of an imminent release. Phyleus came early to counsel his charge, but her ear remained strained for the sound of marching feet. He strived to persuade the fallen neophyte that expectation of rescue was futile, but she shook her head angrily. He stayed throughout the morning, but his words fell on deaf ears. 'I'm leaving you to yourself now,' he said, hoping that silence would bring her to her senses.

When sunset came and Othila had not, Anthia's hope burned on. She refused to believe that the man who loved her, and to whom she had given her all, could stand back and allow her to die. Everyone knew that a Roman always got what he wanted by fair means or foul – so why was it taking so long? Before darkness engulfed Anthia's cell, Phyleus returned bringing some fruit saved from his evening meal, but he found her asleep. Having placed his gift by the water jug he staggered over to contemplate the face that still bore the marks of innocence and purity.

'It was just too hard to resist,' he thought. 'Brute nature won its battle over faith, training and will.' For a long moment he held the palms of both hands over her prone body, beaming invisible strength upon it, but he did not rouse her. He'd be back tomorrow.

The exhaustion of futile waiting had driven Anthia into early sleep, but by midnight troubling dreams tossed her hither and thither. One moment she was sailing with Othila to Rome, the next, peering over the precipice not far from where she lay. Then he was there again; she reached towards him but her arm flailed into emptiness. She opened her eyes. Moonbeams streamed onto the smooth stone floor where a rat scuffled around some bread she had left uneaten. The creature sat on its haunches, whiskers twitching happily as it raised the fortuitous find to its nibbling mouth with its forelegs. 'Only a rat,' Anthia thought, 'but how wonderfully innocent, natural and, above all, free!'

At dawn, neither cocks nor the guardian geese brought Anthia to wakefulness, but a panicky voice, shouting, 'Out! Through the rat hole. Hurry!' She wondered from where the voice had come but, on opening her eyes, realized that it had been her own; her cell was empty and her body damp with sweat. She rose to wash the horror from her face. 'Othila *must* come today,' she murmured, 'or tomorrow I . . .'

An hour later, the bolts of the door were drawn back and Anthia rushed towards it expectantly. But it was Phyleus again with her daily ration of bread.

'You don't understand,' Anthia remonstrated. 'He did not seduce me merely for a night of pleasure. Othila loves me and he knows what will befall me if I stay here. He said he'd never allow such a thing to happen – and he won't.'

As the empty day wore on, Anthia slipped from hope to hopelessness and from there into an impregnable fantasy world of her own. Phyleus tried to shake her out of her stupor, repeating time and time again that the power of Athena prevented Othila from reaching the rock. But such was the ineluctable supremacy of Eros over a woman in love, that his words weren't even heard.

Waiting patiently for a change in Anthia's mood, Phyleus reflected on his pupil's steps to higher consciousness. In spite of all her fervour and good humour, she still had the capacity to choose animal passion over a higher, all-encompassing form of love. Moreover she had tasted this sacred state to some degree for a short period after her first initiation, when it had come to her as a gift. To choose the higher over the lower had been her test; the hardest of them all. Phyleus remembered well his own struggle, and had it not been for his deformity, how easily might he have succumbed as Anthia had done. Eventually darkness fell and Phyleus left Anthia for the night.

The following morning Anthia awoke aware of only one thing. If Othila did not reclaim her that day, it would be her last on earth. The nightmare should have been over by now. If Othila had not come, either he did not love her, or was dead.

Phyleus came at the usual hour and sat quietly on the bench beside her, pondering the pool of sunlight on the smooth stone floor. When it had gone, Anthia broke the silence. 'I shall never see that again in this life, shall I, Phyleus?' The words rose out of her the way a fish breaks surface for air. Phyleus had waited long for such lucidity.

'No,' he said softly.

'If Othila does not come this day, I have wasted my life. You need not remind me, Phyleus, I know it. And,' she continued as though to ward off a blow, 'I am to blame. That is what you want me to say . . . isn't it?'

'No,' Phyleus replied firmly. 'First you must realize that Othilarius should be forgiven for not coming. It is the power of Athena that keeps him away.'

'Why didn't you tell me?'

'I did, many times, but your ears were closed.'

'Is he at the gate, you mean, and nobody will grant him entry? Or are you saying that Athena has turned his mind against me?

'Neither. It is Athena's will that keeps him from reaching

the rock so that you might take responsibility for your actions,' Phyleus repeated calmly.

'But you always said that Athena's power was for protection,' Anthia protested.

'It still is.'

'If it's Athena's power that prevents Othila from coming, then he has not ceased to love me?' Anthia pursued tenaciously, as she searched her mentor's face for the nod she wanted. Phyleus averted his eyes and smiled, but remained silent. Taking this to mean that Othila did love her, Anthia blushed with shame for having doubted his sincerity. She imagined how for three days and nights he'd been struggling to reach her, only to be thwarted by forces he could not understand.

Even if death was inevitable, Anthia clung savagely to Othila's love. How to forgive him for that?

As the day wore on and the inevitability of her situation sank deeper, Anthia knew she was trapped and became agitated. An explosive heat filled her head while her limbs remained frozen. Breathing chaotically, she jumped off the bench to press her burning cheek against the cool wall and remained thus until Phyleus called her back to the bench and covered her shoulders with the sleeping blanket.

'Will death be painful?' she asked, searching her mentor's eyes for assurance.

For the first time ever, Phyleus took her hand in both of his. 'Fear alone is the pain. The passing is painless,' he replied comfortingly, but was pleased that Anthia had at last come to terms with her situation. 'There may be no way out,' he said, 'but there *is* a way through.' Anthia knew what he was going to say, but listened as he said it again. 'Release. Let go. Forgive.' Anthia was listening to her mentor for the first time in three days; his presence calmed her. And from that moment on, he was able to prepare her for the ordeal ahead.

As the sun begun its descent over the western horizon, the bolts of the store-room rasped back. Two sturdy stable hands entered and, keeping a wary eye on Anthia, clasped hands to form a seat for Phyleus, whom they carried along the short passage and up the high staircase. Anthia followed. On reaching the top Phyleus was set down, and for the last time Anthia handed him back his stick.

They were standing at the entrance of the oval hall, with its far portal leading out to the eastern rampart. In the centre of the hall, white-robed and silent, Astraeus waited. Anthia turned a terrified glance towards her mentor. Dumb with emotion Phyleus made no reply, but raised his hand momentarily over his charge's head in a farewell blessing. Anthia had now to approach Astraeus alone, but as she moved forward Phyleus followed, and nobody barred his way.

Behind the High Priest Anthia could see the dreaded portal beyond which two straight lines of white-clad initiates and neophytes stood forming a ghostly corridor to the rampart's edge. Anthia looked into the High Priest's gentle face trembling uncontrollably. 'I'll do services all my life,' she blurted, 'but please . . . please!'

Tension was palpable in the white corridor beyond. Guiding a sister to her death was rare; even the oldest among them had not witnessed it before, but the mercy of this act did nothing to alleviate its anguish. Frantically Anthia searched the High Priest's tranquil eyes, but no response sprang from them. The comforting hand of Phyleus went to her shoulder infusing warmth like a ray of morning sun. When Astraeus spoke the hand withdrew.

'Daughter of Peteos, bride of man, we do not condemn you. The event that is about to be accomplished is, even now, the desire of your soul and the rule of Athena. To continue this life having forsaken your vows, leads only to the loss of spiritual understanding already gained here.' He paused for what he was about to say was crucial.

'You may be grateful to the circumstances that held you back from that loss, meaning that the conscious quest for enlightenment begun many lives ago, may now continue without a backward step, but on one condition – forgiveness! So bear no resentment for the one who failed to claim you. Had he brought the entire Roman army to the rock, he'd not have succeeded in obtaining your release.

'I perceive a certain anger in your heart concerning the sincerity of this man. Unless it is resolved before the sun goes down, the force of it will remain with you until circumstances in a future life provide another opportunity to resolve it.'

'What anger?' Anthia demanded. The thought of Othila betraying her was untenable. Couldn't he see that her feelings were of sorrow, not anger? 'I love the man Athena now keeps from me. He did not intend my death, so what is there to forgive?'

Astraeus ignored these protestations. He knew that Anthia could not fully understand his words until the true extent of Othila's betrayal became clear to her, but the depth of that betrayal was not for him to reveal.

'You will never totally forget The Mysteries,' he continued serenely, 'but you will find them in another time, in another place and in a different way. The knowledge you have gained here will remain as an echo in every future life. As in this school we learn, and advance, by service to our fellow human beings, so in some future time service will be expected of you again. And I tell you that, until the appropriate period of service is completed and forgiveness achieved, the way forward and upward will be withheld. That is why I implore you now, my child, before the sun sinks behind the western hills, let go the anguish and *forgive*, so that once again you may be worthy of white.'

With Phyleus's presence behind her Anthia felt more composed, and refrained from again challenging the High

Priest's conviction that she harboured resentment against Othila.

'If you can fully pardon this man before you go,' Astraeus pursued, looking at the fallen neophyte with supreme compassion, 'then the burden of your future life will be alleviated. You may never re-enter this school, but take another path to perfection. Nevertheless, once chastened by service and freed by forgiveness, it will be possible, if you so wish, to join with a soul destined to share your journey toward enlightenment.' He paused a long moment, then asked if Anthia had anything she wanted to say.

Anthia shook her head, but turned to Phyleus. She was about to fall to her knees, express her gratitude and ask his pardon, but his hand on her arm forbade it. Anthia's mentor, who shunned such acts of formal humility, already knew Anthia's heart and had long since dismissed any need for pardon from his own. In those fleeting seconds, deep caring shone from his eyes, but words defied utterance.

The sun was low. The time come. Astraeus raised his hand in a final blessing before turning to lead the daughter of Peteos, bride of man, towards the far portal. Phyleus followed.

At the portal Astraeus stepped back; Anthia moved on, flanked now by the two living columns lining the 20 yards to the rampart's edge. Her mentor moved closer; she could hear his struggle for breath. 'Look up, look up,' he whispered. Nobody else heard those words, nor saw his tears as he limped behind his slim black-robed charge, whose eyes were fixed obediently upon the sky. Any moment, Anthia's bare foot would meet the void, but before that moment, a sudden blow between the shoulder blades toppled her forward. At once the horizon spun dizzily into the sea, and the sea into rooftops, a flash from the sinking sun, and then velvety blackness as the fallen neophyte rolled the last few yards to the path at the foot of Athena's sacred rock.

In the city streets, the people of Athens gaped up at the pillared Parthenon, holding their breath as the black speck dropped from the eastern rampart. Awestruck and silent they listened as the white-ones chanted Athena's sacred hymn, signifying that her will was now accomplished.

Feeling no pain, and through the eyes of her soul, Anthia observed her earthly body sprawled among the boulders beside the path. She was aware of waiting for someone; a mounted Centurion, or the Governor's litter. But when a heavy plough-horse appeared, bearing a rider wrapped in a peasant's hooded cloak, she knew it was he.

She wanted to rush towards him, but some power held her back. He had to know that it was Athena's power that had thwarted him. And, above all, how greatly she still loved him.

Time was short; the orange orb now touched the distant hills. Slowly the rider approached, his aura a misty gray. But as he neared to where her body lay, Anthia's spirit watched in disbelief.

He did not bare his head, dismount to close the eyes, straighten the corpse, or hold her close to him. From pitiless eyes, no tears fell. From beneath the peasant's cloak no lamp came, and from his stony heart, no prayer said – he did not even move his head. With just one sideways glance he saw, and turned the lumbering steed away. In that gray aura, taken for noble grief, the truth was clear. Fear for his name, his fame and his repute. No trace of love for her was there, and never had there been!

Darts of anger hissed to the rider's ear. He straightened up; the hooded head looked round. Was that her furious voice shouting against the wind, or just his sleep-starved mind deceiving him again? Craning his head to hear, the hood fell back. He waited. It came again. 'Othila, murderer of love, the hand that killed my trust all pardon too has slain. Hades is too sweet a place for thee!'

But then the western hills had swallowed down the sun. And with the vanishing light her spirit too was gone, to cross the Styx, and face her karma in another life.

Chapter Nine

England, 2,200 years later.

Gerald Edmonds had just been promoted Assistant Professor of Classics at Cambridge University, when his daughter was born and he wanted to name her after a Greek Goddess. His wife Norma, however, didn't altogether agree. 'We can't give her one of your Greek names,' she said, sitting up in bed recovering from her recent delivery. 'Every time I so much as mention Diana, Lavinia, Sophie or Athena, she bites my nipple and hollers the house down.'

'Funny. Theo never reacted that way, did he?' Gerald responded, referring to their first-born, now two years old.

'No, but I promised he'd always be called Theo. Theo has a strong harmonious ring to it – Theodore sounds censorious and severe.'

'Nonsense, darling. It means "gift of God".'

'Maybe. But if there *is* a God, the last thing He would be is censorious and severe.'

'Ah, but the Greek Gods managed to encompass all human traits, good and bad, and still have themselves worshipped.'

'They would!' Norma replied, before returning to the point. 'You know Gerald, I didn't sleep a wink last night for thinking of your mother, and it crossed my mind that we might name this child, Anna, after her. Would you like that?'

Gerald gazed up at the ceiling pretending to think, while

hiding the surge of sadness that had erupted on hearing his mother's name; she'd been killed in a London air raid five years previously. But he turned quickly back. 'I'd like that very much – if you would?'

'I was really fond of your mother,' Norma went on, scrutinizing her husband's face to be sure he really *was* happy with the suggestion. 'I think it would be nice to have another Anna around, don't you?' Gerald's eyes brightened.

'A lovely idea. Thank you for thinking of it, darling. Yes, let's settle for Anna, then.'

'What about a christening?' she pursued unbuttoning her nightie for the evening feed. The couple were sincere agnostics.

'Well, I'm not against formality if it keeps our relatives from trying to convert us, and the children can choose their own religion when they're old enough,' Gerald replied, as he lifted his five-day-old out of her cot and carried her over to his wife.

'Anna Edmonds echoes well,' Norma murmured, once the eager little mouth was busy at her breast. 'And as she has neither nipped nor screamed, so it looks as though she has not disapproved our choice – have you, Anna?' this last was addressed to the infant, who was more than happy to get on with her feed.

'I wonder who she'll marry?' Norma said.

Gerald smiled. 'It's a bit soon to speculate on that. But if she turns out half as pretty as you are, we'll have no trouble giving her away to the highest bidder.'

When Anna was born, there was every reason to suppose she would follow in her mother's conventional footsteps. Norma had met Gerald at a dinner party when she was 19, and married him six months later. Life, however, was not to be so clement with Anna, though nobody could have imagined then, the disastrous downturn of events at the very time this pretty baby would need smart clothes, promising invitations and the launching pad of a parental home. Neither did anybody know that fallen neophytes rarely follow the smoothest road.

Both Edmond children went to boarding school. Theo started prep school aged seven, and Anna's convent took boarders at the tender age of six. They had not planned on a convent education for their daughter; it had been a temporary arrangement that had stretched into a permanent one. From then on, and for the rest of their childhood, Theo and Anna saw each other and their parents only when they went home for the school holidays – home was a house in a country village 8 miles from the university city of Cambridge.

Only one isolated memory-bubble brought Anna's mysterious past briefly to the surface. It happened in her first year at school. Mother Christina pointed her ruler, first to a poster of the Acropolis on the classroom wall, and then to Anna. 'Tell the class what you know about this,' she commanded.

Anna looked at the poster, and without a second's hesitation, replied. 'It had a roof with statues, and beautiful white walls, when I was there.' That said, the bubble burst. Anna's memory-fragment of a former life sank back into her soul to await the proper time for its unveiling and Mother Christina's ruler jerked towards a less imaginative child.

After an uneventful childhood, there came a day when Norma took her daughter to buy her first small-cup bra. It was about that time that the notion, seeded in Anna's subconscious mind, began to sprout into her conscious mind. Out there, somewhere in the world beyond the garden gate and the convent walls, lived a man she was destined to meet. She felt sure she'd recognize him immediately, and presumed he would become her husband, but she kept this notion to herself; put into words it sounded so terribly corny.

When 15 candles flickered on Anna's birthday cake, her future looked as rosy as any middle-class maiden could wish for. In a couple of years school would be over and life, with a capital L, begin. She'd have an allowance, choose her own clothes, go to parties, and Theo would include her in his university antics so that she'd be meeting a lot of new people. Nevertheless, like most of her contemporaries, she'd have to suffer a boring secretarial course while living at home. But after that, she envisaged the emancipated life of a shared London flat, a part-time job and a whale of a time. Then, somewhere along the way the man she was destined to meet would appear and that would be that!

Six months after those 15 candles had been extinguished, Gerald was hit by a car and everything changed.

For weeks it was touch and go, but when he finally pulled through, it was with an irreversible memory deficiency and a stammer too pronounced to teach again.

Compensation helped pay the bills, but money was short. Norma coped courageously, always hoping that the university might offer less demanding employment for Gerald, enabling them to see the children's private education through to the end. But times were hard. England was at the height of the interminable post-war employment crisis; young men succeeded with difficulty, a handicapped 50-year old academic stood no chance in any domain.

Theo was the first to feel the rub. He was preparing for his university entrance examinations when the accident occurred, and had to switch to the more exacting scholarship curriculum for the financial backing he would now need. Anna was more fortunate. On hearing about Edmonds' misfortune, the nuns not only reduced the fees for Anna's last 18 months, but coaxed her into passing as many exams as she could.

'I'm telling everyone at supper tonight,' Theo said to Anna the day she got home for the Easter holidays. They were strolling through the woods at the back of the house where primroses peeked up through the dead leaves, and the air smelled earthy and fresh. Anna had wondered about the tension clouding her brother's normally buoyant humour, and was about to hear why. 'I flunked the university scholarship entrance exam, and won't be going to Cambridge,' he said bluntly.

Anna squeezed his arm. 'For heaven's sake, you can try again, can't you?'

'Yes, but with things as they are, I'd rather start earning my own living right away. Our parents don't know it yet, but I followed up on a project offered by the Commercial Bank of Montreal, and they've accepted to take me on as a junior. I'll learn banking from the bottom to the top, and paid as I go.'

'Montreal!' Anna was stunned.

'Look,' he said. 'Even if I'd got the scholarship to Cambridge, or any other university for that matter, I'd still need the wherewithal to keep me going for four whole years until a degree, and a job, came my way. It would be a strain on everyone – I'd rather try my luck in the land of opportunity.'

Anna stopped walking and turned to face him. 'It's a far cry from Geology!' she said. 'Is this what you *really* want, Theo?'

'Yes. This is what I *really* want, Anna,' he said, smiling. 'It's not exactly what I planned, but instant independence is very appealing, you know. As a matter of fact I'm quite looking forward to it.'

'Really?'

'Yes, really – and if you don't stop frowning, premature wrinkles will ravage your lovely face,' he said with a twist of brotherly irony.

To say how dreadfully she would miss him seemed too trite. Instead, Anna slipped her arm through his, and walked on in silence. They had both greatly matured since their father's accident, especially Theo who Anna realized had turned into a man without her noticing. 'Well, fine,' she said after a while. 'We could use a millionaire in the family. Mum refuses to talk money, but I believe they are only just getting by.'

'What?'

'Well, the kitchen cupboard stocks an awful lot of rice, spaghetti and tins of sardines. I believe they save their pennies for when we are home so that we won't realize what's going on. But I overheard Daddy say that things would be easier when the house was sold.'

'Are they planning a move?'

'I don't know.'

'Actually, I was worrying about *you*,' Theo pursued.

'Me? My future won't be affected much. After the summer term I'll stay at home, do a secretarial course which I shall absolutely hate, go to parties, which I shall absolutely love, and then one day, soon I hope – you'll get an invitation to a quiet wedding with a reception in the garden at home. Unless, of course, the prospective in-laws want to make a splash.'

'And presuming we still have a garden!' Theo put in. 'But seriously – you? A secretary! You can't spell for toffee, and shuffling papers all day just isn't your style. You might make a fetching receptionist, though.'

'Well, thanks,' Anna responded sarcastically. 'Everything else I wanted to do, like dancing, or acting, requires training fees and digs in London at the parents' expense. Well, that's out of the question now. Besides, Mum said a long time ago she wouldn't let me go on the stage because it wasn't "quite nice", and wouldn't explain why. Do you remember?'

'Yes, I remember,' Theo chuckled. 'Well, do you know now?'

'Of course. But I hardly see why an actress *has* to be a loose-living lady.'

'No, but temptations and opportunities, my dear . . .'

'Well Mother needn't have worried. I expect to be a virgin when I find the man I'm destined to meet.'

'Oh, yeah?

'Yeah!'

Here the conversation halted. They were at the garden gate and the mirth in Theo's eyes gave way to tension again. 'You *will* back me up when I tell them about Canada, *won't* you?'

'Of course. But you know, I think our parents will be rather pleased. We'll miss you like mad, but they'll admire you for getting ahead on your own. Daddy is always saying how attitudes have changed now, and university degrees aren't as vital as they used to be.'

Not long after that, Theo's leather suitcase was dumped in the boot of family's noisy old Ford, and, they drove to Southampton docks. The goodbye hugs were strong but brief. Norma blew him a kiss and shouted, 'Good luck, darling,' as Theo strode up the gangplank. Gerald was too choked up to do anything but wave, while Anna just stood there waiting for her brother to turn and smile one last time before disappearing into the belly of the *Empress of Canada.*

Soon after Theo's departure, Anna smelled plans fermenting in the parental vat, that hintful questioning failed to disclose. She was back at school when the brew matured enough to be poured into the first of Norma's weekly letters, at the start of Anna's last summer term.

'My darling Anna,
    The weather has been just awful. Damp and miserable. The roses are starting to cheer us up, but Harry the milkman foretells another woeful summer and he's usually right. Gerald's legs do feel the humidity so, and Dr Hendricks thinks he should go to a warm dry climate if he hopes to have the maximum

use of his limbs and his mind – sunshine being the antidote to depression, apparently. We had a good long talk about it last week, and decided we should move to Malaga. Health considerations apart, Spain is fifty per cent kinder to the budget than here – lots of Brits go there for that reason alone. Your father's old professor, Freddy Johnson, lives just outside Malaga – and do you remember the Bennetts? Well that's where they retired to as well. And another thing, Gerald can get his strength back by swimming every day – won't it be marvellous? We shall have to sell the house (heavily mortgaged unfortunately!) and rent something out there. No need to panic about all this, darling, there's no rush. It's early days yet.

'If we go to Spain, of course we'd love you to be with us. On the other hand you may have a better time being among young people your own age in England. Julia McFadden would love you to help her with the horses – the social life there would be good too. Or the Rollands in Devonshire who have just produced child number five, another boy, have hinted that they could use a hand in that huge place of theirs. They seem to know everyone in the county; and that might be a lively start for you . . .'

So that was it! Anna slipped the missive back into its envelope and sat staring at her inkwell with its halo of dried ink on the wood around it. The hammer had struck, and its resonance still shimmered through her when the lunch bell rang. She dawdled to the refectory, but Friday's fish pie couldn't be faced. Pretending a headache, she made her way to the dormitory.

Tears of undefined cause rose as she climbed the echoing stairs. Down the long row of white covered beds she went until she reached her own, drew the curtains around it, and lay down. Before all her sorrow had drained away, however, the rattling rosary and heavy tread of Mother Bernadette striding up the dorm stopped the flow.

The elderly nun poked her head between the curtains. 'Are you ill, child?'

'Just a headache. I've taken an aspirin,' Anna lied. She didn't want the nun going all the way to the infirmary and then coming back again.

Mother Bernadette took a long look, and nodded. She'd known Anna for 11 years. 'All right, deary,' she said affectionately. 'I'll cancel your afternoon classes, but be sure to turn up for Benediction in the chapel at five, won't you?'

After the rattling rosary and heavy tread had faded away, Anna's mood changed to thoughtfulness. She puffed up her pillow, turned it lengthways and lay back to read the letter again. 'Early days' Norma had said, but the move had clearly been planned almost to the last detail. Looking after horses or babies in order to cadge a social life seemed tempting, but with her parents abroad, wouldn't dependence of that kind prove rather precarious? What if she didn't get on with Mary McFadden or that awful daughter of hers? She'd be doomed to mucking out stables ad infinitum! And if, after a year or two the 'man she was destined to meet' did not appear, she might easily be fed-up enough to opt for a marriage of escape. No, that would *not* do.

The alternative would be Spain. But what kind of life would Malaga offer, with Norma keeping her on a short leash because Spain was not England? Unbearable!

Just then the sound of choir practice rose through the dormitory floor from the hall below. '*He who would a Pilgrim be, let him come hither.*' Anna followed the music; it was one of her favourites, but Mother Caroline kept stopping the singers until '*hither*' was given the verve she wanted. The stopping and starting interfered with concentration, and her thoughts drifted to Theo who had 'gone thither' boldly enough. He had faced the situation head on, taken his life into his own hands and written happy letters ever after. 'If I want to do likewise,' Anna thought, 'I'll need a diploma, a qualification to provide independence.' But which? Theo had been right about secretarial work, but his receptionist suggestion wouldn't produce a diploma. Librarian? Far too finicky. Air hostess? Ah, that might be fun. Just then '*Nymphs and Shepherds*' filtered up through the polished parquet. '*This is Flora's holiday. This is Flora's holiday. This is Flo-or-ra's ho-ol-liday.*' All that trilling repetition disturbed Anna's thoughts again. She had never liked '*Nymphs and Shepherds*', but the fact that they danced and sang their way through life, which was what she had hoped to do, made them doubly irritating now. Nevertheless, this was urgent; she had to decide her future before she left school, or somebody else was sure to decide it for her.

In her letter home that week, Anna responded warmly to the Malaga project because it was going to improve her father's health. Proposals for her own future she left uncommented, and when handing in her letter at the headmistress's desk, asked if she might borrow the *Professions for Women Handbook?*'

The astute old nun looked up from her breviary with a wrinkly smile. 'We could go through it together after vespers if you like?'

After Vespers the headmistress and Anna studied the thin *Handbook*'s every page, but it didn't take long. Substantial tuition fees featured in all professions, with the exception of a nursing diploma, where free board, lodging and uniform were an added enticement. 'Hobson's choice,' Anna thought. 'And, if I'm accepted into a London hospital, I'll be living where the action is.' The headmistress naturally urged a week of prayer before deciding; she obviously wasn't aware just how 'Hobson' this choice had to be, nor how important it was that Anna settle the matter before reuniting with her parents at the end of term. By the following evening, therefore, a neatly written envelope addressed to the Matron of St Thomas's Hospital, London, lay on the headmistress's desk ready for posting.

'When a Captain charts his course by the will of Heaven,' says a Chinese dictum, 'an auspicious wind speeds his barque to the celestial harbour.' It must have been just such a wind that filled Anna's sails, because two weeks later a letter arrived inviting her to an interview with Miss J.P. Perkins SRN, RCM, OBE. Matron of that distinguished, though daunting, Nightingale School for Nurses.

On interview day, the headmistress said a special prayer for Anna, who had borrowed Liz's little white hat and Margaret's high-heeled shoes for the occasion. When she got to Westgate station for the London train, she lavished some of Liz's clandestine red lipstick upon her lips too. The colour was more suited to Liz's dark complexion than her own fair one, but she was determined that nobody should guess that a sixth-form heart still throbbed beneath the small-cupped bra.

At Waterloo Station, the number 18 bus panted in its siding like a bull terrier waiting to be let off the leash. 'St Thomas's?' Anna said to the conductor as she climbed aboard.

'Can't miss it luv,' he replied. And when they crossed Westminster Bridge, he pointed to a monumental stone-faceted building covering one straight mile along the Thames opposite the Houses of Parliament. 'The entrances are all at the back in Lambeth Palace Road.' the conductor said helpfully as Anna got off.

Anna turned the corner into Lambeth Palace Road. There were plenty of entrances, but all specifically marked for different kinds of patients – 'Visitors' didn't feature. For a while she just stood, scanning the building from the opposite pavement to make sure she wasn't missing a sign with 'Way in' written on it. This was important, she'd been warned that everything she did, and did not do, would be minutely assessed for worthiness. And rather than be judged inept for blundering through doors clearly marked for other people, it seemed less damning to sneak in through the grand front entrance, even though it was obviously meant for crowned heads on ceremonial occasions.

It was already five to eleven. Anna had dithered long enough; presenting late for an interview would be one notch worse than venturing through the wrong door so she crossed the road and discovered a smaller, humbler door set discretely to one side of the towering ceremonial portal. Once inside, Anna found herself in a sober oval hall, small, and yet too dignified for the vulgarity of arrows, notices, or written directions. Under an arch at the far end, Queen Victoria sat in marble splendor, a delightfully carved baby on her ample lap. But the royal gaze went to the river of uniformed personnel pelting along the hospital's main corridor in front of her. Laundry bins, X-ray machines and portable libraries moved along at the rate of knots while doctors and nurses zoomed in and out as though lives depended upon their every step.

Moving up beside the statue, Anna looked around for someone to direct her. There were plenty who could, but waylaying important persons so obviously pressed for time, might easily be another of those things a candidate nurse should never do! Not knowing whether to turn left, or right, she stood for a moment gazing at the passing crowd trying to imagine the day when she, too, would bustle by with that air of natural confidence. But not for long; Big Ben booming the hour of her appointment called for immediate action. 'Which way?' she wondered, again. Then telling herself that 'Matrons are always "right", made that a reason for turning in that direction.

In a silent, wood-panelled cul-de-sac, a thin, long-legged

woman in black stockings, flat shoes, navy dress and towering white bonnet bore down upon Anna as though she were a bluebottle that had bumbled into her web. 'Miss Edmonds,' she said in a hurried whisper, 'you are almost late!' and without any further niceties, opened an ebony door and ushered Anna into the Royal Presence.

Matron smiled sweetly and edged from behind the bulwark of her desk to offer a white waxy hand, before edging back again. 'Now let me see,' she said pleasantly. 'It's Miss Edmonds, isn't it?'

'That's right,' Anna responded, seating herself stiffly on the edge of the chair opposite. But Matron had been interviewing nervous young women for years, and used a kindly approach, so that after a few casual remarks, Anna stopped quavering and was able to answer the questions on which her livelihood depended, 'What made you choose nursing, Miss Edmonds?'

'Oh. I never considered doing anything else, Matron,' Anna replied more truthfully than Matron would ever comprehend.

'I'm very glad to hear that,' Miss Edmonds. You see, this hospital holds to the very highest of standards, and without a vocation it would be difficult for a young person like yourself to complete the four-year course – and that would be a pity, wouldn't it?'

'Four?' Anna queried.

'That's right. Three years to qualify, and a fourth as a charge nurse after which you are entitled to our badge and full recommendation. It is only fair to tell you, however, that the hours are long and irregular; the work is often distressing, and the discipline strict. Perhaps you should also know, that for three years you will have to live in one of our Nurses Residences where visitors may only be seen in the lounge, and you are expected to be in by ten every evening. In your fourth year you may live out if you wish. But remember, Miss

Edmonds, it is *you* who have asked to be trained here, nobody is forcing you to come.'

In the train on her way back to school, Anna gazed out of the window at a herd of happily grazing cows and couldn't help thinking that they, at least, never bit off more than they could chew. Not that Matron's forewarnings had really intimidated her; they were the price of independence and security, and she was ready to pay it. Besides, if Destiny was pushing her into a medical career it had to be because the man she was destined to meet would be wearing a white coat, or striped pyjamas perhaps. Either way, she was sure she'd not be toiling beyond the training years. Happiness and fulfilment couldn't be further away than that – surely?

As Anna's last school term drew to a close, the auspicious wind delivered a letter welcoming Anna to the Nightingale School. She was to start her training with a set of 30 other probationers in September.

Excitement and laughter echoed in the white-arched front cloister, as nuns and school leavers said their bittersweet farewells. Blank-paged diaries came out of brand new handbags, and telephone numbers were swapped around. At the front door the nuns waved a last adieu as the girls walked away to catch the London train, their school days forever over.

Norma met Anna off the London train and drove her home, as she always had at the end of each school term. On this occasion, however, mother and daughter found themselves uncommonly shy of each other. Their only contact over the past 11 years had been in the fits and spurts called holidays; and without the prospect of another school term, they sensed they would have to get to know each other all over again.

Norma glanced unbelievingly at the offspring who had grown up behind her back. 'Where did you get the lipstick?' she questioned in an amused tone.

'I borrowed some of Liz's. I was going to ask you if I could have some of my own now, and also a pair of high-heeled shoes?'

'We'll get the shoes in Spain. They're better and cheaper there,' Norma replied, presuming without question that Anna had chosen the Spanish alternative. 'We're having a bit of a celebration this evening,' she said as they turned into the drive. 'Daddy is determined to open the bottle of champagne the wine mart gave him for Christmas. He's been saving it especially.'

'How sweet of him,' Anna replied, wishing with all her heart that Theo could have been there too – not only to applaud her milestone, but also to back her up when supper time came. The sooner she got it off her chest, the better.

'So you want to be a nurse?' Gerald responded, after Anna had told of her plans.

'I thought it would be useful. Everyone has a diploma these days, even if they are never used.'

'You never told me about this, darling.' Norma sounded hurt.

'I know, Mum. I just wanted to be sure I'd be accepted first.'

'Well – it's terribly hard,' Norma said hesitantly

'I know, but it won't be for long,' Anna chirped confidently. 'I'm not a career woman, far from it. You know that. But I don't feel that relying on friends for a livelihood is a strong enough handle on life. If you have a diploma you can always move on if you don't like it. See what I mean?'

Gerald nodded. 'Times are changing fast,' he said with a meaningful look towards Norma across the dining table. 'As things are, we won't be able to help Anna much, and she'd best be able to earn a few shekels of her own before marriage.'

Norma said nothing.

With only three weeks before the family's departure for Spain, every waking hour went into the process of clearing up and clearing out. Norma held sway over what to keep and what to throw, what to store and what must go. Rubbish and relinquishable memoralia were wheelbarrowed to a huge bonfire at the bottom of the garden, and on their last evening in England, Norma, Gerald and Anna stood around watching it burn. Not a word was spoken as the flames licked through empty cartons, torn-up letters, jigsaw puzzles, 'Monopoly', 'Snakes and Ladders', and the balding body of a once-loved teddy-bear. Theo's broken cricket bat took a while to consume, and so did his worn out and caved-in rugger ball, but Norma's mildewed pressed-flower album, and the huge rose-coloured cardboard heart that the Girl Guides had presented her with on her wedding day, flared up in a moment and spread to Gerald's splintered guitar, his college rowing sweater, and the stacks of old college magazines that he'd never got around to sorting. They watched it all in silence; words seem meaningless when a volume of your life is burning to ashes.

It was growing dark when they found it safe to leave the pile of smoldering ash. 'Ah well,' Gerald said with an air of jovial resignation, 'What is gone – is gone, and cannot be un-gone!' Then, leaning on his wife's arm he turned up the path towards the house that was no longer theirs. Anna followed, curiously aware that their life lay behind them, while hers lay ahead.

The move to Spain went according to plan. Freddy Johnson, Gerald's former professor at Cambridge and a long-time Malaga resident, was at Malaga station to greet the three weary travellers after their two-day train journey. He managed to get the Edmonds family and their luggage into his spacious car, and drove them to the little *pension* where they were to stay until suitable housing was found. A few days later, Clara and John Bennet turned up with a bottle of Spanish champagne to welcome their old neighbours to the Costa Del Sol.

Very soon a three-bedroom bougainvillea-bedecked villa was found on a small housing complex outside town, ten minutes' walk from the sea. Freddy Johnson and the Bennets spared themselves no effort to ease the three newcomers into their environment, and introduced them to a fair portion of the local English-speaking population.

'You'll never feel cut off,' Freddy Johnson said. 'Ex-pats take care of one another here, and as for the folks back home, you'll discover more relatives than you ever knew you had . . . all dying to visit you.'

The British Costa Del Sol residents shared their visitors with one another so that everybody got to know everybody else and all had a good time. Hardly a day went by without the Edmonds receiving an invitation, and it all led to exhaustive barbequing, swimming, boating, sightseeing in open sports cars, and dancing under the stars. Norma kept a close eye on her ewe lamb, but Anna felt she was getting her slice of life with a capital 'L' anyway. More important still, was the radical improvement to Gerald's health. His depression lessoned, his stammer decreased, and daily swimming strengthened his limbs.

When summer cooled to autumn and russet leaves dropped lightly on the pavements of Malaga, a thoroughly bronzed Anna fluttered down to earth too. It was time to pack and prepare for her four-year training.

There was a watery glint in Norma's eye when she and Gerald stood on the platform of Malaga station to say goodbye. The overland journey back to England would be long and lonesome, but Norma couldn't help saying, 'you won't talk to strangers on the train, will you darling?'

'No, Mama,' Anna replied with sweet sarcasm.

'She'll be fine,' Gerald said, putting his arm comfortingly about his wife's shoulders. 'She's a big girl now.'

Chapter Ten

'Your time here isn't going to be all beer and skittles!' The Sister Tutor said, smiling brightly over a new intake of student nurses on their first day in the classroom. 'And if you were hoping to be "ladies with the lamp" – you can forget that too!'

Anna hadn't come with any fixed idea, except perhaps that she had to go through with it, or muck out stables for heaven knew how long! She was, of course, oblivious to the fact that Destiny had embarked her upon a seven-year maturing process aimed at dispensing enough discomfort of body and mind to eventually ignite an enquiry into the deeper truths of life. Training for 'service to her fellow humans' in a huge hospital with a rigid hierarchy, petty discipline, Victorian attitudes and the highest of standards, was a perfect way of achieving this. But at 19, Anna had the energy to face anything.

The working day started at 7.30 a.m. and ended at 9 p.m., with a three-hour break in between. But as the shifts were constantly shifting, an organized private life was all but out of reach.

£1 a week didn't go far either, but rather than write home for money, Anna found ways to amuse herself for free. She'd take her sketch pad to the park, explore old churches and monuments, listen to the speakers in Hyde Park, or simply walk down Oxford Street window-shopping. Her greatest expense, apart from the black uniform stockings, was a visit to a trendy Chelsea coffee bar where a cappuccino could be sat over for most of her precious afternoon off. There were perks, too. Nurses were grouped with old-age pensioners when it came to cut-price cinema tickets, and Matron's office received complementary theatre tickets for the staff. Boots the chemists generously gave discounts for nurses at their cosmetic counter, and when travelling the London buses in outdoor uniform, bus conductors often 'forgot' the fare. But Anna's navy overcoat and hideous felt hat, did nothing to soften the heart of the man at Cooks Wagon-lit when she purchased her ticket home.

Florence Nightingale's training school lived up to its immaculate reputation and Anna passed through the mill uneventfully. She was 23 when her diploma was placed unceremoniously in her pigeon-hole at the Nurses Residence, and after the fourth year, when she was assigned the emergency operating theatre, she realized that things were not fitting into place quite the way she had expected. It was for this reason she decided to invest another year's study for the sake of a midwifery diploma. This qualification was considered essential for posts abroad, but Anna's motivation was mixed with the feeling that perhaps her lucky star only needed a little more time in London to focus its light upon her. Not that she moped around in the Nurses Residence in her free time, or lacked escorts to the hospital dances and other activities. But Destiny always made sure that Anna's men-friends remained just that – nothing more.

Halfway through the midwifery course, Theo wrote to announce his engagement to Fiona, a Scottish lass he'd had his eye on for some time. A photo came with the letter, showing a happy Theo with his arm around the pretty young sister-in-law-to-be.

'So you beat me to it,' Anna murmured. 'But I'll catch you up – you'll see!' They were planning a spring wedding.

'Just perfect,' Anna wrote back, 'Midwifery ends in April so there is nothing to stop me coming over to see you tie the knot.' She taped the photo to her washbasin mirror so as to see it every day, and be reminded to save money for the event.

Three weeks before the final midwifery exams, Anna peered into the night sky for her lucky star, and found it not. Most of the newly-fledged midwives had plans. Some were to become district nurses, others health visitors. Three were marrying clergymen, and two returning to take charge of a hospital ward. But Anna couldn't see herself doing any of those things. In fact, her train seemed to be nearing the end of the track without her having the slightest idea where she would go when it stopped.

'What shall I do next?' she asked Moora, a school friend who had had the patience to keep up with her over the years. Moora had devoted her youth to doing what comes naturally. So by the time Anna had got her precious diplomas, Moora had a house, a husband on the up-and-up, and three delightful children. Every time they met, Moora always said, 'What about all those super doctors?'

'What about them?' Anna inevitably replied. But when Anna moaned, 'What shall I do next?' Moora became unexpectedly inspired.

'Make the most of your freedom, Anna. The world is your oyster. Haven't you hung around London like a wallflower long enough?'

Moora had no idea that those words unlocked the cage of her friend's stultified mind, and by their next meeting, Anna was amazingly decisive.

'I'm off to my brother's wedding in Montreal next week,' she said, bristling with excitement, 'and from there I intend to travel the world.'

*

The Atlantic lay still for the four-day crossing, and when the ship docked at Montreal, Norma, Gerald, Theo and Fiona were among the upturned faces waiting on the quay. Anna leaned over the ship's railings to wave down at them and found herself swallowing back tears; partly for seeing her loved ones again, but also because it occurred to her at that moment that the first, difficult chapter of her life was now over; freedom and adventure lay ahead.

'That's an awful lot of luggage you've got there for just one week, Anna,' Gerald said after they'd passed through Customs.

'It's everything I possess,' Anna replied casually, but the flash of alarm in Norma's eyes made her go on. 'You see, I plan on taking a short-term job here in Montreal, and then move on to which ever part of the world tickles my fancy.'

'Good for you.' Theo butted in smartly before Norma had time to react. But as the wedding week went by, Norma, with a little help from Gerald and Theo, came round to the idea that her daughter needed to spread her wings before she settled down.

After Theo's wedding, Norma and Gerald returned to Malaga, and Anna acquired a short-term operating room assignment in Montreal's Royal Victoria Hospital. She spent three months catching up on her long-lost brother and his bride, and then it was time to spread her wings and fly.

Anna had indeed turned an important page in her life, but Destiny's seven-year cycle had two-and-a-half more years to run. From Montreal she went to Boston and from there to New York. When a colleague wanted company on a freighter voyage from New York to Cape Town, Anna embraced that challenge too. She had a long holiday in Africa on the ample money saved in New York, and then got a job in the Cape. From there, opportunity led to a contract with the

Red Cross in Geneva. Every new job and each new country demanded a facet of Anna's character and aptitude she didn't know she had, but she thrived on new experiences.

As her year with the Red Cross drew to a close, Anna's seven-year cycle neared completion, too. This was why she felt the time had come to stop circling the earth, and return to her roots. She did not know that the roots she was seeking were not anchored in the soil of England, though she was heading that way when her friends Jane and Christopher Murray suggested she holiday with them in Paris. Christopher worked for a big multinational company that moved him to a different part of the globe every five years. Their time in Paris had just a few more months to run, and they wanted to see Anna before moving on to Nairobi. Anna was delighted.

'I feel I could live here for ever,' Anna said to Jane as they drank coffee in the spring sunshine looking across the Seine to the Isle de la Cité.

'Why don't you? Christopher knows the director of the American hospital in Neuilly. The staff there has to be strictly bilingual, but after Geneva, your French is probably OK. They are always looking for staff. I'm sure an interview could be arranged.'

'What amazes me,' Jane went on, 'is how you've managed to remain single all this time.'

'You can't be more amazed than I am,' Anna replied laughing.

'With all that travel, there had to be *somebody*?'

'Yes – but not the right one.'

'So you hung onto your . . .'

'Virginity? I remained idealistic for ages, but by the time I met Paul in Geneva, I saw my so-called virtue as pure hypocrisy, and decided to enjoy my womanhood to the full and be damned! I lived with him for ten very enjoyable months.'

'And . . .?'

'Well, he did propose. He was kind, attentive and suitable in many ways, but deep down I knew he wasn't the right one either; though I was sorely tempted to give up work and have a family of my own.'

From the look in her eye, Jane seemed to be questioning whether, now almost twenty-seven, Anna shouldn't be considering a lovebird in the hand, worth any number in the bush! But she said – 'Well, why don't you hang around here. In Paris you simply can't miss!'

After the interview came the job. The hospital, though basically a private one, also had wards for state-paid patients and it was to one of these, a male surgical ward, that Anna was assigned. The pay was minimal but a hospital studio was provided gratis, and it happened to be situated just down the boulevard from the Murrays' apartment.

Anna was more than a little flabbergasted at the ease with which all this had happened; no previous move had ever gone as smoothly or as quickly. Her roots would have to wait till her love affair with Paris waned, if it ever did. Walking to work down a tree-lined avenue seemed like heaven, but wherever she went, Paris throbbed like a delighted heart about her. In that city everything invited a closer look, be it a steamy bistro, a flower market, a church, trees, pavements, the river, bridges, quays – everything! This was a place where life went out of its way to beguile the passer by, and *joie de vivre* taken totally for granted.

'Just fill your lungs and blow,' Jane was saying as Anna attempted to extinguish all 27 candles on the big square cake she had baked for her. But it was a sad occasion really, because the Murrays were leaving in a week and had added a farewell party to Anna's birthday celebrations. Anna forced brightness onto her face, as she chatted with Jane's guests, two of whom had sleeping babies parked in the bedroom. She had brought along an unattached doctor from the hospital whom she didn't really know. He had been shy all along and now that the carpet was rolled away for dancing, he said he couldn't dance. But Anna's sadness had nothing to do with this. She was sad because the Murrays were leaving, and because blowing out 27 candles, without having found a partner and family of her own, felt shameful in the company of all those happy couples. Moreover, though enjoyable, life seemed to be leading nowhere; a feeling common to people just before the curtain on their karmic stage begins to rise.

'Like to take my place with the BBSSA ski camp?' a colleague named Barbara asked cheerfully in the cafeteria queue one lunchtime.

'What's that? ' Anna asked.

'The British Boarding School Ski Association, a London-based society that organizes ski camps for boarding school kids. A team of teachers goes with them, of course, but they have to have a bilingual nurse to cope with mishaps. I've done three seasons already, but now my fiancé and I have other plans for our free time. I met him on a BBSSA holiday in Verbier, by the way. Trouble is, I'm signed up for St Hildegard's, a girl's school, going to Austria in February, and can't get out of it unless I find a replacement.'

Anna was curious, and when they'd settled at a table to eat, she pursued the subject. 'You mean the hospital sponsors this?'

'Gracious, no! The time comes out of your annual leave.'

'Have to think,' Anna said cautiously, though the idea appealed.

'The work is negligible, and the school staff are usually good fun. I always had a terrific time,' Barbara said persuasively. 'But if you're not interested I can easily find someone else.'

'OK,' Anna responded, not wanting to pass up the opportunity, 'In for a penny, in for a pound.'

'It's a deal, then?'
'Don't see why not. If you had a good time, why shouldn't I?'

Anna was happily packing for this new venture when her friend Marie-Claire, secretary to one of the surgeons, popped into her hospital studio.

'You do have all the luck,' Marie-Claire said, looking at the pile of ski gear on Anna's bed. 'I wish I could just take off like that.'

'Ah, but it's a working holiday, don't forget. I still have to bandage hands, knees, and you name it. Then there'll be temperatures, coughs, colds, sunburn, overeating, hysteria, homesickness, and perhaps even a call for the helicopter.'

'Yes, but you get free skiing, board and lodging, and your fare is paid.'

Anna nodded. 'That's the whole point.'

'Well, I've brought a couple of English books for you to read in case there's no snow,' Marie-Claire teased, placing the volumes on the bed beside the open suitcase. 'I've no idea what they're about. A grateful patient presented them to my boss just now, and he asked me to get rid of them.'

'Thanks,' Anna replied, dropping the volumes distractedly into her half-filled suitcase. 'Barbara said the night life was terrific. There shouldn't be time for reading.'

'Well, you never know,' Marie-Claire cautioned. But the books weren't her prime reason for the visit; she had something far more exciting to deliver.

Anna picked up one of the books for a closer look, but noticing an unusual glint in her friend's eye, let it fall back into her suitcase again. 'What's up, Marie-Claire?' she asked suspiciously.

Marie Claire swallowed a smile. 'You'll never guess.'

'Don't tell me that Jacques has finally plucked up the courage to propose?'

'*Oui! Oui! Oui!*'

'About time!' Anna exclaimed with a delighted grin. 'Tell me everything. I'll just make coffee, then you can spill the beans.' . . . It was well past midnight before they were all spilled.

Anna was the first of the party to arrive at Chalet Mont-grahl. Poised on a sunny hillock overlooking the ski resort 3 kilometres away, it was more of a hunting lodge that had seen better days, than a ski chalet The fretwork framing gables and balconies showed signs of rot, and the stonework at ground level veiled in moss; only half a pair of antlers hung askew over the impressive front entrance. Inside, once nicely appointed rooms had exchanged tasteful trappings for functional furniture, and every footfall resounded loudly on the scratched and faded parquet. At the top of the grand central staircase, Anna discovered wide landings opening into princely suites now converted into commonplace dormitories. A cherub-painted ceiling looked down upon a row of cheap white washbasins and cubicled lavatories.

No cherubs hovered over the room marked 'Infirmary', which provided only the strict essentials – a bed, a basin and a box of medical supplies. Anna had started to check the latter, when she became aware of two women in overalls eyeing her from the doorway. When she turned, they introduced themselves as the cook and the housekeeper. With a fortnightly change of clientele they knew better than anyone that it takes all sorts to make a world, and were anxious to know what 'sort' was coming next. When Anna explained that she was the French-speaking *infirmiere*, their piercing regard softened, and after a little more talk led her up the creaking attic stairs for first choice of the little wood-lined bedrooms at the top.

'Where do you two sleep?' Anna enquired.

'*Out!*' they chorused vehemently.

The squeak of a halting coach, followed by high-pitched

voices resonating throughout the house, announced the arrival of St Hildegard's.

Anna left her suitcase on the bed of a room facing east, and the trio retraced their steps. At the head of the grand staircase the ladies scuttled away. leaving Anna to go down and introduce herself to the portly headmistress alone. Miss Bindale and her staff of four greeted Anna with little more than a curt nod, but the journey must have stressed them, and she expected smiles when a routine had been established and the fun begun.

The following morning Anna woke early. She opened the little bedroom window, drew in a lungful of crystalline air and gazed at the glory of morning sun on white mountain peaks. Everything seemed set for a perfect holiday. After breakfast, girls, teachers and the nurse trudged off to the ski lifts. The skies were blue, the snow plentiful, and the St Hildegard's sixteen-year-olds well behaved and had all skied before. By supper time the sixth-formers were obviously enjoying themselves, but Miss Bindale and her staff seemed determined to find just everything inadequate, unsatisfactory or unacceptable!

'What do you mean, you don't mind having to walk so far to the ski lifts?' the headmistress snapped, stabbing Anna with a freezing glance as they moved from the dining table to the coffee lounge after dinner. 'It's scandalous! The information brochure stated that ski facilities were on the doorstep, and the village within easy reach. But without private transport, that is nothing short of a lie.' Anna looked surprised. 'You don't seem to realize, Nurse, I have thirty-nine children here, and their parents aren't just anybody, you know. St Hildegard's has a reputation to uphold.'

Anna wanted to say, 'Then hire a bus', but as it wasn't her business she decided to keep her head out of the dragon's mouth. Smiling understandingly, she edged away, only to have Miss Bindale's iron paw grip her arm.

'Furthermore,' she continued sonorously, 'the meals described as "wholesome" are practically uneatable. And the beds! Nurse, really, we feel it's up to you to make an official complaint. There'll be accidents if our children don't eat and sleep properly. You mark my words.'

Anna jerked her arm away from the prong, but kept a light tone. 'No need to worry, Miss Bindale. Walking ten minutes to the lifts warms the ski muscles and that prevents accidents, as I'm sure you know. Then, with so much fresh air and exercise, your teenagers will sleep like logs and not mind what they eat so long as it's food. Look,' she added, nodding towards the rowdy dining room, 'they're having a whale of a time already!'

The headmistress didn't look; she was unaccustomed to being 'told'. Anna went on, 'If, on the other hand, *you* should need a little sedative at night, just let me know.'

Anna's solicitations were acknowledged with a fleeting grimace and a menacing pause ensued while Miss Bindale rummaged her mind for a suitable retort. 'Well, Nurse,' she finally tittered, 'if you find the conditions here commodious, one can only wonder what you could possibly be used to.'

The anger that clutched at Anna's throat came out in a nonchalant laugh. But it couldn't have sounded quite natural, because the four acolytes, sensing a fight, froze in their after-dinner chat and waited for action! If they were hoping to see fur and feathers fly, they were to be disappointed because Anna merely wished the headmistress a courteous 'goodnight', and without waiting for the customary reciprocation, walked calmly to the door.

Obviously the prickly headmistress was to be avoided, but friendly overtures to her four acolytes brought no joy either. The clannish behaviour became clearer when Anna learned that the staff of St Hildegard's had always managed their ski holidays perfectly well without a nurse, and objected to having the BBSSA foist one upon them now. Mealtimes underscored the silent agony of being odd man out, but Destiny's inaugural invitations often arrive in tatty-looking envelopes.

At breakfast on the second day, a courageous student delegate approached the staff dining table to ask Miss Bindale about *après-ski*. The reply came swift and sharp. 'I'm not having my girls running around at night,' she said firmly; and that went for all of them. The acolytes looked complacently at one another, and a resentful groan roared up from the school. But Miss Bindale had spoken, and nobody dared argue! When darkness fell the outer doors were locked, and after the meal, the girls amused themselves with charades, or practised the twist and other trendy dances to the music of an old gramophone and records found in a drawer. As for the staff, they sauntered from the dining room to the lounge like ladies of the manor to have coffee, sample the local brandy and play cards.

For the first couple of nights Anna took her time sipping coffee and struggling to converse. On the third evening however, she felt no inclination to linger in the lounge, still less to accept a round of rummy; she could hardly wait to climb the creaking stairs to her cosy room, and read the books so fortuitously provided by Marie-Claire.

'Well, I suppose you can't win 'em all,' she said to herself as she fumbled for one of the volumes at the bottom of her suitcase. Her hand met with the thick hardback and she pulled it up from under her redundant evening wear. *Dialogue with the Beyond* was the title, and having decided that it couldn't be duller than a dialogue with the people downstairs, she propped herself up on her pillows and started to read. The book was written by an episcopal bishop describing the relationship he had cultivated with his drug-addicted son. Just when the Bishop had succeeded in helping his son conquer the addiction, the young man put a bullet through his brain and later proceeded to contact the Bishop from beyond the grave!

According to the Bishop, communication from the beyond had started in various poltergeistic ways. The dead son's possessions mysteriously began to move from room to room, and books were found open with a message glaring from the page. The phenomena persisted until the Bishop finally, and somewhat against his religious convictions, consulted a spiritual medium thereby making contact with the spirit of his son through her. During the seance, the young man, totally identifiable by the words he used and the memories he shared, told his father why he had taken his own life. He described what it was like to die, and attempted to explain how he continued to live and learn in the dimension of spirit.

With points of Christian doctrine on the line, the Bishop brimmed with questions, among them a sheepish enquiry as to whether sex was at all possible in heaven. Anna giggled, and could just imagine the holy man's face when the answer came back a disappointing 'no'.

Anna skiied with the children in the day and manned her infirmary every evening. She got through supper as one transparent, and spent as little time as possible in the lounge afterwards. If she managed to appear pleasant, it was only because she had the Bishop's tale to look forward to, later.

The esoteric was something completely new to Anna and most other people of her age at that time. Yet the Bishop's story intrigued her because it did not corroborate the type of Heaven, Hell and Purgatory taught her by the nuns, and instead of having to believe, she discovered that life after death could be unequivocally proven. Some might have dismissed the whole fat book as a preposterous invention, but the narrating Bishop had described his experiences with such clarity and sincerity, that Anna was inclined to accept what he had written.

With the Bishop's tale ended, and still one week of ski camp to go, Anna delved into her suitcase for the other book. It had a curious title, *The Initiate (Some Impressions of a Great Soul Written by his Pupil)*. 'Gracious! What have I done to deserve all this spirituality?' she thought. Still, under the circumstances, *The Initiate* was a welcome companion till ski camp ended.

Anna opened the book and started with the Introduction that said the author was a well-known Englishman of the 1920s, who wished to remain anonymous. He was writing this account as the disciple of a Spiritual Adept or Master of Wisdom. The true name of the Adept was withheld too, but he was known by the pseudonym Justin Morward Haig. Haig went about town as a decidedly bourgeois individual, and although Spiritual Adepts are in no way restricted to the puny social order, a gentlemanly demeanour was necessary to gain acceptance in the salons of London's rich and influential. His mission was to temper the rigid and selfish attitudes of those passing for noble, with a deeper understanding of truth, tolerance and love.

The Initiate largely consisted of authentic anecdotes describing behaviour motivated by anger, revenge, jealousy and greed that were considered justifiable, even genteel, by the standards of the day. But in Haig's view, these responses in human behaviour were nothing more than painful, though curable, diseases. He banished the conventional idea that disgraceful immoral tendencies are best suppressed or justified, and claimed that such discrepancies need never occur at all when they are rightly understood.

With every page, Anna's interest quickened. Haig professed no particular religion, but used true stories (cloaked in anonymity) to demonstrate how negative attitudes and behaviour, however righteous in appearance, invariably reap an unhappy harvest. He expanded this topic by explaining a universal principle known as the law of cause and effect: 'As you sow, so shall you reap'. The salient point of which, so little understood and so vigorously rejected by Christian orthodoxy, is the unpredictable time lag between cause and effect. In other words, more than one lifetime is required to balance the scales. This made more sense of life than anything Anna had ever heard before. In the east, they call it 'karma'.

Only hints of this ancient law appear in the authorized Christian Gospels, leaving all Christendom to wonder why unavoidable misfortune can befall apparently blameless people, and villains often go unpunished. But criticism or censure of any religion was not Haig's point; he was above such infantile attitudes. Instead, with the gentlest of breath, he preceded to blow clean the dusty doctrines of Christianity.

Very simply, Haig's anecdotes demonstrated how confusion and unhappiness stem from ignorance of the True Nature dwelling within all humankind. The only reason why people don't know this, is because True Nature happens to be thickly veiled by ingrained erroneous thinking and bad habits. Haig's cure consisted in seeing the truth of what we are doing to ourselves, and letting go of it. Understanding is the key. But as most of us go to our graves with the blueprint for our difficulties unexplored, so it may take many visits to the classroom of earth to detect and root out, all the misconceived desires, hates, doubts and fears that cause pain to others and separate us from the fundamental peace and contentment lying dormant in the core of our being.

This was quite new to Anna, and would have sounded trite coming from anyone other than Morward Haig. For Haig's words, even on paper, bore a magical quality that penetrated her heart. Haig himself had undoubtedly arrived at this enviable goal known as self-realization a long time ago. But he laid no claims to sanctity, or superiority – his message was that everybody can, and eventually will, achieve it too.

Towards the end of ski camp, Anna came upon an anecdote featuring a rather pompous Archdeacon of the Church of England. When the Archdeacon died, Haig's narrative followed him behind the curtain of death to show what happened when the revered cleric left his body. To Anna's amazement, the Archdeacon's 'death experience' corresponded exactly with that described by the Bishop's son in the other book, and the coincidence wouldn't leave her mind.

She was still thinking of it the following lunchtime when somebody was saying, 'Would the Nurse care to come with us?'

'What?' Anna hadn't been following the conversation.

'We, the staff of course, are celebrating the end of ski camp by sharing a taxi and going for an evening in the village,' one of the acolytes explained. 'Would you like to come with us?'

'No thanks,' Anna replied. She wanted to finish her book before returning to Paris. 'But I'll happily stay and guard the girls, if you like?'

After 'lights out', Bindale and Co. clattered upstairs to preen; half an hour later they clattered down again, dressed up, made up and powerfully perfumed. Anna waited by the front door to see them off, and watched as they boarded their taxi, arguing as to who should sit in front and who behind. The house was silent, but when the taxi could be heard no more, dormitory lights blazed on, music from a forbidden radio-set wafted down to the hall, and bare feet thumped on the floor above. A smile of commiseration parted Anna's lips as she climbed the attic stairs to her bedroom.

Having changed into her nightdress and got into her warm bed, Anna looked forward to another friendly evening with *The Initiate*. The anecdotes were finished, but Part Two, 'The Circuitous Journey', remained. 'The Circuitous Journey' was purposely couched in archaic prose. Haig had wanted it so: 'Let the English be flowing and as poetical as possible,' he instructed the anonymous author. 'For occult truths impress themselves more readily on the reader if they are clothed in melodious language.' There followed an allegorical tale of two aspirants, male and female, preparing to climb the 'Mountain of Wisdom'. Their destination was a monastery at the summit; to reach it represented the attainment of enlightenment or self-realization. The thought of 'enlightenment' being attainable by ordinary people surprised Anna.

The valley church chimed midnight. Anna hardly heard it; she was following the allegorical couple from hermitage to hermitage, imbibing greater and greater teachings and submitting to harder and harder tests. Somewhere along the way they fall in love – 'Wouldn't they just,' Anna's thought interjected – and in the end, they had to climb the rocky, snowy, blizzardous Mountain of Wisdom to the very top.

When pausing for a visit to the bathroom, Anna couldn't help wondering if this wonderful couple had any idea how lucky they were having each other for the ordeal. Everyone had somebody in life, why was she still so mightily alone?

The craggy mountain provides the ultimate test of faith and endurance in the style of a Victorian novel. Finally, the story reached its climax when man, woman and a stray dog that had followed them, all arrive half dead at the monastery where food, warmth and loving hands restored their bodies, and illumination transformed their souls. But even this was not quite the end. It was a 'Circuitous Journey', meaning that having attained enlightenment, they were to descend the mountain again, by an easier route this time, to help others to climb and vanquish as they had done. On this note, the book ended.

Silence reigned in the chalet; the children were finally asleep. Still under the spell of Morward Haig, Anna couldn't help wondering if he was still living. His precise age had not been revealed, though the book had said that Adepts and Mahatmas could live incalculable years while keeping the appearance of their prime. All people and places mentioned were purposefully dissimulated, so anyone seeking Haig was doomed to failure.

Placing *The Initiate* on the bedside table, Anna rose and went to the window. White peaks sparkling in the full moon pierced a velvet sky, their majesty breathtaking. She had marvelled at them often over the past fortnight, but now they seemed to return her look with an aura of challenge, daring her to pursue, search, and yes – climb!

'Don't get carried away,' she told herself drawing the curtains briskly. 'It's only a book.'

When morning came, a gust of chill air brought Anna out of sleep. Peeping over her thick duvet, she noticed the curtains drawn back and the window wide open. Had *she* done that? Darkness still brooded outside, though a faint glow was beginning to spread behind the peaks. Soon the first rays of morning would beam into the room, on this her last day at the Chalet Montgrahl.

Chapter Eleven

After her return from Austria, Anna folded back into her hospital routine like the pleats of an old accordion. Mahatmas and Adepts filled her thoughts, but her full-time job, left sparse time to seek them out. In any case, she didn't know how, or where to begin. In fact, the spark of spiritual curiosity ignited in the mountains might well have vanished in the city, but for a series of strange occurrences and odd coincidences impossible to ignore.

The first of these concerned Jane Murray. The Murrays had left Paris for Nairobi as planned. It was a sad farewell, but they would be keeping in touch and Jane had promised to send their address as soon as they had settled into the new home. The move had not been sudden, and Anna was neither shocked nor grieving. It was difficult, therefore, to explain the incidences that followed.

It started on departure day at the Montgrahl. In the entrance hall, milling with pupils and their baggage, Miss Bindale approached with hand outstretched to say goodbye, when suddenly, and for no apparent reason, Jane Murray popped into Anna's mind long enough for her to suppose that there'd be a letter from Nairobi when she got home. When Anna got home, however, no letter waited, but thoughts of Jane returned with greater intensity as she unpacked. This time she connected them with her old habit of phoning Jane after she'd been away, just to say 'I'm back'. It was only when

Jane jumped rudely into her mind the following morning, that Anna wondered if something was amiss, and yet the intrusive thoughts carried no sense of foreboding.

Though mystified, Anna didn't worry. If Jane was in trouble, she had a husband to take the situation in hand. Anyway, without the Nairobi address there was nothing she could do. Had the Jane thoughts ended there, they'd soon have been forgotten; but the phenomena had only just begun.

For the next two weeks, Jane assailed Anna's thoughts in this curiously undefined way with ever-increasing frequency. At first it was puzzling, then intriguing, and finally irritating – Jane just would not go away!

After two weeks without letter or let-up, Anna wondered if it wasn't something she was projecting herself. Turning the spotlight from Jane to herself, she discovered that these strange non-existent messages were not, in fact, assailing her thinking mind, or her intuitive mind, but making themselves felt in another part of herself altogether – a part hitherto uncomprehended; her soul, perhaps? This conjecture quickly led to the alarming possibility that Jane might have died, and if Jane was trying to say she was dead, Anna *had* to get to the bottom of it.

She racked her brains for the name of someone in closer touch with the Murrays than herself, who might know what was going on. Eventually Jane's cousin, Lucy Parker, came to mind. Anna had met her briefly in the Murrays' apartment two months before. She remembered a highly vivacious young woman, recently qualified as a doctor, and engaged to Marco, a much-married painter living in Florence.

The international telephone exchange readily located *la Doctora* Parker, and with the number in hand, Anna was just deliberating how best to introduce herself, when her own telephone rang.

'Long time no see,' came Paul's familiar voice. Anna smiled.

'No see long time,' she replied skittishly to the maturing bachelor banker with whom her relationship in Geneva had been a fine-line experience of the pragmatic and the romantic. They had parted amicably when he was temporarily transferred to London, but Anna had not accepted his offer of marriage because she did not love him deeply enough. He had taken this philosophically, and when he returned to Geneva, their relationship changed. They no longer lived together, but occasionally joined forces for a long weekend, or short holiday. He was calling now from his office in Geneva.

'I don't suppose you'd be free at Easter, would you?' he asked. 'I have to meet our Italian rep in Florence, and I thought it would be nice to combine business with pleasure.' The word 'Florence' sent shivers up Anna's spine, but she hesitated. 'If it appeals,' he continued, 'we could drive down from here and spend a few days nosing about the art world. I've just invested in a brand new Alfa, the latest model, and can't wait to take it out on a long run.'

Anna's hesitation had nothing to do with the Jane-trail, it was the relationship with Paul that troubled her. Paul still wanted marriage and hadn't given up trying to change her mind, so that each post-parting encounter, only furthered false hope making Anna feel guilty.

'Strange,' she murmured.

'Strange what?' Paul echoed. He was a down-to-earth banker, more attuned to the material than the ethereal.

'Oh, nothing.'

'*Surely* you can get Easter off,' he urged.

There followed a moment's silence while Anna reasoned how ridiculous it would be to refuse, when not only would she enjoy being cosseted for a while, but had a specific reason for going to that very place. 'I'll try and wangle it,' she stammered.

'So when will you know?'
Anna stopped beating around the bush. She knew perfectly well she had Easter week off. 'OK, I'll arrange it,' she said decisively.
'That's more like it!' Paul sounded happy. 'My secretary will mail you a ticket tonight, and I'll meet you off the ten o'clock plane at Geneva Airport on Tuesday morning, if that's all right?'
'Fine.'
Paul waited at the Arrivals barrier, but Anna spotted him first. They hadn't met for ten months, during which time he'd slipped discreetly past 43. A slight portliness had crept to his girth, and his hair had receded further up his brow. He was casually dressed, but just missed looking dapper, and scanned the arriving crowd with a foolish, ogre-like intensity.
'I do wish he'd stop hoping,' Anna thought as she waved in his direction. He responded immediately. The old familiar smile turned the lines of anxiety into creases of delight that brought back Anna's lingering affection; the guilt pangs subsided. She would make sure they had a happy holiday; that much she could do. They embraced with a brief hug, and then hurried out to the car park where Paul's magnificent, streamlined bottle-green gadget-filled extravaganza, on four hardly used wheels, waited.
'We should make it by five,' Paul remarked, checking his watch and fairly quivering with pride.
Through the Mont Blanc tunnel they sped, and across the Lombardy plain. The car performed superbly, and Paul was in raptures over it. They lunched off sandwiches and kept going. The further they went, the more buoyant Anna felt, and more than once looked across at Paul, asking herself if she could find it in her heart to . . . but no. It would be like forcing an almost-right piece of jigsaw into the wrong place.

Even so, this did not stop them from chatting like a couple of parakeets from Torino to Allesandria, Piacenza, Reggio around Bolognia and on down to Florence.

It was only when the signs marked *Firenze* began to appear, that Lucy was mentioned. 'Just thought it might be fun to look her up,' Anna said breezily, making the idea seem more like sudden inspiration than a critical plan. Paul was a stickler for detail, and she didn't want him probing into things she didn't understand herself.

They were headed for the Villa San Michaele at Fiesole, 3 kilometres from Florence. 'Almost there,' Paul said as he slowed down so as not to miss the sudden turning up a ramp-like incline, and then into a short drive curving before the old stone portico. Set like a jewel in the hillside, the ancient edifice looked graciously out over the city. Michelangelo had designed it for those embracing poverty, chastity and obedience, but now the old monastery shamelessly enshrined values of an opposite nature.

Once in their room, they threw off their shoes and slumped onto the bed. Paul dropped quickly into sleep. Anna dozed until the light began to pale, then got up, dressed for the evening, and went downstairs to explore.

Passing through the reception hall, she moved into a series of interconnecting salons, each with a wide door leading onto a cloister where columns and sweeping arches framed a spectacular view over Florence. She wandered over to lean against one of the ledges still warm from the afternoon sun, and there looked out over the terracotta roofs of palaces, churches, towers and domes, with the yellowish Arno wending gently under the many bridges. As evening advanced, the air cooled, but the warmth of the ledge held Anna to its side. Soon the orange orb slipped slowly behind the distant hills, and dusk's ever-darkening cloak gently enveloped the city of domes.

It seemed an age since Anna had relaxed like this. She

closed her eyes and took in a deep breath of wisteria-scented air. Savouring the moment, her eyes remained shut until a hovering presence made her open them again.

Paul was at her shoulder, rested, handsome and emanating the subtle fragrance of sandalwood aftershave. 'Penny for your thoughts,' he said brightly, holding out a glass of frosty white wine.

'I was thinking that of the many lovely places you have taken me to, Paul, this beats them all.' And with these words, Jane Murray, who'd been unusually absent all day, made one of her rude intrusions.

'Yes. It's magnificent. I thought you might like it.'

'I most certainly do.'

'Hungry?' Paul asked, maneuvering to face her as they sipped their wine.

'Yes . . . and you?'

'I could take a little nourishment, but no hurry. We're on holiday, are we not?' He moved to her side. 'I mean to savour all this slowly,' he said, sliding his arm around her waist. 'And that includes you.'

Anna smiled, but remained silent.

When their glasses were empty, they wandered along to the far end of the cloister, where a few fashionably dressed guests languished on monastic stone benches drinking cocktails served from a converted baroque pulpit. Without stopping for a refill, they moved on to discover the stone-walled refectory made warm with candlelight and freshly cut flowers.

'My meeting with Poletti is tomorrow morning, darling,' Paul said, when they had chosen the meal. Paul had never dropped this term of endearment after the parting, and Anna liked it that way. 'I thought you might want to go shopping and meet me somewhere for lunch.'

'Sounds fine, but won't Poletti have to give you a big fat business meal?'

'He suggested we both lunch with him. But his wife is in hospital having their umpteenth child, so I let him off.' Anna nodded. Paul went on. 'Once I'm through with Poletti, we'll have all the time for Florence and . . . ourselves!'

'Don't forget Lucy and Marco,' Anna prompted, quickly to make a diversion from 'ourselves'.

'Haven't forgotten.'

'OK. I'll phone her after dinner.'

With dinner over, Paul treated himself to a cigar in the lounge while Anna went up to their room to make the call. Her prior meeting with Lucy had been so brief, she shrank from intruding upon a virtual stranger, but she needn't have worried. 'Come for tea on Thursday,' Lucy said gaily, and then explained how to reach the apartment in the wing of an old palazzo where she lived with Marco and his five-year-old daughter, Camilla. When Anna asked about Jane, nothing spectacular surfaced, but she could probe further when they met.

At five o'clock on the appointed day, foot-weary, eye-strained and thirsty from a surfeit of sightseeing, Anna and Paul walked into the palazzo's courtyard to see a pretty brunette waving to them from a parapet above. 'Come right up,' she shouted. 'Around to your left there's a steep flight of stone steps; we're at the top. By the way,' she added, 'I had a card from Jane today. Have you heard?'

Anna needed her breath for the steps, but when she reached the top, replied, 'How's Jane?'

'Well, according to our postcard she's absolutely fine.'

'Oh good,' Anna murmured, reaching forward to shake Lucy's hand and introduce Paul. As she did so, the shy figure of a little girl appeared in the doorway.

'And this is Camilla,' Lucy said. Anna shook Lucy's hand too, and Paul made a great fuss of her. 'Marco has an exhibition in Venice this week,' Lucy explained as she led the way in. 'I'll show you some of his paintings if you like, then I expect you could use a cup of good old-fashioned English tea.'

The artist's pad was beautifully cool, sparsely furnished but rich in clutter. Paints and half-finished canvases lay about; books and stray papers covered every available surface. They appreciated the paintings, and then looked forward to the promised cuppa.

On her way to the kitchen, Lucy turned to the child. 'Be a sweetie, Camilla, and take Teddy out of that chair so that Anna can sit down, will you please.' Camilla dragged a heavy tortoiseshell cat yowling to the floor, revealing a plain typed pamphlet which, for want of a suitable surface, Anna kept on her knee.

Tea and talk flowed plentifully. The Murrays were mentioned several times, and Anna was handed the postcard to read, but there was nothing in it to arouse concern.

Before her visitors left, Lucy said, 'Why don't we all go for a picnic in the hills tomorrow?' Instant enthusiasm greeted this suggestion. Fun apart, a picnic would provide not only a rest from Renaissance art and architecture, but also the opportunity for an unobtrusive word with Lucy alone; the Jane mystery might well be something not for Paul's ears, or Camilla's either.

It was past six o'clock when they left the palazzo, and made their way towards the car through streets booming and honking with home-hungry commuters. On reaching the narrow alley where the Alfa was parked, a delivery van blocked their exit. With frantic manoeuvres Paul tried to twist the car free, but it was hopeless! Annoyed, he added his horn to the rush-hour cacophony, but nobody came.

'Let's wait a while,' Anna soothed. 'The driver is bound to turn up soon – he wants to get home too, you know.'

'Supposing he *is* home!' Paul moaned.

Just then the deep resonance of organ music reached their ears as someone stepped out of the church behind them. 'Well, I'm going to listen to *that* while we wait,' Paul declared furiously.

'Good idea. I'll keep an eye on the van from the café on the square, and fetch you when it moves.'

Anna found a table, ordered fresh orange juice and had just begun to watch the passers-by, when the unwelcome stare of a man two tables away filtered her awareness. Pretending not to have noticed she looked about for a newspaper to hide behind, then realized that the pamphlet retrieved from Teddy's chair was still in her hand. Holding it up in front of her face, she glanced over the front page. It looked like a boring bulletin put out by an association named the Lucus Trust, intended for members only. Anna hesitated, but the man's attention persisted, so she read on.

In an English country mansion where the Lucus Trust regularly held conferences and retreats, a charismatic Polish priest, Father Glazweski, had died of a sudden heart attack in the middle of the retreat he was giving. This special issue was to relay the Priest's after-death message to those he had so abruptly taken leave of. The written message was transmitted through a medium, providentially attending the retreat also.

'Not *again*!' Anna groaned, looking up to check on the gigolo. He was still there, and half rose when their eyes met, but sat back as hers returned to the page.

For the third time in recent weeks, Anna was virtually forced to read of death and after-death, with all the descriptions bearing an uncanny resemblance one to the other. The subject was becoming familiar – ominously so. She couldn't help feeling that three chance screeds on death, three weeks apart, had to mean something – her own imminent demise perhaps? 'Oh my God!'

'God? I thought you were an atheist.' The voice that made her start was Paul's.

'So did I!' Anna replied.
His forehead furrowed. 'Anything the matter?'
'No, no. Just something I read. How was the music?'
'Wonderful. There was a choir too. Practising for the Easter services. The van's gone. Let's get back to the hotel.'

Anna slept erratically that night, her mind replaying ad infinitum the enigmatic events of the past weeks. She needed to tell someone, but Paul was better at laughing things off than soothing them away.

'How would you like to explore the market?' Paul asked over breakfast the following morning. He wanted some epicurean delights for himself, and add a little of this and that to Lucy's picnic basket.

'Sounds fun,' Anna responded.

So after breakfast, down to Florence they drove, parked on the outskirts of town, and walked on to the lively market-place where the local producers extolled their fish, meat, sausages, cheese, fruit, vegetables, herbs, flowers, clothes and gaudy plastic fripperies at the top of their voices. Some called *Ciao Bella* and whistled loudly when Anna approached. 'No need to encourage them,' Paul growled under his breath.

'I'm enjoying myself,' Anna teased.

'I can see that.'

Having dallied pleasantly among the stalls admiring everything, Paul looked at his watch. 'We'd better go on to Luigi's, now. He's an old friend. Wait till you see his shop.'

Laden with paper bags, they left the clamorous market, crossed the sun-lit street, and plunged into the chill darkness of a cobble-stone alley that seemed to have eroded its century-old path between the tall stone buildings. To Anna it looked like a short cut to nowhere, but after the first curve in its meandering route, they came upon a tiny shop peeping out of a gap in the wall. 'This,' Paul said as they went in, 'is a place known only to connoisseurs of special wines and exquisite cheeses. And this,' he repeated by way of greeting, 'is my old friend Luigi.'

Luigi, his bulging abdomen swathed in a white apron, waddled around the tiny counter towards the door, smiling amiably. 'Paolo, Paolo,' he greeted, then noticing Anna his eyes lit up. 'Ah! You marry at last – eh, Paolo?'

'This is Anna,' Paul replied as though he hadn't heard the question.

'*Bienvenuti, Anna.*' Luigi said, as though he hadn't asked it, and diffused the awkward silence by hastily leading the way through to his Aladdin's cave of wine and cheese at the back of the shop. The two men had quite a lot to say to each other; Luigi, in a jumble of Italian and rudimentary English, Paul, in rudimentary Italian and pidgin English. From the start Paul knew what he'd come for, but the half-hour ritual of choosing, advising and deliberating, was not to be missed. Snippets of cheese were ceremoniously severed and proffered on the end of a sharp knife, and wine poured from several casks for approbation too. With unhurried grace the marvels of the *bottega* were revealed, and after a great many *Bene's, molto'benes and benissimos*, two slightly inebriated customers walked gaily to the car, and then on to where Lucy and Camilla waited outside the old palazzo gates.

It was a beautiful sunny day, and with everyone in high spirits they set off. Lucy sat beside Paul to guide him through the complicated turnings of the town; then out into the hills, where stately cypresses tapered like candles out of the green and into the blue.

They'd been driving for about 30 minutes when Lucy suddenly said, 'Whoops! Slow down here, Paul, and take that farm track on your right.' With due regard for his precious new undercarriage, Paul took the bumpy trail, and a 100 yards further on, parked in the shade of an aged oak.

The perfume of wild thyme and mountain foliage filled their nostrils as they got out; invisible cicadas chirped in the long grass.

Picnic baskets and rugs were extricated from the boot, and they took off along the sunny farm track towards a shady copse. Camilla skipped ahead, picking wild flowers; the adults strolled behind putting the world to rights. Having skirted the copse, they emerged into brilliant sunshine again. Lucy pointed to a bell-shaped hill crowned by a small oratory half hidden in a flurry of trees. 'I thought we might have lunch up there,' she said. 'The view is breathtaking.'

A hot, steep climb led to the top. Camilla was first to arrive and ran straight to the chapel. The others followed. The age-worn little oratory smelled musty and was empty, except for the virgin standing in her niche staring vacantly down at the bunches of wild flowers wilting at her feet.

Here they all stood, recovering from the climb, until Camilla's high-pitched voice shattered the silence. 'Paul, Paul,' she piped, tugging at his sleeve. 'Let's go play Pig-in-the-Middle.'

The hill, with its views across a patchwork of undulating farmland, was indeed a delightful spot to eat. Lucy spread blankets under the trees, Paul uncorked his precious bottle of mellow red wine, and the feast began. They started by plunging their knives into pungent pâté, heaping it copiously onto rough brown bread. Then came sun-ripened tomatoes and cucumber, preparing the palate for basil-stuffed mozzarella wrapped in slices of pink Parma ham. Green salad and fresh figs followed, and after that, an unctuous Talegio, oozing amiably onto its greaseproof wrapping, waiting for a dry rye biscuit to carry it away.

'I've eaten too much!' Anna exclaimed.

'Me too,' Paul seconded, hands poised over his burgeoning paunch.

'You can't give up now,' Lucy protested, placing before them a round tin containing Florentine pear cake. Camilla clapped her hands; it was her favourite.

'We can't,' Anna sighed.

'You can,' Lucy insisted.

They did!

After that they lay back on the grass, listening to a breeze rustling the leaves overhead as they drifted blissfully into slumber.

All too soon, however, Lucy nudged Anna awake, with a mug of tea. 'Better fortify yourself,' she grinned. 'Camilla is organizing Hide-and-Seek.'

Game followed game, and they played like children for the rest of the afternoon.

It was when Paul was hiding, and Camilla seeking, that Anna made her final bid to check on Jane Murray, whose intrusions seem to have subsided since her arrival in Florence. 'I had a strange dream about Jane,' she said. 'Are you *sure* she's all right?'

'You read the postcard,' Lucy replied. 'I don't know any more than that; they'd have phoned if anything serious had happened.'

The air turned chilly as the little party prepared to leave. This time it was Paul and Lucy who walked ahead, Camilla in the middle, a hand in each of theirs. Instead of picking up the picnic basket and following, Anna watched their merry progress. As the path steepened, the trio began to run. 'One, two, three,' they chanted and swung Camilla into the air amid peals and squeals of laughter.

Suddenly, happiness seemed so simple. Why had Anna never quite grasped it? The certainty and optimism of her early years and the notion that there was a man she was destined to meet, came to mind. 'Well I'm pushing thirty now.' The man has not come, and the notion still unchanged! I even imagine that everything would be as easy as rollicking down this hill!'

At this point Anna might have felt bitter, but she did not; her mood was one of bemused detachment. In view of what she had learned from the two books in Austria and from the curious events of the past three weeks, she was beginning to feel there might be a God after all and, fed up with trying to make sense of her life, found herself saying, 'You take it!'

'Take it!' she shouted to the empty sky. 'I've done all I know. If You exist, take it!' She had no idea who 'You' really was, and was even a little astonished by the sound of her own voice. But rolling her life into an imaginary tennis ball, she threw it into the air, indifferent as to whether it descended or not. 'Go on, take it,' she shouted. 'Without love, one has nothing; so what have I to lose?' The imaginary ball fell back into her hands. Playfully she threw it up again, giggling this time. If the others had turned back then, they'd have seen their normally rational friend throwing an invisible ball into the air and . . . laughing!

But they were already halfway back to the car, so grabbing the picnic basket, Anna raced down the hill after them.

'We thought you were lost,' Camilla chirped as Anna sank breathlessly into the plush leather seat of Paul's bottle-green pride and joy.

'Lost? However could you think that?' Anna replied in a voice so gay it almost belonged to somebody else. As the car curved smoothly down towards Florence, something odd began to happen. Anna was conscious of the others chattering around her, but when she wanted to add a comment, words refused to formulate. It was as though her mind was empty; but the sensation was not at all unpleasant.

The strangeness continued as she dressed for dinner, and when it came to applying make-up, she noticed changes. Her eyes seemed feverishly bright, her lips tweaked up at the corners in a semi-smile not of her own doing, and there was a marked glow to her complexion. The day's fresh air and sunshine might have done that – mild sunstroke, perhaps? She recollected that Jane hadn't bothered her for three whole days, but the tears that sprang unexpectedly to her eyes had nothing to do with Jane. They welled with the realization that the 'uncomprehended' part of herself that had hosted the thoughts of Jane, was now brimming over with unexplainable joy.

Nothing in her life had altered to explain this; there was no foreseeable change in view, yet all anxiety concerning her future was gone, and everything suddenly seemed perfect just as it was.

A few heads turned discreetly as Paul and Anna crossed the candle-lit refectory to their table in the corner. The waiters, in their yellow waistcoats and black trousers, fluttered like a flock of butterflies around them with greater attention than usual; they seemed to be sensing Anna's joy. But Paul, kind pragmatic Paul, noticed nothing and just as well, for had he started questioning, she'd have been at a loss for answers. It was like 'being in love' – not with anyone in particular, just 'in love', and Paul couldn't be expected to stomach that. As it was, he chatted merrily in his usual way, while Anna listened with a cool tenderness never felt before. Oddly, this tenderness seemed to pass through him to everything around; her fellow guests, waiters, and even the hot woolly poodle panting under a table. Something quite unusual was taking place, but all Anna could do was relax and, like a marvelling spectator, watch it unfold.

The remaining days of their holiday passed pleasantly. Jane Murray's intrusions never returned; they seemed to have been replaced by the 'sunstroke' glow that grew steadily and showed no sign of departing.

On Easter Monday, they breezed back to Geneva in Paul's wonder car, and spent the night in his apartment. Anna was to start night duty that same evening, so Paul took her to the airport in time for the 10 o'clock Paris flight. With the warm farewells there came no last-minute pleas for permanency. 'It's been perfect,' Paul murmured, 'Just perfect.'

'Thank you, Paul,' Anna said. 'I've had an unforgettable time.' Paul drew her to him in a hard hug, they kissed goodbye then walked together to Passport Control where, with a wave and a smile, they parted.

No sooner was the plane aloft, than white Alpine peaks shone all around, reminding Anna of the Mountain of Wisdom. Sudden sunlight made her close her eyes. She wanted to sleep, but thought intervened. Just three short weeks had passed since reading Marie-Claire's books, during which time her life had swung from the banal to the bizarre. An oasis appeared to be taking shape in the desert of her existence. Something mysterious was happening, like a turn in the wind. An extraordinary thrill was moving through her; from where it came, she didn't know. Furthermore, she sensed that all the frustrations and difficulties experienced hitherto, had brought her to this precise point in time; but were she to tell anyone that, they'd think her crackers. How could anybody understand that ordinary Anna was filling with an overpowering love and gratitude from a boundless source, and imbued with an effortless humility that bore no hint of lowliness.

'Coffee or tea, madam?' the hostess repeated loudly to the window-seat passenger with her eyes shut.

'Oh! Coffee, thank you,' Anna replied, but what she really wanted was someone who could tell her whether this extraordinary state of affairs was natural, unnatural or supernatural. And the only person she knew of who could do that, would be Morward Haig.

Chapter Twelve

With a light heart and a heavy suitcase, Anna struggled into her hospital studio, dropped her bags in the tiny entrance, and surveyed the place which, for want of a better word, she called home.

'So, I'm back,' she said aloud to the empty room, thinking how nice it would be if a familiar cat were to rise from the divan with a friendly greeting. Instead, *The Initiate* lay on her pillow. 'Ah! Mr Haig,' she said, 'I got the last message about death when I was in Florence; that makes three, you know? Something rather thrilling seems to be developing and I'd really like to know what it's all about. If you are still alive, could we possibly meet?' She plumped down on the divan, picked up the book, and leafed through its pages; not so much in the hope of finding a lead as to Haig's whereabouts, but more in an effort to make vicarious contact with him. She had never heard the dictum, 'When the disciple is ready, the Master appears'.

Donning her uniform that evening was like slipping into an alter ego, the one used for the unavoidable real world. On her travels she had made several attempts to escape into lighter employment with normal working hours, but circumstances beyond her control invariably put a stop to it, and back to nursing she'd had to go. She buttoned up her dress, fastened her starched white apron, and then went to the bathroom mirror to brush her hair and secure the little white cap on the top of her head. 'Sunstroke' still radiated her features with serenity and joy, though how they'd weather a busy night on her male surgical ward remained to be seen.

As Anna hurried through the hospital entrance hall on her way to the ward, a large poster depicting a bare-chested Yogi sitting in the lotus position, caught her eye. She was already five minutes late, but couldn't resist stopping for a closer look. The poster announced a lecture in the hospital auditorium on the Yog Sutras of Patanjali, to be given by an Indian swami (monk) in a fortnight's time. Thinking that yogis featured in Morward Haig's line of business, she slipped the pen from her breast pocket and noted the details. She wanted to give the lecture a hearing, but with her work schedule still unknown, getting to it would be a matter of fate. 'Fate has been working over-time just recently, hasn't it?' Anna thought smiling, as she hurried on.

Usually there was a friendly 'welcome back' when someone returned from leave. But one look at the day nurse's face banished the thought.

'*Je n'en peux plus!*' (I've had it) Mademoiselle Perot greeted when Anna reached the desk. Her chignon was on the verge of collapse, her uniform spotted with blood, and her eyes rolled back like a dying horse.

'What on earth has happened?' Anna asked.

Perot looked pointedly at the ward clock. 'You may read the full report for yourself when you have time. *If* you have time,' she said, then rattled off some of the essentials. 'Beds all full. Bed 1, Monsieur Godel, in and out of a coma all week. Bed 8, Duclos, diabetic, left leg amputation yesterday. He is mentally deranged – keeps pulling off his dressing and hopping out of bed. Bed 14, Ticon, hiatus hernia for operation first thing tomorrow –'

'What about bed rails for Duclos?' Anna interrupted.

'Ordered, haven't come.'
'Restrainer?'
'No time. He's had a sedative. He'll sleep.'
'Or so we hope,' Anna added, as she glanced quickly round at the ensemble of 30 patients before turning to look at Monsieur Godel's curtained cubicle. She'd not expected to see him on her return. 'Have his people been called?' she asked.
'*En route.*'
'I can read the rest for myself. Do go,' Anna urged.
'I'm off. *Bonne soirée.*'
'*Bonsoir,*' Anna echoed as she dimmed the lights and started on her round. Thankfully Duclos was snoring. With luck he'd sleep till morning. She then crossed the ward to look down upon the pale, moist face of Monsieur Godel. The acrid smell of death filled his narrow cubicle. He'd been dying for over a week now, but his last dose of morphine was keeping him out of pain. Gently lifting his hand, Anna felt for the pulse. A feeble squeeze met her touch, and his eyes fluttered open with a brief glimmer of recognition.

'I'm back, Monsieur Godel,' she said softly in French. 'Back to look after you. Your wife will be here soon, too.' The response was another weak squeeze before his eyes slid up under their lids again.

Perching on the edge of the bed, Anna kept her fingers on the flickering pulse; it could cease at any moment. Monsieur Godel's death might reveal something she'd never noticed before, or verify something of what she had read.

According to the three accounts so recently pushed under Anna's nose, Monsieur Godel was about to slide out of his physical body, the way a snake sheds its skin. He would then find himself in his etheric form, which is the insubstantial part of the physical body, resembling it in every way, though exempted from the usual physiological needs. According to the books, the etheric body becomes the vehicle for a person's soul after the material one has been vacated, and is needed to transport consciousness to other realms of existence. In this form the departed can observe his or her own lifeless physical body. The Bishop's son had hovered over his own dead body, the Archdeacon witnessed his own funeral, and Father Glazewski gone through a similar process. All three had expressed wonderful relief in leaving their earthly carcass, and Monsieur Godel had every reason to feel likewise.

Anna was just gathering the courage to tell Monsieur Godel that he had nothing to fear, when a clatter at the ward entrance attracted her attention. His relatives and a priest stood awkwardly by the door, while from the gloom at the end of the darkened ward a hand waved frantically. Vanquishing shyness, Anna bent her head to the patient's ear and whispered quickly, '*Laissez vous allez, Monsieur Godel. Suivez la lumière. Il n'y à rien à craindre.*' (Let yourself go. Follow the light. There is nothing to fear.) Then, beckoning to the relatives, she dashed off to the waving hand of a man desperate for *le pot*.

After *le pot* had been given and taken, Anna's steps turned briskly back towards the curtained cubicle where muffled sobs suggested that it was perhaps too late. An ominous thud stopped her in her tracks. Monsieur Duclos was on the floor, a malicious smile wrinkling his whiskery face as he waved his bandages in the air like a stationmaster's flag. Thoughts of death fled before the quandary of how to get this hefty one-legged lump back to bed before the night superintendent arrived to charge her with negligence. But the night superintendent's heavy footsteps were already creaking up the ward half an hour earlier than usual. She had come to say that all the private beds were occupied, and Mademoiselle would have to make room for a private patient with a fractured tibia. The words were hardly out, when her torch beam struck the grinning moon-face eyeing her from the floor at Anna's feet.

'*Mon Dieu*!' she exclaimed, jumping back. ' 'Ow did zis 'appen? I am obliged to do a report, you know.'

'Yes, yes, I know,' Anna replied impatiently; her chances of getting to Godel at that crucial moment slipping irrevocably away. Together they heaved the one-legged man back to bed, and then more precious moments passed as they laced him into a jacket restrainer that they tied loosely to the bed. 'Monsieur Godel hasn't much longer,' Anna said anxiously when the job was done, 'I must get back to him now.'

'*Non*!' snapped the superintendent. 'You prepare for ze tibia, ees English, and me, I do zem.'

With a possible negligence report hanging over her, Anna didn't argue, and it was well that she did not. The private tibia in a public ward was Destiny's way of offering the opportunity she'd always longed for.

The lift doors clanked open and a casualty bed a trundled noisily into the ward. It bore a lean, long-legged man in his middle fifties. He had a well-shaped head rising from a sinewy neck and shoulders, a high forehead mounting to a balding crown, and a froth of gingery eyebrows shadowing intelligent hazel eyes. He appeared to be taking his predicament with a mixture of disgust and humour.

'I'm afraid I'm being an awful nuisance,' he said in French, but his accent, sentiment and intonations were as English as could be. Anna picked up his medical file. This was David Greening: '*Age*. Fifty-six. *Occupation*. Chief of Personnel, Organization of Universal Education. *Diagnosis*. Simple fracture of left tibia. *Treatment*. Fracture to be reduced under general anesthetic as soon as possible.'

Though stoic about pain, Greening openly deplored being 'messed about' in hospitals. Having a compatriot remove his clothes and shave his leg eased the tension considerably, and even engendered a certain empathy.

'How did you manage this?' Anna whispered.

'Doesn't your report tell you?' he whispered back with a touch of ire. 'I fell over our cat in the kitchen.'

Anna swallowed a smile. 'How's the cat?'

'Missed the cat. How else do you suppose I broke my leg?' The emotion of this last statement erupted in decibels incompatible with a sleeping ward.

'Hush,' Anna admonished.

'Sorry!' he whispered rueful as a naughty schoolboy, bringing a surge of nostalgia for England to Anna's heart. The leg may have been fractured, but his sense of humour most mercifully was not.

With Greening in the operating room, and Godel's relatives huddled round the night superintendent in the glass-fronted office, Anna went over to the curtained cubical again. Godel had left his body, but for a moment it looked as though breathing had recommenced. She stepped closer. No, he had gone. Focusing her gaze above his vacant body she addressed him in thought. 'Are you still there, Monsieur Godel? Can you see me? In case you didn't realize, you've died, but don't be afraid, there is a light waiting to guide you when you're through looking at your old body. You must be feeling relieved already? They say it's a lot nicer where you are, than down here, and I can quite believe that!' She paused before making her request. 'If you can hear me though, Monsieur Godel, would you give me some kind of a sign? – Please.'

Silent, intent, Anna watched. Had the bed-light flickered, the curtain rippled, or if she'd suddenly gone hot, cold or hungry, Anna would have known he had heard, but nothing happened. She was about to repeat the request, when a voice behind her interrupted.

'Zis is not ze time to dream, *Mademoiselle*! Prepare 'im for ze mortuary *vite, vite*, before ze tibia come back.'

Happily, Greening's fracture was a simple one and the anesthetic relatively light, so by early morning he was awake and quite himself again. 'Now,' he said with an air of natural command, 'would you be kind enough to get me a wheelchair and some crutches? Then I'll ask you to phone my chauffeur, so I can get back to the office as soon as possible. Ah yes, and ask him to call in at home and bring a clean change of clothes. Don't bother about breakfast, my secretary will arrange for it at my desk.'

'Not so fast,' Anna protested. 'Your plaster is hardly dry, and patients usually stay in a full twenty-four hours after general anesthetic. Doctor Dubois will be here soon, you can ask him.'

'I'm expected in New York tomorrow.'

'Is that wise? ' Anna asked diplomatically.

That was how the conversation started, but as it went on Anna sensed that Greening had taken an innocent shine to her, and before Dr Dubois arrived, he was encouraging her to consider the opening for a SRN in the medical unit of the Organization of Universal Education. Anna was extremely flattered, but couldn't imagine what they might need nurses for there.

'Oh, there's plenty to do,' Greening replied. 'We have over five thousand staff to see to, and visiting delegates galore.'

'But aren't they all healthy?'

'They have to be vaccinated when we send them abroad, and they would need you when they fall up the escalators, down the stairs and walk through glass doors – that sort of thing.'

Anna laughed. 'Well, I guess I could manage that.'

'Good! I'll get an application form posted to you today,' he said. 'But my recommendation won't be enough, you'll have to make yourself agreeable to Doctor Roch, Director of that unit. He's French,' Greening added. 'Came to us from the military. Competent administrator. Keeps a low budget, runs a tight ship.' The practical implications of this passed over Anna's head. 'Ever worked for a French Director?' he pursued.

'Doctors, yes. Directors, no,' Anna replied. 'Are French directors so different from other kinds?'

'Not really,' Greening said thoughtfully, 'but they do rather enjoy being "*Monsieur*".'

This remark tickled Anna on and off until midday, when she went to bed and slept. Thoughts of the French Director came up again when she awoke, and she looked forward to another conversation with Greening that evening. But when she appeared for duty at eight, there was only a space where his bed had been.

A day or two later, a long buff envelope waited for Anna on the ward desk. It contained a brief thank-you note from Greening and the promised application form, which she filled in when the ward was quiet. Getting this job would mean normal working hours and money to spare; in fact, a new kind of a life altogether, but it was too soon to speculate. The wheels of big organizations turn slowly and, although Greening's recommendation was an advantage, she'd have to give three months' notice to the hospital, during which time the French Director might easily select a candidate without such a long time lag. However, as 'sunstroke' was incompatible with anxiety, Anna found she could want the job, and yet remain unruffled even if she did not get it, and in the meantime there were the Yog Sutras to look forward to.

Not in the least surprised to find that the Yog Sutras fell plumb in the middle of her 'nights off', Anna made for the hospital auditorium wondering what destiny had in store for her this time. At the door, a bearded student handed her an information sheet describing the 62-year-old Swami Sat Anand as a renowned expert on the Yog Sutras of Patanjali, an erudite scholar, author of many books, and much loved personality among Paris's Hindu community. The Yog Sutra's were described as 'aphorisms that cut to the very heart of truth'.

There was much more, but the lights were dimming, and hush descended as a tall, orange-robed Indian with a mane of white hair walked confidently onto the podium. He nodded amicably to a brightly clad bevy of Indian ladies in the front row, and after a brief introduction from the bearded student, took his seat on a velvet and gold armchair placed beside a low microphone. He greeted his audience with the word 'Friends', and gave his discourse in impeccable English.

The discourse, that lasted almost an hour, was lofty and theoretical; Haig's practical examples, easy logic and humour, had no part in it. Anna supposed that she was not the only one having difficulty understanding it, because when the lights went up and questions called for, nobody dared open their mouth.

The Swami stood smiling over a silent audience for a while and finally said, 'Well, if anyone wants to deepen their understanding on this, or any other subject, they are welcome to come and see me at the centre. Mrs Gupta, here present, makes the appointments.' Then, having thanked everyone for coming, he walked quietly from the stage.

The Swami hadn't impressed Anna one way or the other, but determination to start somewhere gave her the courage to go forward and find Mrs Gupta.

Two weeks later, Anna sat in the Metro speeding towards a villa in the suburbs that served both as the Swami's residence, and the venue for meetings and meditations. In her handbag was Mrs Gupta's hand-drawn map to help find the house, and soon she was standing on the front door step feeling foolish. The Swami himself, almost unrecognizable in a roll-neck sweater and gray flannel trousers, opened the door and with a friendly greeting, ushered her into a spacious hall smelling of incense and floor polish. Two sari-clad matrons looked up from their sweeping and dusting as the Swami led his new visitor past them down the narrow corridor to his book-lined study at the back of the house.

Still wondering what she was doing there, Anna sat on the upright chair facing the Swami across the expanse of his untidy desk. To her relief the conversation started with the weather, the traffic, and the garbage collectors' strike, giving time for Anna's galloping emotions to slow to a manageable trot.

'So how did you find the Yog Sutras?' Swami asked.
'A little puzzling.'
He smiled benignly. 'You are a Christian, I take it.'
'No. That fell by the wayside.'
The Swami's eyebrows rose. Whether from interest, or surprise, was impossible to tell. Either way, he made this his cue to begin a lengthy discourse on the fundamental differences between Eastern and Western religious concepts. Evidently most of the Swami's visitors came to enhance their knowledge of oriental philosophy.

'It's awfully interesting,' Anna interrupted. 'But I didn't come to see you about that, exactly.'

'Oh?' The Swami seemed surprised. But before he could ask the reason for Anna's visit, the door burst open and a short round woman in a flowery sari swayed in under the weight of a fully laid, tea tray. Her elbow had opened the door, which her foot now slammed, and she staggered towards the Swami's desk turning the prevailing calm into a whirlwind of confusion. In his haste to clear a space for the tray, the Swami sent papers into the air like butterflies, and pencils rolling noisily onto the floor. While he swooped to save a pile of pamphlets from cascading into the waste paper basket, Anna found herself catching flimsies in mid-flight and harvesting pencils, rubbers and paperclips around her feet. By the time the tray had been firmly set down, and Lakshmi thanked, the Swami was more concerned about Anna's preference for milk and sugar than the reason for her visit.

'Just milk,' Anna replied, but her desire to speak of 'sunstroke' had passed. She was sure she had knocked at the wrong door, and was wondering how long it would be before she could politely leave. She was thankful when he didn't say 'Where were we?' the distraction having jolted him onto another track altogether. He spoke now of a Hindu Saint named Rama Krishna whose portrait hung on the wall. Anna listened respectfully, but sensed that the benign erudite Swami was no substitute for Morward Haig; Haig would have known immediately why Anna had come.

'And where is Rama Krishna now?' Anna asked, thinking that perhaps *he* was the person she should see.

'Rama Krishna left his body back in 1896,' the Swami replied with an indulgent smile. 'But I see you are new to all this. You might like to come for our Sunday morning teaching and devotions and I will give you a book on the basics.' He did not wait for Anna's response, but swivelled his chair gleefully to consult the bookshelf behind him, leaving Anna with a view of his venerable back. In the moments of silence that followed, Anna found herself smiling at the thought of what her mother would say if she could see her now. But the smile quickly faded as the Swami spun back to face her again. 'Yes, this will give you grounding,' he said, holding up a well-worn hard-cover volume.

'Have you ever meditated?' he asked.

'Well, I'm not sure you would call it meditation,' Anna replied hesitantly. 'But since this thing occurred, it seems to kind of happen quite a lot.'

The Swami nodded, and without questioning 'this thing', pushed on. 'How do you go about it?'

'Well, when I'm just sitting quietly, I sometimes feel myself slipping into a deep velvety well. It's rather frightening, really, like drowning, and I quickly pull myself out.'

'Is that all?'

'Yes. Except occasionally there comes a diffused light, as though sunshine is penetrating my eyelids. If I open them to see where the light is coming from, it goes, and on shutting them again, the light does not return.' Anna knew she was not imagining this, but to draw the Swami out, added, 'Do you suppose this is all imagination?'

'Perhaps,' he replied blandly, confirming Anna's feeling about having come to the wrong door, and making her wish she'd kept her experiences to herself. She saw no point in revealing the other developments that had come with 'sunstroke', either.

After a thoughtful pause, the Swami went on. 'Just sitting isn't quite all there is to it. What about thoughts?'

'What about them?'

'Thoughts have a habit of getting in the way, don't they?'

'Getting in the way of what?'

'Discovering what lies behind the mind,' he replied, as though it were the most obvious thing in the world.

'Well, what *does* lie behind the mind?' Anna asked.

'Ah!' the Swami chuckled. 'I'm afraid you have to do the work and find out for yourself. When you have been with us for a while, I'll give you a mantra. That is to say, words, or sounds, which will help you deepen into things.'

Deepen? Hadn't her velvety well been deep enough? All Anna had wanted to know was what her experiences meant, and now she was getting uncomfortably embroiled.

Glancing at his watch, Swami handed Anna the book. 'I don't have time now to show you the shrine where we do our teaching and meditations, but it would be good if you read this before we meet again,' he said opening his diary. Anna tried to field what was coming by pleading the irregularity of her free time. But insensitive to the hint, the Swami insisted on a tentative appointment anyway, so Anna noted the date, and decided to cancel later.

Lakshmi then clattered in to remove the tea tray, and the Swami accompanied Anna to the front door where he repeated his invitation. 'Why not come along to the Sunday morning gathering, and meet our dear devoted group of friends?'

The book intended to give 'grounding', rested on Anna's bedside table where the dust that it gathered bore witness to her disappointment. Ten days later, when she was about to cancel her appointment and wrap the book for posting, she made a quick tour of its pages. One of the chapters was devoted to karma and rebirth, and curious to see if it corresponded to what she already had learned from *The Initiate*, Anna soon found herself deeply absorbed

The subject of karma was treated in the simplest possible way, the progress of lives on earth likened to a kind of knitting. In each life we have to pick up the stitches (mistakes) dropped in former incarnations, but in our ignorance cannot help but drop a whole lot more! The problem is that we feel a nagging incompleteness that comes from within, and try to satisfy it from without. Sensual pleasures and ego satisfaction make life bearable for a time, but are never totally fulfilling, and woefully short lived. The nagging incompleteness continues and the frustration of seeking satisfaction in the wrong place gathers momentum, driving motivations and actions further and further from safe anchorage into a choppy sea.

Eventually there comes an incarnation when the garment of life that we are knitting with thoughts, words and actions becomes unwearable and unbearable. And at this point, the pilgrim seeks another way. If the seeking is sincere, an expert knitter comes along with a pattern based on three truths. Firstly, that true joy lies hidden within a cluttered self. Secondly, every action inexorably returns to its sender: 'As ye soweth so shall ye reap'. And thirdly, the incalculable time-lapse between the sowing and reaping make it impossible to know, unless told, that the wounding darts were in fact released from one's own bow.

The world is never without inspired teachers who know, and recommend, perfectly good knitting patterns, though tenacity is needed to follow the intricacies every stitch of the way. It may therefore take more than one lifetime to unravel and let go the unconscious habits of countless lives.

Abject misery and failure is as effective at setting the seeker on his path as is the futility derived from a surfeit of luxury and ease. There are fast knitters, and slower ones. As more stitches are picked up, fewer and fewer get dropped and the garment becomes recognizable. When the whole garment is seen and recognized, understanding dawns. The sowing automatically stops, and there is nothing more to reap. For those arriving at this point, called *moksha* (liberation), worldly pleasures are no more appealing than childish toys. After Moksha, the knitting class ends, but some compassionate souls, such as Buddha, Jesus, Lao-Tsu and a number of others, return to the earth plane to help knitters untangle their lives and find joy.

Anna finished the chapter, and reached for the wrapping paper. Yes, everything she had read affirmed the little she already knew. As she started to make the parcel, however, she wondered if dropping the Swami off-hand with nobody else to go to, was such a good idea after all. Wouldn't the Swami's centre offer an opportunity to move into a milieu where people were already familiar with the subject that was becoming of compulsive interest to her? She reached for her diary and laughed; the rendezvous fixed by the Swami fell right in the middle of her next 'nights off' – again!

Chapter Thirteen

On Anna's second visit to the Swami, an elderly French woman in a plain cotton sari came to the door. '*Entrez,*' she said dryly, and without further ado, led Anna straight through to the book-lined study.

The Swami got to his feet and introduced the woman as 'Sudah, my right-hand man – Mother to us all here – we don't know what we'd do without her.' Sudah made no retort, but edged politely to the door, looking as though she'd heard all that before.

Tea was not served on this visit but during the initial small talk, Anna learned that the Swami was not the only person living in the centre; it was a home-from-home for a number of Asian students and countless visitors passing through Paris. Again the Swami rattled on, assuming Anna to be a student of Eastern philosophy, something she was perforce becoming. When she could pierce the monologue, however, she pushed straight to the key of what she now saw as the crux of all life's predicaments, karma. She wanted to find out what she had done to deserve an apparently unending delay in finding her beloved – though dared not put it quite like that.

'Can you see into past lives?' she asked. The Swami's jaw stiffened. 'Even if I could, I most certainly would not,' he said severely, but as this had sounded harsh for a beginner, he went on in softer tones. 'Understanding comes with time.

I'll lend you a book I've written on the subject if you like, and perhaps you would reconsider coming to the Sunday morning devotions when I give a short teaching; that would certainly hasten your familiarity with these difficult concepts.'

The following Sunday, Anna was there along with 40 others sitting cross-legged on the floor of the basement shrine looking around in amazement. On a low dais at the far end of the room, stood an awe-inspiring portrait of the Hindu saint Rama Krishna surrounded by night-lights in lotus candleholders. From an ornate brass incense burner, the solemn aroma of benjoin filled the air and there were flowers everywhere. Off to one side, three musicians sat on the floor in front of their weird-looking instruments, and then Swami appeared in a long orange robe, to sit on an ornate cushion in front.

First there was chanting in an Indian language, and then recitations, which Anna couldn't understand either. After that, the Swami stood to give a discourse in English which was as complicated as his lecture in the hospital auditorium had been. Boisterous singing livened things up towards the closing stages, and a blessing brought devotions to an end. Anna watched, and listened, and again shuddered to think what her parents would say if they could see her now.

When the devotions were over, the congregation went upstairs to a room where an urn of spicy tea and some bright yellow cookies had been laid out. Feeling excruciatingly shy and out of place, Anna followed. Swami's dear friends comprised smartly dressed Indians passing for European, a bunch of unshaven Europeans looking as though they'd just run out of dope, ladies in saris fluttering hither and thither, and a sprinkling of intense-looking women of different nationalities seemingly at home in the place. Anna was about to slip away when the Swami appeared and like a great orange spoon, scooped her up and stirred her into the soup of his multifaceted followers. It was not the time to speak of the serious subjects that united them all, though some looked as though they had an unusual tale to tell. It may have been this that tempted Anna back on the following Sunday.

After a few visits to the centre, Anna was allowed to borrow books from the Swami's library, but as he never taught on a one-to-one basis until after the devotee had attended devotions for at least one year, Anna hardly caught sight of him. As a book borrower, however, she became an accepted face around the place and often came across a visitor, a student, or a devotee who was interesting to talk to.

Then there was Sudah, but her reputation for fierceness kept Anna from making the first move. Sudah was a Buddhist nun of French nationality who had run an orphanage in Bangalore for many years. Ill health had forced her back to France just at the time when Swami's centre needed a housekeeper, and she'd become the pillar of the place. Anna was as fearful of the Swami's 'right-hand man' as anybody, but when Sudah invited her to help cook lunch one Sunday, she eagerly accepted.

Little by little Sudah became less daunting. 'If I have to scream sometimes,' she said gruffly after scolding a young student who'd burst into her kitchen, 'it's only to stop those greedy little fingers from pillaging my fridge.' The twinkle in her eye belied the gruffness.

One Sunday, when Anna turned up in the kitchen with a bunch of rosemary and thyme she'd bought on the way to the metro, Sudah smiled broadly. 'That reminds me of something that happened when I was fourteen years old,' she said, putting the bunch in a jar of water. 'I had been sent to spend the summer holidays with my uncle and aunt in Athens – I had a passion for Greece at the time. In those days a girl couldn't go anywhere alone, and I was always begging my cousins to take me up to the Acropolis. I must have listened to those tourist guides dozens of times, but never got tired of it. My cousins couldn't understand what I saw in the place, I don't think I knew myself.

'Anyway, at the end of the holidays, before returning to Paris, they let me go up one last time. I remember very clearly now. It was late evening, and those wonderful white pillars were aflame in the setting sun. I had a pocket full of toffee wrappings, and as workmen were burning rubbish over a small fire, I decided to burn them. A young tourist guide with a bouquet of rosemary and thyme in his hand stood chatting to the workman, and as I dropped my toffee wrappings into the fire, he looked at me and said, "Here again?" Then dipping his bouquet in the fire he waved the wonderfully perfumed smoke around. I felt I ought to have recognized him, but I didn't. Then he said, "You'll not find it here, or even in Elusieus any more; India still has it though." Of course I knew of the ancient Elusieus Mystery School, but had never heard of one on the Acropolis, so I supposed he must have been referring to the thyme and rosemary in some way.'

'How very strange,' Anna responded. 'Was it because of what the man had said, that you went to India?'

'*Dieu non*! I only remembered the incident twenty years later – in Bangalore. I'd been shopping for the orphanage, when a bearded sage waved his empty bowl at me. My basket was full; I could spare him rice, and as I poured some into his bowl, he said, "Thank you, lady of Athena." I asked him what that meant, but he shook his head and moved away saying that I had more than enough to do here – meaning Bangalore.'

'Perhaps you had a past life in Athens,' Anna said. 'What made you go to India?'

'What makes you come here?' Sudah answered sharply.

155

'Now, those chickpeas have soaked long enough. You can put them in boiling water and add some of your rosemary and thyme later, when they are almost cooked.'

The marble floor of the grandiose entrance hall of the OUE shone like glass as Anna walked across it to the reception desk. A smartly uniformed receptionist pointed to the lift, and as it rose silently to the eighth floor Anna inspected her appearance in the mirror. She was wearing a smart gray suit, and expensive new lipstick bought especially for the occasion. Yes, she approved of herself – but would Mr Greening?

'Ah, my night nurse!' Greening hailed from behind his desk as Anna was shown into the softly carpeted office. 'Good to see you again. Forgive me for not getting up,' he pointed to a pair of crutches leaning against the desk beside him. Beneath the arch of his desk, an upturned waste paper basket and cushion couched his plastered leg.

Their meeting in the hospital had been so brief that Anna was surprised when Greening treated her more like a friend than a trembling candidate. She remembered, however, that in their earlier conversation he had mentioned her resemblance to his only daughter, and supposed this could have something to do with it. At the time the comparison was purely physical, but when Greening's daughter entered the conversation again, he expressed his perplexity at her having slipped past 30 without acquiring a wedding band. 'I wanted to give her away ages ago,' he said with a little laugh. 'But she set her heart on archaeology, of all things! Now how the devil do you suppose she'll find a fine upstanding male, down some obscure hole in the middle of an uncharted desert?'

The question was of course rhetorical, but his look called for comment. 'Things usually work out the way they're meant to,' Anna replied sweetly, with karma at the back of her mind.

'Well, if she doesn't buck up,' he blurted with feeling, 'she'll miss the boat and all the best blokes will be booked.' That said, he turned the conversation back to Anna, her qualifications, aims and interests. At the conclusion of what had been more of a merry chat than a formal interview, Greening reached for his crutches and made towards the outer office. His secretary stepped forward to take Anna down to the medical unit for her meeting with the Director, Dr Roch, but Greening decided to do the job himself.

They took the corridor slowly, for although Greening despised his crutches, he still needed them. 'New York was a bad idea!' he said jovially, pressing the lift button with his elbow. 'Should have listened to my night nurse. But it's too late now – damage is done, and I'm paying with ten extra days in plaster, and who knows how long on crutches?' The elevator came.

'Where to?' Anna's finger hovered over the button panel.

'The bottom, I'm afraid.'

'The basement, you mean?'

'Not quite. The one just above marked Rez. Inf.' Greening hesitated before going on. 'Your quarters aren't perhaps as modern as you would wish. You see, in the bad old days, a medical unit wasn't considered necessary at all. But as the organization expanded, it became statutory to have first aid on the spot, and from then on the medical service grew into a sizable unit – Doctors, nurses, a laboratory, secretaries, 'Old Uncle Tom Cobbly and all!' When the new wing went up though, I voted the medical unit out of those badly converted offices and into something more appropriate, but Dr Roch seemed satisfied with the way things were. I'm afraid the chance won't come again. Because for one thing, there's not a square inch of working space left in the building, and for another, I'll not be here to plead your cause. I'm being posted to our Asia headquarters in Hong Kong at the end of the year.'

The lift came to an upswing halt; Anna's heart made a similar movement at the thought of losing Greening so soon. They stepped out into a lengthy, neon-lit corridor punctuated with dead-looking doors on either side marked 'Archives'. Away in the distance, a partition daubed with an enormous red cross, reminiscent of army ambulances in the First World War, left no doubt as to what lay beyond.

'That's the main unit,' Greening said, nodding ahead. 'There's another infirmary on the first floor of the conference wing also. Just a small joint, so that folk over there don't have to walk miles for their medical needs. It serves the various conference arenas too. Sizeable conferences go on all year round, you know. Conference factory, that's what I call it.' He paused a moment to catch his breath before moving on. 'Then every five years we have the WEA – World Education Assembly – a marathon comprising three thousand delegates from every country in the world. Quite a jamboree! So you see, medical facilities are needed in both places.'

As they neared the Red Cross panel, Greening halted again, this time to face Anna with an air of seriousness and concern. 'Look,' he said. 'You mustn't be intimidated. Roch isn't a bad bloke at heart; only a little conservative, that's all. Just remember that all staff members have to pass through the medical unit for their statutory check-up at one time or another, so you'll be meeting a lot of healthy people for a change.' Anna nodded, and had the distinct impression she was being saved from the uncharted desert of hospital nursing.

A yard further on, Anna stepped ahead, opened the door for Greening to pass through, and found they had entered a continuation of the corridor turned into a drab waiting room. Two rows of mock-leather seats, placed side by side with their backs along the opposing walls, left a narrow space for movement through the middle, and at the far end, looming over whoever chanced to be waiting, was a bald-faced uni-sex WC.

'Here we are, then,' said Anna's knight on shining crutches. The chairs were all occupied by people flipping through tattered magazines. There was a bell that could be rung for attention, but the moment they arrived a tall nurse of mature years appeared out of nowhere. She wore an old-fashioned *blouse blanche* that started as a dog collar at the throat, and stopped just six inches short of the white clogs nurses often find more comfortable than ordinary shoes. But there was no cap, no make-up and not much of a smile either. Having cast a fleeting glance over the candidate, she greeted the Chief of Personnel with, 'Dr Roch is expecting you, sir.'

'Good!' Greening responded crustily. The nurse then walked over to the boss's door, pressed a bell, and waited for the reciprocating buzzer before pushing it open. Anna cast a puzzled look towards Greening who returned it with a wink as all three trouped into *Monsieur le Directeur*'s spacious, though strictly functional, consulting room.

A man of middling height and age, with a pale complexion and a neat gray moustache, rose slowly from his chair and leaned across his desk to shake hands with the Chief of Personnel, murmuring '*Bonjour.*' Anna couldn't see his eyes; they were focusing on the blotter. Greening hastened to introduce Anna, but instead of a handshake, Roch merely nodded in her direction, and gestured them to chairs on the far side of his immaculately ordered desk.

Pointing to his plastered leg, Greening declined a seat, and after a few inconsequential remarks gave Anna's shoulder a fatherly pat and said he had to be off. The nurse who had ushered them in was at the ready to let Greening out, and after he'd staggered away, she bustled up to Dr

Roch's desk for some signatures and a word in conspiratorial tones. While they spoke, Anna, who felt she'd been transported from the Tropics to the Pole, used these moments to acclimatize, and focus on Roch before he focused on her. He was reaching for a file and listening to the nurse without looking at her. Observing every gesture, Anna groped for some feature or endearing mannerism that would allow her to feel they were going to get along, but his face gave nothing away. The thin mouth tweaked up at the corners, though whether from humour or tension, she couldn't tell. His eyes might have supplied the answer, but they concentrated on the file that the nurse had handed him; his voice remained lowered too.

When the nurse had hurried away, Dr Roch slid Anna's application form in front of him, and without looking up went through its contents detail by detail. Monsieur's interest was confined to qualifications and experience. The candidate's personality was not an issue; she clearly wasn't expected to have one. Neither was Anna expected to have questions for him; she only knew that the interview was over when he rang for his two nurses, Mademoiselle Maude, and Mademoiselle Lisette, and ordered them to show Anna around. Anna thanked Dr Roch for seeing her and followed Maude and Lisette into the small room they claimed was the infirmary.

That evening Marie-Claire dropped by oozing curiosity. 'How did it go?' she asked, and listened as Anna covered her misgivings by making her morning's exploits sound amusing. Having listened to the description of the boss and his henchwomen, Marie-Claire asked about the work.

'It's an outpatient department for the huge staff, and certain members of the diplomatic corps. They send delegates and experts all over the world, so there is a great deal of vaccinating to do, otherwise it's small stuff. Oh yes, Roch also mumbled something about giving advice and mopping up tears!'

Marie-Claire laughed. 'Think you've got it?'

'If David Greening bears weight, perhaps, but I don't think I'm Dr Roch's *verre de vin*.'

'Why not?'

'He neither looked at me nor smiled during the entire interview. He was only just polite.'

'Doesn't sound very French to me.'

'Me neither. We'll just have to wait and see.'

Greening's influence did bear weight, for in due course a letter arrived on official notepaper, informing Anna that she'd been selected for the post, and that she must go to Personnel to sign her contract. She was expected to report for duty in three months' time.

'Thank you so much for your help,' Anna wrote to Greening, and ended her letter with best wishes for his mended leg.

'Who will I laugh with when you've gone?' Marie Claire moaned in the café where they met after Anna had visited the huge OUE Personnel Service to sign her contract.

'Don't be silly. It's office hours. We can meet any time. I'll be as free as you are. Not only that, pay is based on the American scale – double what I'm getting now. And, you'll never believe it – six whole weeks' holiday a year!'

'And you say the department is headed by an ex-military man who neither looked at you nor smiled?' Marie-Claire pouted dubiously. 'What about colleagues?'

'Three plus me. I only saw the two in the main unit, Maude and Lisette; both past their prime. Maude is the snooty one who greeted us. Lisette looks a shade older with fizzy white hair, bright little eyes, and speaks with the velocity of machine-gun fire. They mentioned a married one too. She runs the conference infirmary in another part of the building, but I didn't get to see her. They were polite, I suppose, but not exactly chummy.' Anna paused before saying, 'Oh, don't look like that, Marie-Claire. I'm sure it will work out beautifully when I get to know them.'

'With all those advantages, it'll have to. Where will you live when you leave the hospital studio?'

'A one-bedroom apartment not far from the Organization goes with the job. '

'Wonderful! Think of all the new people you'll meet, and healthy for a change.'

Anna smiled. 'Mm – so I'm told.'

Chapter Fourteen

July that year was wonderfully sunny, and after the labours of the night Anna found that a brisk walk in the crisp morning air cleared the cobwebs and made for better sleep later on. No city in the world offers greater beauty than Paris on a bright morning. One of her predilections was to stroll along the quay where long black barges converted into houseboats with gaily painted woodwork and flower pots on deck were moored. She would hang over the wall watching them awaken to the day, hear the clatter of pots and pans, smell the brewing coffee, and dream of living in one of them with the man she was destined to meet. Then she would wander into a nearby covered flower market and linger in the perfume of a thousand freshly sprayed blooms before buying a small bunch to take home. Some mornings she'd take off in another direction to drink coffee among breakfasting tourists at a pavement café; which made her feel human again and gave her a whiff of holiday mood.

It was on one such sunny morning on the Place du Tertre, that Anna's quest for one such as Haig led her into unexplored waters. She had just begun to enjoy her coffee and watch the world go by, when a book on the adjoining table magnetized her attention. The glossy paperback had *Initiates of the Planet* embossed in gaudy gold letters right across the cover, and its presumed owner was a young man slouching on the chair beside hers, cocooned in a daydream.

When the waiter appeared he sat up, ordered coffee, and then noticed Anna's eyes on his book. Given that the volume was written in English, he hazarded conversation in his mother tongue. 'Hi, I'm Terry Miller,' he said. 'Are you into this stuff, too?'

'In a casual kind of way, I suppose.' Anna replied evasively.

He pushed the tome across onto Anna's table. 'Go ahead – have a look if you like.'

'Thanks, I'd like to,' Anna replied, and reaching for the book, started to look for Morward Haig.

'You sound English,' Terry pursued. 'Are you vacationing here?'

'No. Are you?'

'No. I'm from California, on an art student exchange programme at the Sorbonne. My real interest, though, is esoteric studies. I didn't catch your name.'

'Anna.'

'Well, what brings you to Paris, Anna?' With the book in her hand, Anna told him what she was doing in Paris, and then tactfully turned her eyes to the fat volume again. All the great religious founders were there, and a number of lesser-known names too, but no mention of one who could have been around in the 1920s. Finally she closed the book and gave her full attention to the young man who seemed eager to converse. 'Are *you* taken with all this?' she asked.

'You bet I am,' he said, and went on to tell how he came from San Francisco, where oriental philosophy, mysticism and all manner of psychic phenomena known as 'New Age' were fast becoming the rage. He described it as a 'hodge-podge' that was neither religion nor philosophy, but borrowed from both. Nor could it be identified specifically as a sect or a cult, though numerous sects and cults – sublime and ridiculous – had sprung out of it. 'Call it a spiritual cocktail, if you like,' Terry concluded.

'And it has intoxicated you!' Anna added, smiling, as she

slid the volume back to its owner. It was time she made a move, but with the sun warming her shoulders, sparrows chirping over crumbs at her feet, and an accordion playing Viennese waltzes up the hill, she felt inclined to linger. 'This New Age thing hasn't reached France yet, has it?' she pursued.

'Not in quite the same way as back home.' Terry acknowledged, but explained he had, nevertheless, stumbled upon an unorthodox group in Paris whose epicentre was an incredible man named Michel. The group was still in embryo, but would one day have *immense* importance for the future of the planet. This 'embryo' as Terry called it, was now gestating in an old farmhouse in the throes of renovation on the outskirts of Paris. When the renovations were completed, the farm was to become a place of healing, spiritual development, organic farming, and a haven of refuge for the group, when things got tough.

'Tough?'

'We are entering the Apoco.'

'The *what*?'

'I guess you're not familiar with the jargon. Apocalypse.'

'Oh, that.' Anna was far too immersed in the pursuit of consciousness taught by the Swami on Sundays, to worry about the end of the world.

'We are perfectly above board,' Terry went on. 'I'd be happy to drive you out to the farm and see for yourself.' Anna shook her head disparagingly. 'Well, why not come to the Wednesday meditation in town, first?'

'Thanks, but I don't think I can manage that,' she said, signalling the waiter for her bill. Terry babbled on. It was only when he tapped the glossy cover of his book, stating proudly that Michel was one of *them*, meaning an initiate, that Anna changed her mind.

Michel's meditations were held in the gym of a small primary school. On the appointed Wednesday, Terry turned up at Anna's apartment building in a battered *Deux Chevaux* excitedly chewing gum. Anna got in, and as they jogged along she was briefed on essentials. Michel apparently spoke all the terrestrial languages but always communicated in his mother tongue, French. The group's main purpose was to prepare for the 'Apoco', of which they had no fear because the farm was a spiritually protected space, and if things got badly out of control they'd all be airlifted to safety anyway.

'After the planetary clean-up,' he continued, spitting his gum out of the window, 'we're due to move into the Golden Age.'

'Really?' Anna replied. She'd been only half-listening in her excitement at the thought of meeting a real live initiate, and wondering if he would already know of all the mysterious things that had happened to her as Haig would have done.

They mingled with the 30 or so others at the gym. Terry introduced Anna to right and left throughout the room. They only halted when a short, dumpy man, well into middle age, wearing a coarsely knitted sweater and baggy corduroy trousers, approached. He shook Terry's hand while his watery gray eyes veered towards the newcomer.

Terry introduced them. 'Michel, this is Anna.'

Anna shook the man's hand, wondering if this was *the* Michel? She knew initiates sometimes disguised themselves so as to meld with their disciples, but expected the handshake of an initiate, to feel more like an electric shock than a depleted chamois-leather beanbag.

'Terry tells me you are a nurse,' Michel commented with a note of approval.

'That's right.'

'*Très bien.* We shall be needing nurses sooner than you may think,' he remarked wryly, and then moved on. A pale young creature with long red hair, who had stood demurely behind him all the while, followed.

Soon everyone gathered in a circle around a thick wax candle flickering on the floor in the middle of the room. They joined hands and closed their eyes. 'You will feel the energies in a minute,' Terry whispered. But all Anna felt was the clammy grip of the person on her right. After a while, everyone dropped hands but with their eyes still closed, sat cross-legged on the floor. Michel commanded all present to visualize Planet Earth shrouded in brilliant white light. This was the group's magnificent healing gift to soothe the apocalyptic rage of Mother Earth. A rage of which the recent devastating earthquakes were but a tame beginning! A knowing titter went round the circle. Puzzled by such heartlessness, Anna half-opened her eyes to scrutinize the mediators.

They seemed unassuming folk; the average age was about 35 years, and twice the number of women to men. Next to Michel sat Miriam, the slim redhead who had trailed him earlier. There was something childishly angelic about the girl's face as she sat with eyes closed, her left hand resting delicately on her fiancé's right knee. According to Terry, Michel had spiritually outgrown and divorced his first two wives, and was now engaged to Miriam. The fact that he was old enough to be her father mattered not. They were 'soul mates', which explained and excused everything.

Michel began to speak again. Anna hastily closed her eyes. 'Potent cosmic forces proceeding from The Christ and Buddha are pouring upon the earth at this very moment,' he said to the motionless assembly. 'Oh, wonderful! These mighty cosmic forces are turning now on each and every one of you. Lift up your arms and receive.'

The meditation ended with Michel stretching his hands in a gesture of blessing over the circle of bowed heads. After that, everyone got to their feet and started reconnecting with themselves and each other in conversation.

'Well,' said Terry, 'how d'you feel?'
'Same as before,' Anna replied.

'That's just fine. It often takes a while for things to filter through.'

It was gone ten-thirty, and although nobody seemed in a hurry to leave, Anna wanted to be taken home.

The initial impressions of Michel and his group weren't in the least inspiring, but Anna knew that hasty judgements sometimes prove false; initiates were inscrutable people, and as her next lot of nights off fell on a Wednesday, she decided to attend another meditation and see if she felt more positive.

When the day of the second meditation came, Terry turned up like clockwork to drive her to the gym, chewing his gum with all the congeniality of an experienced convert-maker. Anna didn't mention her regular attendance at the Swami's centre; it belonged to a different world.

This time the candlelit meditation brought forth the crystal power of Atlantis, people from Venus, the Egyptian dynasties, Hermes, Jesus and Pythagoras all rolled into one. According to Michel, the entire human race was a colossal genetic experiment that had gone wrong. Again Anna studied the group unobtrusively as they hung on Michel's every word, but try as she might, she could neither see nor feel anything special about Michel. She was even beginning to think that the subjects he extolled had a superficial, *Readers Digest* quality to them.

By the end of the second meditation, Anna knew she wanted to quit. But just in case Michel really *was* an initiate testing her spiritual stamina, she went to the gym one more time to give him the benefit of a heavily weighted doubt. Terry picked her up, she mingled with the group, observed Michel as deeply as she could, and went through the usual motions. But no compelling insight emerged to change her mind, and she left wishing she'd trusted her first impressions.

On the homeward journey, Anna told Terry that Michel's

group was indeed a wonderful thing, but not for her – thanks all the same. She expected a barrage of argument, and encouragement to give it a longer try, but the 'New Age' lion took it like a newborn lamb, and they said an amicable, though definitive, goodbye.

That should have been the end of it, but it was not. Two weeks later a panic-stricken Terry was on the phone. 'Miriam needs an injection. They told me to drive you out to the farm presto.'

'Out of the question. I've just washed my hair.'

'Have a heart,' Terry whined.

'The nearest hospital, local doctor or nurse, would be just as good and a deal quicker,' Anna reasoned.

Minutes later Terry was at her door and brushing past her into the living-room. Anna was furious.

'I've already said no. As you can see, my hair is dripping wet.'

But Terry just stood there, arms folded, a look of dire determination on his face. Anna stood in front of him, equally adamant.

'You can't do this to me,' Terry moaned. His problem, the real problem, was that he'd forgotten to tell Michel that Anna had bowed out of the group, and he had already promised to drive her out to the farm without fail. His loyalty and standing with Michel was at stake. Would she please, please, please help him out – just this once? Anna still shook her head.

'You don't understand. Miriam is in *pain!*' Terry yelled, as though stricken himself. 'She's in bed – can't be moved.'

Anna wasn't duped, though nurses have trouble ignoring the word 'pain'; it sets up a troubling reflex demanding action. Terry noticed the momentary effect his words had had, and before she could harden up, he drove in with, 'If I don't keep my word to them, they'll expel me. Please! I'll never bother you for anything ever again.'

Anna went to the bedroom and wrapped a scarf around her wet head. 'Be warned, Terry,' she said. 'If I don't see a proper prescription for whatever has to be injected, you are taking me straight home. Understand?'

Darkness had fallen, so it was by the car headlights that Anna first saw the isolated stone farmhouse frowning in the shadows at the end of a long muddy trail. This 'spiritual haven' belonged to Michel, but the renovations were undertaken by specially chosen members of the group, labouring for free. Others had the privilege of sweating ardently from dawn to dusk farming organic vegetables.

They entered by the front door, passed quickly through a labyrinth of bleak, candlelit rooms, and finally climbed the stairs to Michel's attic apartment. Here Terry knocked reverently on the door, and Michel appeared, wearing carpet slippers and the same baggy corduroy trousers Anna had seen on two previous occasions. He seemed pleased to see Anna, but instead of an apology for the imposition, he merely declared Anna's vibrations to be the only ones compatible with Miriam's healing process. After a dismissive nod to Terry, he led Anna into an apartment that, in contrast to the rest of the house, was a model of warmth and comfort.

In the bedroom, the redhead smiled wanly from an electrically operated multi-poise double bed hooked up to a profusion of electronic gadgets. These, Michel said, directed cosmic forces and healing energies into the room. However, it seemed strange that, against this backdrop of futuristic therapeutics and esoteric know-how, they had stooped to consult an ordinary doctor for Miriam's ills.

'Hello, Miriam. Terry tells me you have a lot of pain,' Anna said kindly, though suffering was not in evidence at that moment.

'Oh, it's not really pain,' Michel butted in, 'just discomfort caused by her body's slow attunement to my own high-frequency vibrations.'

'I see,' Anna replied, starting to feel an atmosphere she really did not like. 'If you would just show me the prescription, I'll get started.'

'Can I offer you something to drink – tea – cognac?' Michel said, producing a crumpled prescription from his trouser pocket.

'No, thanks. I can't stay long.'

The prescription was genuine enough; all it amounted to, though, was aspirin, but to be given intravenously. Intravenously! Anna was not expecting that. Intravenous injections carry the risk of a sudden reaction, and should one occur in Michel's apartment, she would be helpless. What was the doctor playing at, or had he intended going to the house and giving it himself? Anna was uneasy. She wanted to refuse, but at this juncture, the only way out – was through.

'OK. Where's the syringe?' she asked, forcing a spurt of brightness into her voice.

'All in the bathroom,' Michel replied, leading in that direction. Once beyond Miriam's hearing, he whispered, 'You've been drawn to this group for a *very* special reason, Anna. You have one of the brightest auras I've ever seen. Really *very* bright.' Anna remained dumb; but the flush that rose to her cheeks stemmed from fear, not flattery.

Into the tastefully refurbished bathroom they went. On the marble-edged washbasin, a large bottle of expensive toilet water, a gold chain and a good-sized diamond ring had been pushed aside to make space for a packaged syringe, disinfectant, cotton wool and the ampoule. Anna immediately inspected the engraved label on the ampoule, hoping it would not correspond with the prescription, thereby giving her an easy let-out. But there was no discrepancy.

Michel moved up close to peer over Anna's shoulder; she could smell his breath. 'I can manage alone, thank you,' she snapped. 'Go back to Miriam, I'll be along in a minute.' Michel jerked back, pursed his lips, and went.

When he had gone, Anna breathed deeply to quell her racing heart. 'When this is over,' she told herself while filling the syringe with a substance she'd no intention of letting into Miriam's vein, 'the bright aura will be out of here like a shooting star!'

After more deep breaths, Anna returned to the bedroom and suggested Michel leave the room while she gave the injection. He obeyed. She then checked Miriam's arm and, using a dressing-gown cord for tourniquet, she found the vein.

'This won't hurt, Miriam,' she said with a confident smile. 'No need to look – just focus on that picture of the pharaoh over there.' While Miriam's eyes focused on Tutankhamun, Anna expelled both air and liquid from the syringe and, having slid the needle into Miriam's vein, withdrew the patient's own blood, released the tourniquet, and then slowly returned the contents of the syringe to its unsuspecting owner.

On the way home, frightening conjectures raced through Anna's mind. Miriam must have been to a doctor's office to get the prescription, though what she had said to solicit one isolated dose of intravenous aspirin was difficult to imagine. It was easy to see why Michel wouldn't want strangers in that house, and had opted for the "bright aura" instead of a gossipy nurse. But could they have forged the prescription, and put some other substance, an illicit drug perhaps, in the vial instead? No. That would be difficult. 'Or could they have suspected my withdrawal and set up the scenario to make me feel important?' Whatever the reason for that expedition, Anna knew that future entanglements had to be pre-empted at all costs.

If Michel had something to hide – Anna sensed that he had – an abrupt break might scare him and lead to unimaginable trouble. For a while she felt at a loss, but then thinking back over her conversations with Terry, and the few words she'd exchanged with other members of the group, she realized that she'd never mentioned her impending change of job and residence to any of them. So, by the time Terry's jalopy squeaked to a halt in front of the hospital's apartment building, Anna's strategy was clear.

'Terry,' she said. 'You know, I'm rather glad you forgot to tell Michel I was no longer interested in the meditations, because he has made me change my mind.'

'Jeez, that's just great, Anna,' Terry replied, circulating his gum with centrifugal speed.

'Yes, I feel it would be really worth giving it another try – when I'm not on late shift, that is to say.'

'Far out! How about Wednesday next?'

'Late shift, I'm afraid.' Anna replied to eke out the time. 'But the Wednesday after should be fine.'

'I'll pick you up. Thanks for being such a sport this evening. No regrets, eh? Michel sure knows what's cookin'.'

'Sure does,' Anna responded gaily. But the meditation she had agreed to attend would fall on the eve of her move to another part of the city, distant enough not to brush with the group again. She would go as promised, but let it be known then that bad news from home was forcing her back to England – for good.

173

Chapter Fifteen

Bright-eyed and bushy-tailed, Anna presented herself at the main medical unit on her first morning at the OUE. She opened the door of the little infirmary on the dot of eight to find Maude and Lisette waiting for her. They stood shoulder to shoulder behind the infirmary desk; an unlikely combination of hawk and sparrow. Anna was first to say *bonjour* and they broke ranks to move forward and shake her hand. 'Nerves,' Anna thought, 'only nerves. It's bound to take a while for us to get to know each other.'

For the first week Anna trailed either Maude or Lisette, learning what they did and how they did it. She discovered that the congested little room she'd seen at her interview and taken for an antechamber really *was* the infirmary; and the overall shabbiness she had observed before, only the tip of a very tawdry iceberg. Good pay and generous vacations belonged to staff rules and couldn't be denied, but everything else was at the discretion of the unapproachable ex-military Director, whose unopposed attitudes were demonstrated by the state of the terrain.

Greening had been right. Only cursory effort, and even less expense, had gone into converting a row of offices into a functioning medical unit 30 years previously. Since then the medical staff and their functions had tripled, but the space to accommodate them had not. The square metres were plentiful, but the will to convert them into something efficient and comfortable, considered unimportant. *Monsieur le Directeur* and his two full-time doctors enjoyed decent consulting rooms, but they remained totally indifferent to the plight of the three secretaries, who had run out of filing space and managing with cardboard boxes on the floor; the two laboratory technicians, producing haematological profiles and other analysis in an area little larger than an alcove; and the three nurses working in an infirmary with just one desk, two chairs and one typewriter between them. After a while, when Anna got the hang of 'Administrations', she realized that a low budget went with high prestige in the lofty boardrooms where Angels fear to tread.

Patients fared no better. Of the two examination couches crammed into the infirmary, one was jammed up against a filing cabinet, ostensibly hidden by a flimsy cotton screen, and the other squeezed into an open-ended cubicle plainly visible to all who entered the room. Anna had never seen a wartime field dressing station, but she now knew what they must have been like. Maude and Lisette refused to admit that anything was amiss and warned Anna that complaints were always rebuffed with an invitation to work elsewhere. Employment with international status and conditions was hard to come by, so Dr Roch's boat was never rocked.

Had Anna's colleagues been young and gay, the shortcomings might have created camaraderie, but Maude and Lisette had been there since the First Aid beginnings and melded with the mind and attitudes of *le Patron*. Their catchphrase was, 'So it was in the beginning, is now, and ever shall be.

There was one exception, however – the bright and friendly Elizabeth Dapi who appeared from the conference infirmary every afternoon to work alongside Anna for a couple of hours, to replace Lisette's off-duty, and Maude's hospital visits. Elizabeth was a happy, companionable woman, who had married late in life and was expecting her first baby aged 40.

'Take no notice and enjoy your pay,' she'd say consoling. 'You can't change anything, I've tried; you can't talk to a brick wall without getting bricks in your face.'

When Anna was more or less accustomed to her new environment, 'sunstroke' began to wane. The joy and confidence that had pervaded her life over the past months was fading slowly away. She wondered if perhaps her less than docile attitude towards the medical unit was choking it, and confided her work-story to Sudah one Sunday morning as they were shelling peas at the kitchen table.

'Tricky karma, probably.' Sudah declared.

'How long does *that* last?' Anna enquired.

'Till understanding comes.'

Anna fell silent. Sudah went on. 'It's a question of scrutinizing whatever is rubbing you up the wrong way from the inside, rather than fighting it on the outside.'

'Oh?'

Sudah stopped shelling to gaze across the half-filled bowl. 'The quickest way through is total acceptance, you know.'

'What!' Anna exploded. 'And join the doormats? Never! Besides, if acceptance were the way to enlightenment, the entire medical unit would have reached Nirvana ages ago.'

Sudah laughed. 'To say "*oui Monsieur*" is not the kind of acceptance I'm referring to; nor the "grin and bear it" kind either. Acceptance that carries one through, is the one you bring yourself to take – not swallow. It is the art of allowing yourself to coexist, without fear or animosity, with an unalterable situation, however humiliating, unfair or uncomfortable. Fear and animosity hold a situation in place, you see. It's natural to suppose that people will take advantage of you, and animosity springs from that fear. But if you can somehow detach from the outside and welcome what is happening within yourself, a kind of strength oozes out that prevents people from walking all over you. It takes practice, but when you have mastered that, circumstances usually change for the better. Not easy, I grant you, but in my experience the outer doesn't improve until the inner changes.'

'Well, if I just sit accepting *le Service*, as they call it, all I'd attain to would be spiritual bed-sores.'

Sudha laughed again. 'Your situation isn't *that* bad.'

'But the facts *are* negative, Sudah. Very. And I really doubt that anything would change just because the new nurse dropped her fear and animosity.'

'You've missed the point. It's not them, or the situation, it's *you*, Anna, who have to change. Just for a while you might stop applying your idea of "good" and "bad" to everything that happens.'

'Because it doesn't exist?'

'No. But you'll be interested to see the result in your own mind. Think of it as a little experiment.' Sudah added sympathetically.

At this point they'd finished the peas. Sudah went to answer the telephone in the hall, and when she returned, Anna had to go.

As the city Metro rattled Anna home she mulled over Sudha's suggestion, thinking it would take a huge detonation to disperse her objection to 'As it was in the beginning, is now, and ever shall be'. But if this would bring 'sunstroke' back it would be worth it. In any case she had nothing to lose and there was the comfort of having Sudah to report back to.

The experiment was difficult. Anna's fear, antagonism, and a multitude of other emotions erupted each time Lisette's verbal Kalashnikov sprayed *le Service* with forceful, fussy words; and again when she had to vacate the desk and perch on the radiator so that silent superior Maud could write up her report on hospital visits. Anna's antagonism was particularly acute when overcrowding in the infirmary led to a pile-up in the waiting room, and the only other place in which she could give an injection or replace a bandage, was the stuffy staff changing room. Anna practised Sudah's suggestion. She tried – she really did, but nothing seemed to halt the departure of 'sunstroke'.

At six o'clock on a gray November morning, Anna awoke and knew that indescribable feeling was not there. 'Sunstroke' was gone. She could, of course, ask the Swami why, but didn't think he'd know. Which reminded her that it was a special Sunday at the Centre and she'd promised to arrive early to help Sudah in the kitchen.

Hordes of devotees dressed in their glittering best were arriving as Anna reached the Centre, and more swarmed around the house bearing flowers, food and exciting little packages for Swami, whom they affectionately addressed as Swami-ji. He greeted them all with magnanimous affection.

On these occasions Sudah opened her heart and her kitchen door to everyone. Just before noon, the gathering descended to the lavishly decorated basement shrine for a grand ceremony. Candles flickered, flowers overwhelmed the eye, their perfume melding with a fog of incense swirling thickly around the fire censer in the ceiling. Paris seemed to have poured its entire Hindu population onto the floor, where they sat shoulder to shoulder clapping, swaying and chanting *Bijans*. Then there were prayers led by Swami-ji, resplendent in a robe of orange silk. Offerings were blessed and respectfully laid before the portrait of Rama Krishna. The culminating moment came when Swami-ji stood and circled a flaming candelabrum majestically before the crowd to the tinkling of little bells. Anna sat discretely with Sudah at the back, observing it all with sympathetic fascination. But nobody stepped out of the crowd to tell her why 'sunstroke' had come and gone, or why it was taking such a time to find her beloved. Wise old Sudah had been helpful, but neither she, nor the erudite Swami, was a substitute for the enlightened Morward Haig.

Anna practised Sudah's suggestion, for several weeks, but Maude and Lisette were wearing her down drop by drop. All the healthy people she was supposed to be meeting were not inclined to linger in the medical unit, and wouldn't have done so even if Bridget Bardot were on the receiving line. Nothing was turning out the way Anna expected, and she was seriously contemplating returning to the poverty and friendliness of a London hospital, when Lisette bustled into the infirmary, eyeing Anna with a faked look of doom.

'*He* wants to see you *immediately*,' she said, cocking her head towards the boss's door.

'Good,' Anna responded dryly. 'I need to see him, too.'

Anna rang the bell, waited for the buzzer, and then pushed the directorial door open. Roch looked up from his papers.

'*Entrez Mademoiselle*,' he said, and without offering a greeting or a seat, went straight to the point. 'Madame Dapi is now on sick leave. She'll not be back until after her maternity leave, so you are to work in the First Aid post until her return.'

'First Aid post?' Anna enquired. 'I thought she worked in the Conference wing, carrying out the same duties as here in the main unit.'

'The statute defines that infirmary as First Aid post,' he said, dryly.

Anna didn't care what it was called; elation defied description. This was the wisest, noblest and possibly kindest decision that Roch had ever made. He had unwittingly contrived an undreamed-of solution to Anna's dilemma. She almost wanted to embrace him – but not quite. Moreover, this masterful move would satisfy everyone. Lisette would be happy because she would have a new replacement to boss around. Maude, because Anna would be taking her 'improvement methodology' with her, and Anna, because she'd be working solo; Destiny must have been grinning too.

Another First World War Red Cross daubed the door of Anna's First Aid post. It gave access to a small but comfortable waiting room, from whence a connecting door led directly into a compact modern infirmary. The privacy and tranquillity of the place drew prayers of deepest gratitude, and Anna knew that once she'd reclaimed her personality from beneath the suffocating atmosphere of the main unit, the flame of optimism would rekindle.

One fine morning, only days after settling into her new surroundings, Anna answered the buzzer to find sunlight personified standing in the waiting-room. The woman, in her thirties, was of medium height with straight blonde hair and dressed from top to toe in radiant orange. Her pink and white complexion bore no embellishments; the only adornment was a long necklace of dark wooden beads.

'Hi!' said the bright one, her smile as broad as her American accent.

'Come in,' Anna replied, walking briskly through to her desk in the little surgery. 'What can I do for you?'

'Vaccinations for Delhi.'

'OK, but I'm expecting someone in five minutes, so perhaps we could make an appointment for this afternoon. What's your name?'

'Virya,' she replied, with another enchanting smile. 'My appointment *is* for now, actually.'

Anna's agenda read: 'Veronica Silverling (Economic advisor). One-week mission to India.

'I'm expecting a Miss Silverling,' Anna said.

'That's me.'

'You mean you're taking Miss Silverling's appointment?' This young woman's appearance didn't fit with the title.

The orange one laughed. 'No, I *am* Miss Silverling.'

'So Vera must be your nickname,' Anna said, drawing her card from the filling cabinet.

'Virya,' the economist corrected. 'It's a Sanskrit name. Most people get confused. I changed my name. It's a long story.'

'So you're going to Delhi on official mission.'

'That's right – but I take annual leave in India every year, so all my vaccinations are valid except for cholera.'

The infirmary card verified Virya's words, and after the usual preamble, Anna prepared the shot.

'So Virya is a Sanskrit name,' Anna said casually to distract from the jab. 'Sounds fascinating. How did you come by it?'

'It's a long story. Do you really want to know?'

'Yes. Unless you don't feel like telling me.'

Virya rolled up her sleeve and seemed happy to remember the event. 'Well, after getting our PhDs in Sacramento, my boyfriend and I decided to take an open-ended vacation to India. We'd heard that India was famous for 'holy men,' and just for fun, decided to track some of them down. We had a great time. But on the night before we were due to fly back to the US, we slept in a small Bombay hotel where we came across a book of Shri Nakshatra's discourses left behind by a former occupant. After reading some of the discourses, we decided that this was a holy man we simply had to see. So we cancelled our flight to Los Angeles, and made the three-hour train journey to the Nakshatra Ashram near Lonavala.' Vyria rolled down her sleeve. 'Thanks – didn't feel a thing.'

'Yes, but how did you get the name?' Anna insisted.

'That was more than five years ago, when the Ashram was very informal and one could speak with Guruji, every evening if one wanted. Well we went along with a handful of others, not knowing what to expect. But the moment we saw him, it was like we'd known him forever – kinda love at first sight. After a week of listening to his morning discourse, he asked if we wanted to follow his teaching, and when we said yes, he put a *mala* (a string of 108 wooden beads) around our necks, and gave us a new name. Mine was Ma Anand Virya. So that's how I got this name.'

'Interesting,' Anna mused, staring at the beads around Virya's neck. 'Does the name have a special meaning?'

'*Ma* is the prefix for "woman" – mother, if you like. *Anand* means "bliss", and *Virya* is a Sanskrit word for "valour". After that, Guruji insisted we meditate every day and wear the traditional sannyasin colour, orange – though it can be stretched from ochre through to burgundy.'

Anna was amazed. 'Is this what's-his-name an initiate, I wonder?'

'Shri Nakshatra is an Enlightened Master – a realized soul. One who has come full circle and has no further need to incarnate, but has chosen to do so to help others. Are you into these things?'

'In a way,' Anna replied. 'Does all this make you a kind of nun, and your boyfriend a kind of monk?'

'No. Hindu sannyasins are supposed to be celibate, but Guruji calls us neo-sannyasins, he gives the *mala* to all who ask, and we grow gradually under his guidance. I'll send you a book of his discourses in the internal mail if you like. Then, if you want to talk some more, we could get together when I'm back from this mission.'

'I'd love it.'

A week later Virya left for Delhi, and the promised book lay on Anna's desk. When the morning's first patient called to cancel his appointment, Anna opened the book and plunged into the Zen discourses given by Nakshatra at his regular morning talk. Although the verbatim transcription of these discourses came in prose, poetry filtered through, sweeping Anna into a current of understanding she had never experienced before. While discoursing on nothingness, something ineffable swelled in her mind. And when the subject slid from form to formlessness, the thrill was such that tears welled. On a wave of elation Anna picked up the phone, dialled the main unit and, holding the receiver a precautionary three inches from her ear, waited for Lisette's staccato.

'I need all the leave I'm entitled to as soon as possible,' Anna said.

'*Comment? Non! Impossible! Le Patron . . .*' etc., etc. Lisette rattled away, But when Destiny calls, even the medical unit is powerless to obstruct, and the following day, after the request had been macerated in the minds of permission-givers, Anna had five days' leave attached to two weekends, amounting to nine days in all.

A few days after Virya's return from Delhi, Anna stood at her front door, grin on face and flowers in hand.

'Come right in,' Virya said. And after hugging her guest as though they'd been lifelong friends, Anna was led into a room furnished solely with chintz-covered mattresses and cushions on the floor. Poster-sized pictures of Nakshatra hung on the walls and a delicious smell of cooking filled the air.

Virya's New Delhi mission became the focus of conversation to begin with, and then Anna said; 'Virya, you're not going to believe this, but I'm off to Lonavala in ten days' time.'

'Holy smoke! That soon?'

'Yes, I simply have to meet your Guruji.'

Virya looked up at the ceiling, grinning broadly. 'I knew it, man! I just knew it.' she hooted. Her delight was curtailed by the hiss of milk on the stove and she spun away to turn off the gas. Anna followed the smell of burning. 'How long will you be there?' Virya asked.

'Seven days, plus two for travel.'

'Kinda short, don't you think?'

'It's my leave quota for the months that I have worked. However, if this Nakshatra is what I think, I can anticipate next year's vacation and go back for a month in February.'

'That would be great. I usually go in February, too. But I have to warn you, the Ashram has filled up considerably since my first visit and, if you want to speak to Guruji – it's called *darshan* – you will have to go to the office and book it the moment you arrive.'

Over the meal, Virya offered more advice on everything a girl should know about going to an Ashram in India. 'And if you'd like a preview,' she said, 'I have a taped discourse followed by a potluck supper here, on Thursday evenings.'

Anna shook her head. 'It's the dentist next Thursday and the Thursday after that, I'll be gone.'

'Well – plentia time when you're back.'

Warmed by this new friendship and a wonderful vegetarian meal, Anna left Virya's apartment loaded with Bhagwan books, an orange robe, a list of Poona hotels and a consignment of useful information.

Anna dared not mention her Indian impulse to friends knowing they'd take her for crazy, but her project drifted into a conversation with an Indian patient, Nirmala. Nirmala thought it *very* unwise. 'Women just don't travel alone in India,' she said primly. 'I'll cable my uncle in Bombay to be of assistance.'

'No!' Anna protested quickly. 'Thanks, but everything is already organized and it would complicate life terribly to alter plans now. I'm very used to travel and would rather go alone.' Nirmala's reply was a surreptitious smile, and one that might have been worrying but for the fact that Nirmala's injections were a daily event, so any further mention of assistance could be scotched immediately; fortunately there was no need.

The following week Virya drove Anna out to the airport. The Bombay flight would be leaving on schedule. 'Bon voyage,' Virya said as she hugged Anna goodbye. 'You won't forget to order those taped discourses for me, will you?'

'No problem. Big thank you,' Anna replied. Then turned towards Passport Control.

Chapter Sixteen

After nine long hours, the Boeing touched down at Bombay airport. A landing stairway was wheeled against the exit, and a stream of weary passengers poured down the steps. Anna followed the crowd, but no sooner had she moved onto the tarmac than a uniformed chauffeur touched her arm. He asked if she was Anna Edwards, and when she nodded, he put a letter from his employer into her hand. Nirmala's worrying smile was not at the forefront of her mind, so she shook her head and prepared to walk on.

'Read, read, read,' the chauffeur insisted, barring her way; Anna opened the envelope.

Under an impressive Ministry of Health letterhead, the writer started 'Dear Doctor,' and then introduced himself as Dr Gopal Mehta, Nirmala's uncle. Dr Mehta, however, seemed to think that Anna had come to India on official business for the World Health Organization. And after profuse apologies for not greeting her personally, said that his chauffeur, Banda, would drive her to Victoria Station where Leela, a house servant, was to accompany her on the train journey to his residence in Lonavala. He hoped she would have a comfortable journey, and looked forward to joining her when he drove up with his family for the tennis championships on the following day. Would Anna have time to give them the pleasure of attending the championships with them?

Highly amused, Anna put the letter in her purse and followed Banda like Mary's little lamb.

Dr Mehta's trusted chauffeur, waving his master's diplomatic pass, made short work of airport formalities and in a matter of minutes ushered Anna into the back seat of a king-sized limo, where she sat like the last pea in a pod all the way to Victoria Station.

Banda pulled up right in front of the station's grand entrance as though he were delivering royalty. He opened the door for Madame to alight, and then went round to the back to lift her very un-regal canvas holdall out of the double-bed sized boot. Looking over his shoulder to be sure Anna was following, Banda and the holdall then plunged into the oven-like heat of Bombay's teeming railway station. Once inside Anna immediately shortened the royal distance between herself and Dr Mehta's chauffeur, in fact she all but hung onto his jacket as he waded into the thick shoal of human beings. Losing Banda would make her a 'missing person' long-term – and she had not told her parents where she was going. When they reached the appointed spot, a matronly figure emerged from the crowd smiling pleasantly.

'This is Leela. She take you now,' Banda said curtly, before touching his cap and dissolving back into the shoal.

'Good afternoon, Miss Edmonds,' Leela greeted. She was obviously used to the relay system set up by her boss for honoured guests, for she had two first-class tickets in her hand and a porter standing by for luggage. 'Our train is on platform six, so we might as well board right away.'

'Do you think we could get some bottled water?' Anna asked, after they had settled into a compartment all to themselves; she was dreadfully thirsty.

'No refreshments on the train,' Leela replied in a sing-song accent. 'But I've ordered tea along the way.'

'I see,' Anna said more from acceptance than understanding, for the unaccustomed heat was making her dazed and disconnected. Before the train pulled out, however, and without really meaning to, she fell deeply asleep.

An hour later, just as the train was coming to a halt in a good-sized station, Anna returned to consciousness to see Leela leaning out of the window. When the carriages came to a complete standstill, she leaned out even further, waving frantically. Intrigued, Anna sat up and noticed a heavily laid tea tray with thick gray railway crockery zigzagging over the heads of the milling crowd in the direction of Leela's outstretched arms. After some debate with the bearer over payment, she shut the window and set the tray down on the empty seat opposite.

'You had a good long sleep,' she said handing Anna a cup of very dark brew. 'Are you feeling better now?'

'Yes, thanks.' Anna replied, taking the cup that a closer look showed to be white, with a railway-grime mottled design. 'Aren't you going to have some?'

'I simply can't digest station tea,' Leela said. And after a mouthful of the tepid, bitter-tasting concoction Anna understood, but rehydration had to take precedence over taste and she was glad of a full pot to herself.

The tea ritual was performed at two major stations along the way. At the last, however, came with a farewell gift of a lipstick-decorated cup and stale coffee grounds at the bottom of the teapot. But Anna drank it gratefully through to the last thick blob.

The noise of the train as they set off again, made conversation a struggle but Leela persevered. 'You must have come for the tennis championships,' she said.

'I'm afraid there has been a misunderstanding,' Anna replied. 'I wasn't expecting Dr Mehta's kind hospitality at all. He was right in thinking I work in a medical unit, but with the OUE, *not* the WHO as he has been led to believe.' Leela looked perplexed. Anna continued. 'As a matter of fact I've come on a short visit to the Nakshatra Ashram near Lonavala. Perhaps you could show me how to get there?'

Leela's smile evaporated, her expression darkened. 'It's a 3 kilometer ride from us. You'll need a taxi.' Her tone betrayed disappointment, if not mistrust, and she pulled the veil of her sari protectively over her head. The conversation then swerved to another topic before petering out into uneasy silence for the rest of the journey.

A white, king-sized limousine with net curtains in the back window waited outside Lonavala station to drive Dr Mehta's guest to his very pucka bungalow down by the river. When they arrived, Anna and her holdall were taken to the guest bedroom and Leela bustled away.

Wondering what kind of an evening it would be in a house without a host or hostess, Anna went to freshen up in the adjoining bathroom. When she returned to the bedroom a tray of fresh tea awaited her, and whoever had brought it had left the door ajar. She was about to shut the door, when the grinding of a dial-telephone in the hall captured her attention. After a series of pings and clicks came Leela's voice asking to speak with Dr Mehta, and when she got him, an excited conversation in her native tongue ensued. Hindi lessons weren't needed for Anna to understand that Leela was informing her boss that his honoured guest was not a distinguished doctor from the WHO, but a common-or-garden nurse from the WEO – whatever that was. Worse still, she was heading for the infamous Nakshatra Ashram!

Dr Mehta's orders probably consisted of one sharp word, but the barefooted manservant who appeared shortly afterwards in Anna's room, pleaded a litany of unforeseen and unfortunate circumstances that made it imperative that Anna move out immediately! 'Mr Mehta, he really very, very, sorry,' said the man with a marvellously pained expression.

'No problem. I already have a hotel booking,' Anna

replied sweetly reaching for the teapot that slid from her grasp because the tray was being whisked away by someone passing behind her chair. Surprised, she turned and saw a bare-footed servant scuttling through the door with the tea tray, followed by a houseboy, her holdall on his head. 'Nothing happens quickly in India you know,' was one of Nirmala's many warnings, so getting her out of the house must have been considered a dire emergency. In the hall Leela waited with an awkward smile. Anna thanked her for her help, and they went out into the driveway where the white limousine with the net curtains waited – doors outstretched to welcome her away.

Fifteen minutes later, Anna arrived where she'd originally planned – the Lotus Hotel – and plumped down on the hard little bed, happy that things had worked out the way they had. She'd not come all this way to give unto Caesar the things that are Caesar's; but to explore the things that are God's. And staying in the wealthy Mehta's domain, sidetracked by tennis championships and social events, amounted to sabotage. Well, heaven had saved her from that, but what else was in store?

Early next morning, a rickshaw dropped Anna off at the Ashram gates in time for the eight o'clock discourse. She advanced a few yards to find herself at the end of a higgledy-piggledy queue of mostly European disciples, clad in every shade of orange, ochre and burgundy. They resembled a gypsy multitude, crumpled but clean. Everything seemed to flow; the men wore flowing beards, the woman flowing hair, and all wore flowing robes. Bras seemed to have been thrown to the wind. Hugging, hand-holding and kissing among the young was commonplace, but a fair number of white heads and gray beards stood quietly in line as well. Almost everyone wore the dark *mala* beads, even the numerous children playing tag in and out of the line that straggled right through the Ashram grounds, and up to the gate of a leafy garden. Beyond the gate, a narrow path curved to the roofed patio stretching from the back of Nakshatra's bungalow. It was open on all sides, and floored in white marble.

Dressed in one of Virya's robes, Anna blended with the crowd. She had also taken the precaution of washing her body and hair in fragrance-free soap. Nakshatra had a severe allergy to all forms of aroma, so two 'sniffer' sannyasins stood either side of the gate to detect any untoward odour as each person passed through; the slightest hint of smell was enough to bar its perpetrator from entry.

The queue began to move, and quickly gathered speed. Having passed the living perfume detectors, people threw off their shoes and jostled along the winding path till they got to the patio where they dashed for a place as near to the front as they could get. Bewildered by all this, Anna found herself sitting near the back.

About 300 waited for discourse that morning, and soon the rustle gave way to silence. It was just five minutes past eight, and having slapped yet another mosquito, Anna looked up and suddenly – he was there.

A tall white figure with a high forehead and a long gray beard, stood on the low rounded dais in an aura of silence. His tapering hands were joined in the *namaste* greeting as slowly, slowly, he pivoted in a semicircle blessing everyone sitting on the floor in front of him. Shivers of recognition ran up Anna's spine, and tears of indescribable joy coursed unashamedly down her cheeks. The sun-suffused foliage surrounding the patio became a hazy blur as she focused on the tall figure in his immaculate white robe, settling into his discourse armchair and positioning the microphone at a comfortable distance from his face.

It seemed an age before he spoke. When he did, it was in a quiet voice that spanned the silence of the universe to say, 'Truth is. It simply is.'

The shattering simplicity of those words dropped like a stone to the depths of Anna's heart, sending out ripples to the confines of her being. With this, all had been said. A discourse entitled 'Life and Death' followed, but Anna was too overcome to realize that death was still in pursuit; not bodily death now, but that of the ego.

After discourse, it was *chai* time at the outdoor cafeteria. In addition to Guruji's bungalow, the Ashram consisted of 3 acres of garden belonging to a spacious, colonial-style house that served as its administrative headquarters. At the back, good-sized kitchens opened onto a patch of garden where a few rustically constructed palm-leaf parasols provided shade for a stand-up snack. This was the secular hub of the Ashram, where orange people met to talk, drink, cry and laugh. It was here that the orange river flowed after discourse to drink *chai* (spiced tea) and eat Ashram-made cakes and biscuits.

Following the stream, Anna found herself standing next to a sannyasin whose neck-length hair was white, his face clean-shaven. 'How does one get to see Guruji?' she ventured.

'Just go to the office and ask for a *darshan*,' came the blunt reply in an accent that sounded distinctly Dutch. 'Are you coming or going?'

'Arrived last night.'

'First visit?'

'Yes.'

'The office is over there,' he said, pointing to the front entrance of the house. 'I'll take you after *chai*, if you like.'

'Thanks. How come no beard?' Anna pursued as they moved slowly forward.

'Not Father Christmas,' he quipped. 'Where are you staying?'

'The Lotus, down by the station . . . and you?'

He pointed to a corner of the garden where Anna could

see a makeshift bamboo hut roofed with coconut matting. She looked at him questioningly.

'I'm Sangeet, by the way,' he said. 'I've lived in that hut with my girlfriend for more than six months now.'

Anna introduced herself and, reassured by Sangeet's joviality, asked what had drawn him to the Ashram. 'Guruji, of course,' he replied. Then unreservedly described how he'd abandoned a lucrative psychiatric practice in Amsterdam and come to India. His adult children had flown the nest and his wife, vehemently opposed to his new discovery, had flown it too. He had recently been given the honour of becoming an Ashram group-leader specializing in different growth groups. Resident workers weren't paid, Sangeet said, but like many others, he wanted nothing more than the privilege of living and working in that indescribable sphere of energy known as a 'Buddha field'.

'A Buddha field?'

'It's the vibratory atmosphere that pervades in the vicinity of an awakened one.'

'Meaning?'

'When you hang around Nakshatra you get every kind of insight. Un-asked questions find un-thought-of answers. Loves and hates burst into flame, waking you up to who you really are. Things happen here – it's quite extraordinary.'

Once they reached the head of the queue, they took their mugs of *chai* and made for a fallen tree trunk in the shade. 'Are you taking sannyas?' Sangeet enquired.

'After this morning's discourse, I feel I've always been a sannyasin,' Anna replied.

Sangeet smiled. 'It's not the first time I've heard that!' They sat for a while sipping their *chai* and watching the queue advance till Sangeet looked at his watch. 'Come on,' he said, 'I'll introduce you to the office and get you booked for a *darshan*. Then it'll be time for my shift in the lavatory block, and you might like to sample Sufi dancing.'

Anna's *darshan* could not be arranged before the eve of her departure. 'Can't be helped, the Ashram's pretty full at the moment,' Sangeet said.

'Why did the person in the office call you Swami?' Anna asked as they walked back into the garden. 'Isn't that a reverential term for a Hindu monk?'

'Yes it is. But here, it's a general term for male sannyasin, as Ma is for the female.'

Looking around the free-and-easy Ashram where Swamis and Ma's unrestrainedly gave vent to their affections, Anna understood why the Mehta ménage didn't hold with Nakshatra's neo-sannyasins. The very word sannyasin means one who lays aside the world, and Swami, meaning lord, inspires deep reverence and an almost patriotic place in every Indian's heart. An Indian Swami is a celibate, owning nothing more than his robe. His arduous pursuit of the infinite is often apparent on his face and in his eyes. He lives an aesthetic life in the world, but not of it, and he commands the deepest respect and love from people wherever he goes. Unless confined to a monastery, these true celibate renunciates have roamed the country for millennia and by so doing, distinguish India from every other nation of the world. Anna could well understand the adverse reaction of respectable Indians to these wild Europeans, dressed in orange and demonstrating a life of sexual freedom while dressed and addressed as Swami. Were a Christian monk and nun to be seen wandering, arm in arm, down the High Street, wouldn't westerners react similarly? Why did Guruji allow such sacrilege? Where was the necessity? And what had senseless provocation to do with his exquisite teaching? She glanced at Sangeet with these questions, but found him looking anxiously towards the one and only newly installed lavatory block, and its perpetual queue. 'Two cleaners work round the clock there,' he said, 'and my shift started five minutes ago.'

'But I thought you were a psychiatrist, orchestrating groups.'

'Yep. I do that too. Toilet cleaning's great for the soul, you know. When you start getting rid of your own shit, you'll understand,' he chuckled.

Virya's liberal use of this trendy word, signifying unwanted psychological traits barring the way to enlightenment, had prepared her ear perhaps, but she didn't find it particularly funny. Sangeet did, and his mirth roared out towards her as he backed away to his eight-holed sanctuary.

Anna wandered back to the office door, to glean what information she could from the notice boards standing outside it. There was a long list of therapeutic growth groups with interesting names; enlightenment intensive, Zen, mysterium, and a whole lot more. Her eyes then slid over to another sheet listing the different meditations taking place throughout the day, with a short explanation for each. Meditations could be practiced by humming, dancing, spinning and sitting quietly watching the breath. Anna remembered Swami Sat Anand saying she had to discover what lay behind the mind, but now Guruji was showing how. Beside the meditation list, a 'health bulletin' informed sannyasins that entering a Buddha field could have a cleansing effect upon the body, presenting as headaches, coughs, urinary and bowel disturbances, sinus congestion and skin eruptions. Several sannyasin MDs and accredited acupuncturists were on hand to help.

The sound of singing floated across from the roofed meditation area, where Sufi dancing had begun. Forty or so sannyasins moved slowly in a circle singing a Blake poem set to music: *'If I to myself would bind a joy, it doth the winged life destroy. But if I kiss the joy as it flies, then I live in eternal sunrise.'* Anna hesitated, was shy, felt foolish, glad her mother couldn't see her, but shit notwithstanding she joined in.

When the excitement and newness of the first day had

passed, fatigue and jetlag set in. *Farniente* time was needed so as to acclimatize. Energy for the eight o'clock discourse came easily, but that was all the spiritual nourishment Anna could take in one day. Meditation in the sweltering heat was for the aesthetes. Towards evening however, when the temperature waned, Anna went to the Ashram gates where a queue of scooterized rickshaws waited to slalom neo-sannyasins into town.

Rickshaw slalom is a sport practised only by the robustest of rickshaw-drivers in the sturdiest of vehicles; rickety rickshaws can't compete. The game consists in last-minute swerves around potholes, bumps, bicycles, other rickshaws, pedestrians, stray dogs, holy cows and the occasional elephant; the passenger hangs on for dear life!

The part of town favoured by Ashramites was the long straight Pancha Road where incongruous brick vestiges of Victorian England rub shoulders with the concrete of modern India. Here, in the late afternoon, *chai* is brewed over gas burners on the pavement, and ladled out to tousled customers just awoken from a long siesta. Scrawny dogs with drooping tits nose around the meat shops for scraps, and holy cows feed off bananas skins and paper bags lying on improvised rubbish dumps. Naked wide-eyed babies take their evening bath in aluminium buckets, and tailors treadle their sewing machines with bare feet listening to sports' commentaries blaring from transistors plugged into the light socket.

Anna usually shared a rickshaw with someone going in the same direction, and learned where to go for what. All she needed from the shops was presents to take home. Shopkeepers welcomed neo-sannyasins with rupees in their pockets, and offered them tea and Coca-Cola. Anna loved to linger in their shops, lured by the calming smell of incense and usually a chair to sit on while deliberating over a purchase. There was a cloth merchant she had a particular liking for. His shop was too narrow for a window. No chair. No incense. But he would lean his tall, handsome Kashmiri body nonchalantly outside the door and inveigle the passer-by with a flashlight smile and a chant, 'Cheapest and best – cheapest and best'.

The days fled by, and soon the long-awaited *darshan* was upon her. In the cool of the evening, Anna sat before the white-robed sage and he spoke to her. During the short exchange, she felt her story about 'sunstroke' to be quite unnecessary; his eyes and smile plainly conveyed that he knew whom she was, and why she'd come. Comparisons with Morward Haig never entered her head. He asked the usual questions – 'Where are you from?' and 'What do you do?' – then moved deeper.

'You search the beloved,' he said. Anna nodded vigorously but the mystic meaning of those words passed over her head. 'There is still work to be done, so you will come back soon.'

'I was thinking to make it in February,' Anna replied timidly.

'Very good. Very good,' he chuckled. 'You *will* make it. Mm.' He then placed a hand on Anna's head, while hers instinctively reached for his sandalled foot. Something passed.

'When the disciple is ready, the Master appears.'

Chapter Seventeen

The morning after her return from India, Anna caught herself humming as she unlocked the infirmary door. No mental wrangling beset her; Master and path lay straight ahead. The yearning for husband and home remained undiminished, but now she presumed that Destiny wanted her settled on her spiritual path before presenting the man she was destined to meet; and the obvious place to meet him would be in the Ashram.

The effect of Nakshatra's presence lingered in her memory and started to grow roots into her thirsting soul. She resisted the idea of belonging to an outrageous orange-clad sect, and yet could not deny or reject that penetrating voice ringing with humour, wisdom and a mystic truth. It was said that some of Nakshatra's disciples had sat at his feet in past lives too, and Anna might well have been one of them for she perceived the Ashram experience as an echo of something already known.

This whole discovery so deeply involved the heart, that half-heartedness would seem impossible, and for this reason Anna intended to become a sannyasin. And now she had three months to prepare her second visit to Lonavala.

'Becoming a sannyasin will probably turn your life upside down and inside out,' Virya told Anna one day. Anna was not deterred, but had no intention of wearing long robes as Virya did, and had decided that her classical clothes would change only in colour. The reaction of her family and friends was to be dreaded, however. The Swami would have to be told too, and no great blessing could be expected there, though Sudah, who always advocated following one's heart, would be pleased. Anna's straight, respectable acquaintances would certainly cool off when they realized her *mala* wasn't just a bit of junky jewellery, and her nursing colleagues, were cool enough already, so what had she to fear?

On Virya's discourse evenings, Anna was always there. The discourses seemed like choice music of which one never tires, and it wasn't just the depth and diversity of their content – something ineffable about the sound of Guruji's voice held meaning for her too. The individuals gathered *chez Virya* for this event were as varied as chocolates in a box – some wrapped in orange, others not. They ranged from highly educated to unmistakably marginal, though drugs and drug-users were firmly excluded. Psychotropic substances capable of inducing states similar to enlightenment had brought a number of disciples to Nakshatra's feet, but once there, the drug had to go.

Now and again Virya would drop by the infirmary for a quick chat, bringing coffee for both of them.

'I've had the strangest of dreams,' Anna told Virya one morning, as the latter handed her a carton cup of the dark reviving brew.

'Really?'

'Yes. The same one twice this week.'

'Guruji is usually disparaging about dreams,' said Virya. 'But if it won't go away I guess there's a reason. Let's hear it.'

'Every detail remains so clear. Perhaps you can make something of it.'

'I doubt that very much. What was it about?'

'Well, I find myself the reigning Queen of a country

recently defeated in battle by a General from another land. Tradition demands that the vanquished monarch be beheaded before the crowd, and the victor mount the throne. Well, standing in the empty throne room I wait for the victor to arrive. Marching steps enter the palace and pound up the stairs. Then a tall, powerfully, built man dressed as a Roman Centurion – clean-shaven, brown hair, dark eyes – appears. To my surprise he is courteous, civilized, and not at all in any hurry to drag me off to the scaffold. In short, most attractive.'

Virya raised an eyebrow.

'He stops at the entrance to the throne room, introduces himself as Othila, but makes no attempt to enter. He simply stands there with an amused look on his face. I walk towards him saying, "I'm ready. Let's go." But he replies, "What's the hurry? Let's go for a walk." The mutual attraction was palpable; and still there when I woke up.'

'My, oh, my! Love at first sight?' Virya sniggered, then paused, 'Just a minute – Othila? That name rings a bell.'

'Well I've never heard it before.'

'It'll come to me in a minute. Go on, don't keep me in suspense.'

'Well, arm in arm we walk the paths of the palace garden. There is a deep narrow canal on the left, and tall trees spreading over an expanse of dazzling water on the right. My feelings are bittersweet. Why do I have to die when here is someone who feels so right? All of a sudden he is naked and walking down the bank into the canal to swim underwater and against the stream.'

'So you escape?' Virya interjected.

'No. I keep pace along the bank. When he emerges fully dressed I know for certain he won't kill me, and we start climbing a steep dusty road to a crumbling citadel where a bunch of ragged children appear. I want so much to be alone with this man, so I say to the children, 'When does your mother cook your supper?' He squeezes my hand disapprovingly because these children have no mother and no supper. Then I wake up.'

Virya thought for a while. 'Othila! Now where have I heard that name before?' Her reflections were cut short by the waiting-room buzzer. 'You've got a customer. I'd better get going,' she said. 'I was just wondering if you'd be free for a movie on Friday. *The Spy That Came In From The Cold* is showing at the Odeon Champs Elysées.'

Anna pressed the Engaged button, leafed through her diary, found Friday and said that would be fine. They then walked to the waiting room door which Anna opened, but instead of walking through, Virya stepped back with a horrified gasp. Before them stood a tall African clutching a heavily bleeding hand, a pool of blood spreading at his feet.

Backing briskly into the infirmary, Anna grabbed a wad of gauze and, applying pressure to the wound drew the patient into the infirmary, sat him down on a low stool, and raised the hand above his head. For a moment Virya stood mesmerized, and then made to leave.

'Just a moment,' Anna called to the departing flame. Virya turned. 'In the second drawer there's a box marked "tourniquet". Could you bring it to me, please? We'll probably not need it, but just in case.'

While Virya obliged, Anna applied yet another wad to the hand. The patient remained mute but his eyes swivelled like marbles to follow the action. 'Don't worry,' Anna reassured. 'Pressure seems to be doing the trick. We'll wait a moment.'

Virya then smiled at the patient, and again made to go.

'Oh. Just one more thing, Virya, please?' Anna said.

'Sure.'

'Would you mind taking a paper towel and seeing to the pool on the waiting-room floor? The DG has an appointment in five minutes, and there'd be a top-level enquiry if he slipped up here.'

'There'd be a top-level enquiry if he slipped up anywhere,' said the patient cryptically.

Virya mopped up the pool, and when she returned to dispose of the blood-soaked towel, the patient murmured something that Anna missed, but Virya exploded with laughter and seemed less keen to leave. An exchange of banter ensued between them, then Virya said, 'This is Mr Mapeta, by the way. His office is just down the hall from mine.'

'I was wondering when you were going to introduce us,' Mapeta retorted. 'We've been holding hands for the last five minutes in case you hadn't noticed.'

Anna smiled. 'I think we could risk a peep at it now.'

'Well, I'm outa here,' said Virya, scuttling to the door.

Anna slowly lowered Mr Mapeta's arm onto the glass-topped trolley, and eased off the gauze. A deep jagged wound, the length of his thumb, came into view. 'I guess I should leave sardine cans alone,' he said, looking up at Anna with a tweak of a smile.

'When did this happen?' Anna asked.

'Yesterday evening, but I ripped it open again fighting with the window in my office a moment ago.'

'In that case it's too late for stitches, though I should send you across to the doctor in the main unit.' His response to this was an uneasy silence. Anna washed her hands and reached for the phone. 'I'm sorry – I didn't catch your name?'

'Konsu Mapeta,' he replied, looking anxiously at his watch. 'But Sister, I don't have time to go all the way over there now. I'm fifteen minutes late for a meeting as it is. Just patch me up – I'll live.'

Anna put down the phone. The wound was ugly, and Roch would unhesitatingly return her to purgatory if he could fault her in any way. On the other hand, there wasn't much to be done except re-apply a compressive dressing, put the arm in a sling and give a painkiller. All this and a tetanus shot she could perfectly well do herself. Antibiotics could be prescribed the following day – if necessary.

'OK,' Anna conceded. 'I'll spare you the journey on condition you let me check the dressing and give you a tetanus shot before you leave the office this evening. We'll take it from there.'

Mr Mapeta relaxed. Anna padded the dressing to the size of a lollipop and then produced a sling.

'Oh no! I'm not facing the board looking like a war veteran,' he protested, backing towards the door. 'Thanks a lot. See you this evening.'

As she tidied up, Anna found herself puzzling over where she'd met this African before. Not in the infirmary, she was certain of that. Looking him up in the office telephone directory, she saw DDG (Deputy Director-General) after his name. Dignitaries were always received by Dr Roch, making it unlikely that they had met in the medical unit, and all the people she knew out of it, were white. However as the cut thumb was the first of several accidents that day, the question was forgotten until a quarter to six when the waiting-room buzzer announced Mr Mapeta, true to his word, the lollipop intact.

'Bet you attracted some attention with that,' Anna commented.

'Yes, I've been sticking out like a you-know-what all day. And you?'

'Me what?'

'How have *you* been?'

'Oh, busy!' Anna replied, surprised that he should ask. She gently removed the blood-soaked dressing and inspected the wound. 'I don't think you'll need to show this to Dr Roch tonight – unless you'd prefer to,' Anna said. 'Daily dressings should do it from now on.'

The expression on the patient's face seemed so familiar, that again Anna leafed through her memory files in search of when, where and how she could possibly have met him.

'You'll be glad to know that this dressing need not be quite so bulbous as the last,' Anna said, starting to bandage. 'But it should be renewed first thing tomorrow morning.'

'Right, Sister,' he responded with an approving smile, and that too seemed disturbingly déja vu. Or was she imagining things? She went to the filing cabinet to check the date of his last tetanus shot, and found her eyes veering to 'Date of birth'. He was 11 years older than she. His tetanus booster was still valid.

The next morning, Anna had hardly unlocked her cupboards and drawers when Mr Mapeta turned up with a beaming smile. To be helpful, he started to unravel his bandage while Anna washed her hands. The dressing and wound needed to be soaked apart in a bowl of tepid disinfectant, and while this was in progress, Mr Mapeta began to tell Anna something about himself – his three unforgettable years at Cambridge, an economics degree followed by a scholarship to an American university for his PhD. It was in America that he had met and married Conchita, a Brazilian art student from the same university. They had three children, of whom he was extremely proud. The two boys had just started at London university, and the youngest, a girl, was still at home studying for her baccalaureate.

'So they're all brilliant, like you?' Anna said.

'More luck than brilliance,' he replied. 'When I was a boy we happened to live near a Catholic school run by the White Fathers. Fortunately for me, and a few others, they took a number of black students every year aiming to get as many of us as possible into university. You see the monks of that community understood the need to educate us locals, even though independence seemed a long way off then.'

'Did you enjoy your school years?' Anna asked.

'I had to prove myself, of course,' Mapeta replied. 'Being good at football and boxing helped.'

'Boxing?' Anna was surprised; he didn't look the pugilistic type.

'Yes, they used to call me "Iron-fist". It kept the bullies at bay. But I was grateful for the opportunity of a solid education. Had our family lived up-country this would never have happened and I'd be tending somebody else's cattle now.'

'A far cry from Paris,' Anna commented.

'Indeed. Do you live here by choice, or do you have ties here?'

'Choice,' Anna cut in, steering their attention back to the soaking thumb, and Mapeta, curious though he seemed, accepted the diversion. Soon a smaller lollipop completed the job.

'And my next appointment . . .?'

'This should hold till tomorrow morning. If it gets loose or uncomfortable during the day, come back.'

Having thanked her, Mapeta walked purposefully towards the door, then paused as though wishing to say something further. Anna waited, but after a moment he jerked the door open and strode out without a backward glance.

By five to six, the infirmary drawers and cupboards were locked and Anna about to leave, when the buzzer sounded. Wearily she pressed 'Enter' on her desk.

'I'm afraid I've come rather late,' Mapeta said, hesitating on the threshold.

'Well, come in.' Anna replied as she started to unlock again, but Mapeta didn't move; he just stood in the doorway, watching in bemused silence. 'I'm ready,' Anna said decisively. But as he still hadn't entered, she looked questioningly towards the door to see the smile that had puzzled her earlier.

But when he said, 'What's the hurry – let's go for a drink,' Anna's heart missed a beat. The keys in her hand clattered to the floor and she remembered. Mapeta swooped to recuperate the keys, and handed them back; his lollipop looked brand new.

'Go for a walk?' she mumbled.

'Drink,' he corrected.

'Drink?' Anna looked back mutely wanting to say yes, then no, then ... but Mapeta masterfully interrupted the silent volley batting back and forth in Anna's brain. 'The dressing will hold. Meet you by the parking elevator on the sixth floor in five minutes,' he said, and left.

'What a nerve!' Anna thought as she relocked everything. But she wanted to go, and they both knew it. She slipped into her coat, and while checking her make-up, spoke to the washbasin mirror. 'He who sups with the Devil needs use a long spoon,' she said, picturing a line of copper spoons hanging in a line from a kitchen beam, and herself reaching for the one with the longest handle. 'No supping,' she admonished. 'Just one quick drink!'

When the lift came, they entered without a word. It was Anna who broke the unbearable silence. 'I hope you won't mind if we make it a quick drink, I have something planned for later.'

'Of course not. As a matter of fact, I mustn't get home late myself.'

Reassured, Anna hung her spoon back on its imaginary hook and relaxed.

They drove to the Latin Quarter and entered a quaint bar off the Rue Jacob. The old oak furnishings and polished brass gave it a nautical air. Electrified hurricane lamps shone on a dozen or so tables, and a grand piano stood on a low dais at the far end of the room. 'A perfect Devil's lair,' Anna thought, mentally summoning her row of spoons.

The black barman, decked out as a Venetian gondolier,

stepped forward to greet his fellow African. 'Not seen you for centuries,' he hailed. 'Where've you bin all this time, K ol' man?'

'Working like a Nigger,' Mapeta jested. 'Napoleon, meet my nurse,' he said holding up his lollipop and grinning. They ordered drinks, and were shown to a table up near the piano.

'Do all your friends call you K?' Anna asked.

'Not all,' he replied. 'Just the ones I've known for a long time – like you.'

'Me? But we've only just met.'

He studied his whisky intently for a moment before saying, 'Konsu's a mouthful for most people. I'd like you to call me K.'

'Well, I'm calling you Othila,' Anna declared.

His brow wrinkled. 'Othila! Where did that come from?

'Just dreamed it up. Do you mind?'

'Well, as I see it, you've made me a cross between Attila and Othello – murderers both! You are a funny girl. Do you often invent names for your friends?'

'Well, no. But let's face it, I did meet you standing in a pool of blood!'

Othila laughed. 'And what may I call you – Sister?'

'Anna.'

Conversation flowed easily. Othila's principal interest seemed to be Africa's struggle to catch up with the fast-moving industrial world. He felt he owed it to his country to get back and contribute in a more personal way as soon as the political climate there allowed him to do so. When Anna's interests came into focus, philosophy, art and Indian cookery swept them away on alternating waves of agreement and controversy till the ship's clock over the bar read seven.

'I've really enjoyed this, but I'm afraid I have to leave,' Anna said.

'Me too,' Othila agreed. But as he reached for Anna's

coat draped over the back of her chair, Napoleon approached wearing street clothes.

'My shift is over,' he said. 'Would you like me to play something before I go?'

'Well, that really *is* an invitation!' Othila enthused. 'Nap's an incredible jazz man when he's in the mood, which isn't half often enough.'

'You don't come here half often enough,' Napoleon quipped. 'So, what would you like?' He looked at Anna.

There was a modish piece Anna loved. ' "Petite Fleur". Do you know it?'

'Know it? Of course!' He walked over to the piano. Wispy clapping rose from the tables behind.

Napoleon made languorous work of 'Petite Fleur', and by the time the last notes had faded the place was full, and a crowd had gathered by the door waiting for a table. Applause rang loud. Anna caught the pianist's eye, mouthed a thank-you, and struggled into her coat sitting down, because they were waiting for the bill.

A double bass had joined Napoleon now, and someone was walking towards the piano, clarinet in hand. The lights dimmed and feet started tapping to the effervescent tunes of New Orleans. Anna regretted her invented engagement. Othila too seemed reluctant to tear himself away. The bill came just as the players had begun to make 'Old Man River' sparkle and splash.

'What about a quickie for the road?' Othila said.

'Well, all right,' Anna replied, spoons forgotten. 'But won't your wife be waiting behind the door with a rolling pin?'

'No. It's her rehearsal night – she's acting in a play.'

'Your daughter?'

'She's quite old enough to fix herself a hamburger when she gets in.'

A fat saxophonist joined the impromptu musicians and

further enticed them with yet another arrangement of 'Petite Fleur'. Drinks came. Anna slipped out of her coat and conversation resumed. It circled around Othila's wife, Conchita, who not only acted in the English Drama Society but kept herself busy teaching Spanish and English as well. After a while the decibels made conversation difficult. Anna drained her glass, stood, put on her coat and was about to make for the exit when suddenly the jazz stopped and an elderly maestro, violin under his arm, appeared by the piano to boisterous applause.

'You can't leave just yet,' Othila whispered. His hand went to her arm and she sank back into her seat. The maestro lifted his bow and with an energetic little sweep launched deftly into a familiar Paganini étude. Time melted into the beauty of those notes. But the piece was short, and after it ended an enraptured audience clapped wildly; the tables reverberated and lights flickered.

Regretful but resolute, Anna stood. Othila took her hand so as not to lose her in the crowd, but before they reached the door, the maestro had moved suavely into Beethoven's irresistible romances and it was Anna's turn to stall. 'Just a minute,' she said, turning to face the room. Othila moved up behind her; close, immobile, protective and warm. They stood thus until the last ecstatic stream of sound had faded, and then stepped outside.

The cold January air jolted Anna back to reality, and her hands to her pockets. They hardly spoke on the way home, and when the hospital apartment building came in sight, Anna reached for her long-handled spoon. 'Thank you for a very pleasant evening,' she said. 'Please don't bother parking in this impossible district, I'm old enough to see myself to my own front door.' He put on the brake, stopped the engine, and in the silence glanced at Anna in that strangely familiar way.

'I've had a wonderful evening too,' Othila said. 'But

before the "big girl" sees herself to her own front door, perhaps she could just tell me where we have met before?'

'I told you. In a dream.' Anna teased, fumbling for the door handle. Othila leaned across to release the catch. Their faces came dangerously close but what might have happened did not, and with laughable formality they wished each other a very good night.

Daily dressings continued for a week, each visit marking a stride in the relationship. Anna knew the attraction to be mutual and recognized a near miss in the car that evening, but her real focus was the second visit to Lonavala in three weeks' time. Quite apart from the fact that Othila was a husband and father, an emotional entanglement now would be detrimental to finding a like-minded soul travelling the same enlightened path. Nevertheless unavoidable contact in the infirmary engendered compelling subterranean currents held in check by the need for professional formality.

Ten days after the accident, Anna cut a strip of Elastoplast, covered Othila's jagged scar and said, 'Well, Mr Mapeta, your thumb doesn't need me any longer.'

'No, but I do,' came the not altogether unexpected reply as he stepped nearer to surround Anna with his arms. She looked apprehensively towards the door and reached for the 'Engaged' button on her desk; people did sometimes bumble in.

Othila shook his head and held her a little closer. 'It's gone six. Nobody'll come now.' They stood thus for some time, silently savouring a long-desired moment. Firm intentions and long-handled spoons melted in a pool of feeling that was deep and warm and comforting.

Anna felt his lips brush the top of her head as he echoed her thoughts. 'Darling, I feel I've known you for a long, long time.' Then, as though it were the most natural thing in the world, his lips met hers, and she welcomed them.

When time recommenced, Othila regretfully backed away.

On reaching the door he changed his mind, returned to where Anna stood and enfolded her in his arms again. When eventually he stepped back, Anna felt as though part of herself had been ripped away. But he had to go home . . . to somebody else.

The infirmary seemed to chill after he had left, but an inextinguishable smile lit Anna's face as she peered into the washbasin mirror. All the signs were there – eyes like stars and the beauty of a woman desired written all over her face.

'You're mad!' she said aloud. 'He's forty and you are twenty-nine. He's married. He's black. He has a top job and an impeccable reputation to uphold. And God help you, Anna; he's the man you are destined to meet!'

Chapter Eighteen

Just four months after Anna had taken charge of the First Aid post, an important memorandum topped the pile of mail on her desk. The signature and style belonged to Dr Roch, but Destiny must have been behind those three factual phrases. '*This is to inform you that Elizabeth Dapi has given birth to a son. She will not be returning to the Medical Unit after her maternity leave as she has resigned her position with the WEO. Miss Edmonds will therefore remain at her present post until further notice.*'

'Thank you. Thank you!' Anna murmured, feeling as thrilled for Elizabeth as she was for herself. 'Further notice' might have sounded intimidating, but Maude and Lisette weren't likely to stray far from *le Patron*'s beck and call, and Elizabeth's replacement, when she came, would hardly be allowed to stray far from theirs. 'Further notice', therefore, stretched to a sunny horizon. Suddenly Anna had everything a girl could ask for in a job: good pay, long holidays, normal working hours and a self-regulated working atmosphere – so where was the need to resign? Furthermore, this pivotal piece in the jigsaw of Anna's life had fitted into place a week before her second visit to Lonavala, enhancing her morale still further.

The rest of the mail was the usual OUE notices with no relevance to the medical unit, and she started throwing it into the wastepaper basket, when an envelope with Paul's handwriting appeared. Paul usually phoned. It had to be important for him to write, and when she read the letter she understood. Paul wanted her to be the first to know that he had 'finally found the girl for me'. He was planning to marry Valérie; a young French widow whose husband had been killed in a car crash leaving her with a son aged two, and a daughter of five. But as Valérie was only thirty-two, they hoped to have children of their own as well. Anna was sincerely delighted; all his kindness and generosity deserved a better pay-back than Anna had given him, and she hoped Valérie would fill his heart completely.

On the first of February, with five weeks of freedom ahead of her, Anna left for India. Virya had departed the week before and would greet her at Lonavala Station when she arrived. They'd agreed to share a hotel bedroom because accommodation within easy reach of the Ashram was now both scarce and expensive. If educated Indians abhorred neo-sannyasins desecrating their time-honoured traditions, hoteliers and room-letters grew fat on them.

Another Paris sannyasin, Anand Dharma, was booked on Anna's flight, and Virya had told him to look out for her. 'He's been to Lonavala dozens of times,' Virya said, 'but this time it's for good. His Spanish fiancée is an Ashram resident, and now he's hoping to become one too. You may find him a bit short on conversation, but good to travel with as he knows all the dodges.'

Anna had not come across Dharma before and their seats weren't together on the plane. But when she noticed a tall, bony man with a stubbly beard, stringy blond hair, a *mala* and cheap orange clothes – who else could it be? They met up at the Arrivals hall at Bombay airport, and after a casual 'Bonjour', shuffled silently though immigration and customs together. Dharma immediately picked out a taxi with a driver willing to reduce the fare, and at the station found a shady dealer for first class tickets at second class prices.

They boarded that magnificent piece of old rolling stock named the 'Deccan Queen' with time to spare. Anna bumbled down the narrow corridor behind Dharma's bulbous backpack, peering into the occupied compartments where the worn velvet seats and white antimacassar squares still managed to exude a frayed notion of colonial gentility.

'Keep going,' Dharma muttered. 'Less crowded further down.'

Eventually they found what they'd been looking for, and entered an airless compartment filled with a cloud of rose perfume. It emanated from the oil-embalmed head of the only occupant already seated by the window. He was short and tubby with a sallow complexion. A gold and diamond ring winked brightly from a pudgy finger, but the dark globes under drooping eyelids reflected only weariness. He'd been staring idly out of the window, but after the invasion of his privacy, he lifted the newspaper draping his lap and pretended to read. Dharma sniffed rudely and opened the window that admitted more noise than air, so he banged it shut again. He then heaved his backpack and Anna's holdall onto the netted luggage rack and finally sank heavily into the corridor seat, leaving the remaining window free for Anna to look out of.

Sitting in a steam train dredged up Anna's childhood memories of the pin-striped commuters travelling between Cambridge and London. Except for the heat, that tangy Indian smell, and a morass of lightly clad people, she might have been going somewhere in England's green and pleasant land; the girders and glass roof of Victoria Station Bombay, was the image of its English namesake.

Across the teeming platform, a bottle-green locomotive screeched slowly to a halt. On the bodywork, 'Great Western Railway' was still visible under a veil of grime and green paint, but 'Indian Rail' retaliated boldly in white further down.

'So this is where the unpunctual trains of England go to when they die,' Anna mused. She glanced at her watch, but before she could calculate just how off-schedule the train would be, the staccato of banging doors, a shrieking whistle and the sight of the turbaned stationmaster walking slowly up the platform waving his green flag, told her they were off. Slowly, slowly, the ten-ton wonder backed out of the station snorting steam like a horse reluctant to leave its stall.

After axle-defying jolts on the intersecting rails, the torrid city was left behind and gaiety infused the rhythm of the wheels. The train sped merrily across the coastal plain then up into the hills. For a while the three travellers gazed intently at the sunny landscape racing by, but as their eyes began to tire, they slipped into sleep. Dharma was the first to blot out, then the rose-scented head began to nod and finally Anna shut her eyes, and recoiled into an Othila-filled reverie.

The time between the healing of Othila's thumb and Anna's departure for India had been an obligation-packed ten days, and the rush of activity had forcibly taken precedence over everything else. But assuming her return as a sannyasin would end the amity anyway, she had accepted one last quick drink, over which they had agreed it best not to meet again. This left Anna trying to convince herself that Othila was *not* 'the man she was destined to meet'; but the notion stuck.

Adultery! Adultery! That's what a relationship with Othila would be. It ranged among the least forgivable of sins; a crime for which woman in some countries could be stoned to death! And in view of such appalling consequences, Anna had often wondered why those concerned didn't nip their passions in the bud. 'Cut the drama, Anna,' she admonished. 'Nothing untoward has happened or is going to happen. Here I am, thousands of miles from the man in question, and going to where infinitely more suitable partners exist by the dozen. Now if this isn't nipping passion in the bud, what is?' But these thoughts rang hollow; who did she think she was kidding? But she was too hot, too tired, and it was all too complicated, to come to terms with on the 'Deccan Queen'. The train raced on and Anna too slipped into sleep.

A jarring jolt and a loud hiss brought Anna to full consciousness. The train had come to a halt in virgin countryside. Hush descended. No silence is more penetrating than when the wheels of a steam train stop turning. Dharma and Weary-Eyes changed position and slept on, but Anna got up and leaned out of the window. Poised on a half-moon curve of track, she had a panoramic view of the entire train. Just beyond the engine, a brick hut daubed with peeling advertisements seemed the only reason for a halt. Unless, perhaps, the stop was to avoid a collision with a down-coming locomotive? The torrid plain was far behind them now; they had climbed into the hills where the air was fresh and tinged with the fragrance of earth after rain. Just then, the thump of an opening door up near the engine brought faces to every window.

All eyes focused on three women as they climbed perilously down onto the grassy verge. They had the deeply lined features and the darkened skins of field workers, but moved with the grace of queens in their plain cotton saris of vivid orange, shimmering green and glowing magenta. Gold dangled from their ears and bangles glittered and jangled as they reached up for the cotton bundles dropped down to them from a window. They waved up at their companions in the train and, having balanced the bundles on their heads, ambled happily down the track chatting raucously. Along the narrow verge they went keeping in the shadow of the train, while the faces at the windows turned like sombre sunflowers watching their progress. Where the shadow of the train ended, dazzling sunlight engulfed them and a highland breeze ballooned the orange, green and magenta saris like the sails of a mythical ship. The colours merged as they sailed away, growing smaller and smaller till a bend in the track hid them from sight.

With unexpected smoothness the train moved on again, gathered speed, and plunged into a long tunnel. Only one of the reading lights worked – the one illuminating Weary-Eyes, his face mournful even in sleep. Anna hastily shut the window and returned to her seat for more reverie.

Tunnels. 'What is life if not one long tunnel!' she reflected as the sudden blackness behind the rattling window touched her thoughts. Sudah had lauded tunnels for the insights they bring. 'What insights? Stay in a tunnel too long and what do you get?' Anna fumbled for a truly execrable adjective, but 'sunstroke' popped up to shame her. How could she be such a cry-baby when all those tunnel-filled years had led specifically to the extraordinary phenomenon of peace and serenity that had lasted three whole months, and now an enlightened Master to guide her on the most fascinating adventure of her life. 'Really Anna! What more do you want?' Yes, just one thing more – but she'd exhausted that subject, and that subject had exhausted her. So she let the throbbing train rock her into sleep again.

There was a terrific jerk before the train began to slow. Darma's backpack fell from the luggage rack and Anna lurched up from the depths of nowhere, saliva dribbling from her mouth but she felt rested. They were almost there.

Dressed in her brightest saffron, Virya waited beside Dharma's Spanish fiancée. When Dharma's head appeared above the throngs of arrivals, his fiancée ran towards him and he swung her around and around before whisking her away without saying goodbye. Vyria and Anna hugged warmly and then hurried for a rickshaw.

'It's not the Ritz,' Vyria declared as they entered a dark hallway and up some well-worn wooden stairs. A narrow corridor led to the bedroom they were to share. The window looked down onto a tiny garden, where a holy cow stretched its neck over the fence, and was feeding on the greenery.

Anna freshened up at the washbasin while Virya gave her the lowdown. 'Our arrival *darshan* is booked for tomorrow evening. It took me a full week to get mine, so I included your name while I was at it.'

'Thanks.'

'The place has grown, it's hardly recognizable. The cafeteria has tables and a staff of seven now, and the organization has seriously tightened. You'll need to get an ID card from the office. Well, the rest you'll see for yourself. Make yourself at home. I'll be back later.'

The following morning Virya and Anna jumped into the rickshaw waiting outside the little rooming-house. Rickshaw drivers had a flair for knowing when and where sannyasins were likely to need them, and this one needed no orders to deposit his passengers at the Ashram's gates. There wasn't far to walk; the discourse queue filed all the way back to the Ashram's arched portal and even a way down the road outside.

'We'll have to get here a lot sooner if we want to sit anywhere near the front,' Virya commented.

The queue moved forward, and minutes later they were shuffling between the two fragrance detectors, slipping off their sandals, and making for a space on the cool marble floor. People poured in behind them until every inch of floor was covered, and the hall transformed into an undulating sea of orange. At eight o'clock sharp, all eyes focused on Guruji in his immaculate robe emerging, silent as a cloud, through the door at the back of the dais. He advanced to his chair, then stopped and joined his hands in *namaste* before pivoting slowly in a semicircle until his invisible beam had covered the whole assembly. Silence was tangible; the birds in the trees surrounding the open sides of the hall ceased their twittering, as though they too wanted to know 'The Way'. Guruji then sat, adjusted the microphone, and a disciple read a sutra from the Zen mystic Sosan:

> 'The Great Way is not difficult
> For those who have no preferences.
> When love and hate are both absent
> Everything becomes clear and undisguised.
> Make the smallest distinction, however,
> And heaven and earth are set infinitely apart.
> If you wish to see the truth
> Then hold no opinion for or against.
> The struggle of what one likes and what one dislikes
> Is the disease of the mind.'

'We will be entering the beautiful world of a Zen Master's no-mind,' Nakshatra began, his voice soft and penetrating. And you should remember that the words of Mystics like Sosan are not merely factual, they are also seeds of knowing. You listen. You nod. You think, 'Yes Guruji is right. Sosan is right. We know detachment is the name of the game. But love and hate are natural – necessary even, for survival in the world.' So what to do? I am telling you one thing. It will be enough. Just listen. No need to agree or disagree. Allow the words to fall into the dark soil of your inner being and one day they will rise as tiny sprouts of understanding. Nobody knows where, or when, this will occur. You may even be sitting on the toilet at the time. (Laughter) Yes – this has happened.' (Pause) 'And will happen again! (More laughter,)

After this discourse Vyria and Anna looked at each other with something to say, but words didn't come, so they joined the *chai* queue in silence.

The following evening, 40 orange-clad disciples sat in Darshan on the floor in front of Guruji's chair. Most would be simply sitting in the Master's presence, for Nakshatra's time was now fully taken with giving sannyas to the newcomers and exchanging a few words with those who had either just arrived, or were about to leave. Everyone waited for the hushed moment when Guruji would appear, and again, shivers ran up Anna's spine at the sight of him.

Virya was first to be called. Guruji asked how she was getting on in Paris. She had a question. Was her comfortable and lucrative lifestyle compatible with sannyas?

Guruji chuckled. 'Nothing in life is to be spurned, Virya,' he replied. 'Rich or poor, it's a gift. What matters is the awareness and love you bring to everything you do.' He spoke a little longer, and assured Virya that she would soon be ready to join the Ashram for good. This last remark brought a tremor of excitement visible to Anna sitting a yard behind her. Guruji then concluded, 'Very good, Virya. Very good.' Anna was next.

More than a little awed, Anna sat before Nakshatra, close enough to see the sparkle in his eye and the smile shining out from behind his moustache and beard. As before, he asked where she was from, and what she did there. But after that he seemed to have remembered, and wanted to know if she'd thought about becoming a sannyasin. Anna nodded happily, and when a *mala* was handed to Nakshatra, she leaned forward that he might slip it over her head. He then reached for the clipboard to write the new name on Ashram notepaper.

'Ma Deva Sabda,' he said, handing Anna the paper. 'Will you be able to pronounce it?'

'Yes.'

'Deva means "Divine", and Sabda "sound".'

Trembling slightly, Anna took the paper. Guruji continued. 'The Divine sound has no beginning and no end, Sabda. That is the Mystery – the greatest that is. There are multiple manifestations of the Divine, and all lead back to the eternal source. The nearer you grow to the source, the more silent you will become; only in total silence will you hear that sound. Do you have any questions?'

Anna wanted to ask how, when, and would it be with her physical ears, that she would hear the Divine sound. But all this seemed so far in the future, and time with Guruji so limited, that she decided to stick with the present. It was now or never.

'Yes,' Sabda answered. 'When I was here three months ago, you told me to search the beloved. Well, I believe I've found him!'

'Already!' Guruji chuckled, as peals of laughter rose from the gathering behind her.

'Yes, but it's not straightforward at all,' she answered, her candidness provoking even greater mirth from the assembly.

'What is the problem?' Guruji asked without smiling.

'He isn't free!' The listeners restrained their giggles so as not to miss the reply. There was silence. Guruji answered.

'Love, as you know it, is a way of expressing the Divine in human terms. It is a poor replica, of course, but we can only start with what we have and we have to start somewhere. No opportunity for deep love should be rejected. Anything repressed will rise again and again until it is expressed, and nothing implores expression more urgently than love.' Opening his eyes very wide and looking deeply into his new disciple, Guruji continued, 'When love is elevated from passion to a natural state of being, Sabda, the true beloved is found. I say to you again, search the beloved.' He then suggested she follow several different growth groups, and ended the conversation with, 'Very good, Sabda. Very good.' Another name was called.

When Darshan ended, Virya hugged the new sannyasin and, as they walked out into the garden, said, 'Who's the guy?'

'Nobody you know,' Sabda replied gently.

'Not from the OUE, then?'
'No.'
'Hope it works out for you.'
'So do I,' Sabda replied as they joined a crowd of friends waiting to celebrate with a meal in town.

When they got back to their room after supper, Sabda suffered a little more probing about 'the man who wasn't free'. She said she wasn't ready to talk about him just yet, and the subject was dropped. Virya had her own embroilments to worry about. She had split up with the student fiancé she had come to India with the first time, and was still fancy free, except now she was greatly attracted to a handsome Italian group-leader who was not responding with all the fervour she would have liked.

Nakshatra's words had moved Sabda, though her perception was still too limited to really understand them. Othila buzzed like a fly in her mind; the kind that lands on the same spot repeatedly, defies all swatting, and will not go away.

'Be totally yourself and harm no one,' Nakshatra said in his discourse one morning. He illustrated this by speaking of a musician who wanted to play his flute in the middle of the night. 'Perfectly good,' said Guruji. 'Everyone needs to express their inner being – it should not be denied. But go out of the town, where no one will be disturbed.' On hearing this, Sabda immediately projected these principles onto her own life-screen, wondering if they might be applied equally well to a clandestine love affair. After all, her feelings for Othila *were* the needful expression of her being, and if nobody knew, would anyone be harmed?

Nakshatra's discourses were always nourishing, not only for their spiritual content, but also for the jokes he was sent from all over the world.

He loved to see his orange crowd rocking with laughter. 'When you are both relaxed *and* attentive,' he often said, 'then something of the beyond can be transmitted to you.' And although the jokes were often extremely raw, he claimed that the higher the truth he wanted to convey, the lower he had to go in search of a joke.

Sabda's next chance for words with her Master would be at her farewell *darshan*, but a letter was another way of getting his attention. Many a time she sat at the rickety table in her room to pen a query, but by the time she'd condensed her thoughts succinctly enough to write them down, the question had usually answered itself, or become irrelevant.

When not engaged with growth-groups or communal meditation, Sabda would wander out of the Ashram gates, along the tree-shaded avenue, and then turn off right down a dusty road, till she came to the path that followed the river. A short distance from the burning ghat, there was a spot that was cool and green and silent. Now that her stay in the 'Buddha field' was coming to an end, it was there that she went to sort her thoughts before going home.

'Othila is the man I'm destined to meet,' she said to herself, settling on a crumbling wall beneath a shady thorn tree, 'and my feelings for him are as fresh as ever. Guruji has been clear about not blocking energies with repression, but the choice seems to be that, or suffer the ache of handing my heart to a married man.'

Sabda's mind had played this melody for a month now; but her thoughts lifted a full octave when she remembered that Masters of Truth see further than their disciples, and if Guruji had encouraged her to love regardless of the apparent absurdity, he must be looking further ahead. In that case, where might an equitable solution lie? One – Divorce. Two – Legal separation. Three – Conchita falls for her leading man. Four – My leading man turns up as a sannyasin. At this point a huge green and turquoise dragonfly swooping about her shoulders distracted Sabda's attention, and while watching its exotic flight, she noticed a tall, lanky Swami with curly brown hair striding along the river path towards her. Just what she did not want!

'Ah, so you've found my favourite spot,' he said, drawing level with the wall on which Sabda sat. His face and arms were deeply bronzed, but his legs, glimpsed through the slits of his straight orange robe, were as white as the day he left England. 'Meditation?' he questioned rather charmingly.

'Cogitation,' Sabda replied.

'Would you mind if I joined you?' Sabda moved along the wall to make room for the stranger, and they sat for a long moment silently contemplating the wide, gently flowing river. On the further bank a man and a buffalo tilled the soil, while a boy of about 12 fished from a rock in midstream. Tall rushes rising out of the pastel green marsh at the water's edge trembled in a light breeze.

'I'm Deva Tarika,' the Swami said after a while. 'What name did they think up for you? Your *mala* looks new.'

'Deva Sabda. Yes, I got it recently. You've been here for a while, I see.'

Tarika had been living near the Ashram for three months. Like Sabda, a book of the discourses had lured him to Lonavala, and before that he'd earned a secure living as an architect in his father's London firm. The family lived in Surrey, but bachelor still, Tarika preferred the independence of a Chelsea flat. Anna guessed he was just into his thirties.

'How come. Not married?' Sabda asked.

'Long story. No tell,' he replied, amused.

'Happy ending?'

'Don't know,' he replied, a hint of exasperation in his voice.

Sabda had a horror of the Ashram's trite expression, 'Want to share it?' so they just sat gazing at the river until a loud splash disrupted the stillness. The rock was bereft of the child, and when no head reappeared over the ripples, they sprang off the wall and hurried to the water's edge. Tarika waded in up to his knees, eyes scanning the empty surface ahead. He was about to strip, when the child's head popped up and, lithe as an otter, he swam back to his rock.

Relieved, they returned to the wall, and Tarika resumed the conversation. 'I really don't know,' he repeated. 'I wish I did.' It sounded as though he wanted 'to share it' after all.

'What happened?' Sabda asked, happy for the distraction.

His story went back six years, when he had fallen in love with a superficial, immature opportunist named Olga. He knew her for what she was, 'But love,' he emphasized, 'is not only blind but barmy.' Sabda giggled. Yes, she knew.

'Olga could be very loving,' he continued, doodling in the sand with a stick. 'Particularly at bed-time. And because of this, I foolishly thought she really cared as much as I. I assumed that marriage and children would soon iron out those immature little traits, but all she really wanted was a good time. I'd only recently finished university, you see, and money was tight to start with. Well, to cut a long story short, there came a day when she aimed the engagement ring at my head, and walked off with a better catch.'

Sabda nodded north south, while thinking east west.

'I knew I was a complete fool to go on wanting her, but I simply couldn't help it. About a year after the break-up, however, I came across this book of Nakshatra's discourses, they made more sense of life than anything I'd ever read before. So here I am.'

'Did she marry the other man?' Sabda asked.

Tarika looked up from his patterns in the sand, and laughed sarcastically. 'If only karma were a fairy story, Sabda. No, her affair with him disintegrated, and now she's back wanting to move in with *me* again.'

'... And you?' Sabda pursued.

'Yes and no.'

While he spoke, it flashed through Sabda's mind that had she met Tarika six years earlier, neither of them might have paid so much attention to a book of discourses. And it was not without anguish that she speculated on the possibility of his becoming the focus of solution number 4.

'What does Guruji say to all this?' she asked.

'Stay here as long as possible and allow the alchemy of meditation to work for me.'

'And you've been here three months?'

'That's right. It's a lot better – but perhaps not totally cured.'

'Sounds like tuberculosis,' Sabda mocked, eyeing him quizzically.

Tarika laughed. 'Then at least there'd be a pill – but strange things happen here, so who knows?'

'I sincerely hope so,' Sabda commented. 'Because, like you, there's someone I have to pluck from under my skin too!'

Tarika grinned. 'Yes, I know. I was at *darshan* when you mentioned it.'

'And you laughed, I'll bet.'

'I must confess, I did.'

They sat silently for a while, watching a white heron moving among the reeds. Tarika turned and looked speculatively at Anna in much the same way she had looked at him. 'How long are you staying?' he asked.

'Just a few more days. Tomorrow I do the Zen group, and immediately after, "Enlightenment Intensive". Then the farewell *darshan*, and straight back to Paris.'

'Pity.'

'Why?'

'Not long enough for two minuses to make a plus.'

Sabda laughed. The shade had slipped beyond the wall, and the sun was in mid-heaven.

'Better get back,' Tarika said. 'I'm hungry, aren't you?'

Sabda speculated on Tarika's story as she lay tossing in the heat that night. If his problem were karmic, there'd be no alternative but to live and learn his way through it. Poor Tarika! But supposing Othila was karmic too? She'd never considered that! Getting to know Tarika was tempting, but time didn't allow. In any case, Sabda wasn't really interested in a romantic involvement with anybody else.

The next morning, Virya was booked on the early train down to Bombay for the first lap of her journey back to Paris. A taxi waited outside the rooming house. Farewells were short, because Sabda would be home herself in a matter of days. As she got into the taxi, Vyria said, 'Oh, by the way Sabda, remember that dream you told me about in the infirmary?'

'Yes.'

'Well, I learned last night that the name Othila comes from the old *Nordic Book Of Runes*. It means "radical severance".'

'Really?' Sabda replied, kissing Virya goodbye through the taxi window.

'Yes, a group of us were discussing runes last night and it came up then. I knew I'd heard it somewhere, and that was it. Well, 'bye. See you next week.'

'Right. Right. Right.' Sabda murmured as she stomped up the wooden stairs to the empty bedroom. Life with Othila would certainly mean severance – A break with family, race, culture and country; what could be more radical than that?

After discourse that morning, Tarika found Sabda in the *chai* queue, and while they drank he pulled a rather creased business card from his robe pocket. 'That's my legal name,' he said. 'If ever you should find yourself in London, do get in touch. My home phone number is on the back.'

'Oh, I don't have a card to give you,' Sabda said regretfully. 'But if ever you find yourself in Paris you know where I work, and the switchboard will always be able to locate me.'

'I'll remember that,' Tarika said. They walked together to the Zen group room, and there parted, wistfully, as ships that pass in the night.

Zen was yet another attempt to discover the forgotten 'True Self' buried within each and everyone. To this end, a hand mirror had been placed by every cushion on the Zen-Room floor, because group members were to spend many a session peering at their faces finding the 'true me' behind the delusional appearance. The 'true me', say the Zen Masters, reveals itself when the logical mind dissolves, and to dissolve the logical mind, Anna and her group-mates turned their cushions to face a bare white wall, and were given an unsolvable riddle known as a Koan to solve. A Koan is a conundrum purposefully devoid of logical sense, for example, 'what is the sound of one hand clapping?' Being forced to look for a meaning or imagining the sound, is so mentally draining that eventually the logical mind drops of its own accord, and the experience of 'no mind' arises. With long practice Zen monks sometimes reach enlightenment this way, but Sabda, and a number of others, attained mostly to sleep. Another ancient technique in the exploration of what lies behind the mind is the practice of being 'a watcher on the hills'. This implies mentally detaching from personal matters and simply watching all that is happening without so much as a whispered thought.

At the end of those three days Sabda had not found her watcher, but had one more technique in her pocket for when she got home. Next morning it was to the basement that Anna went for her last group, 'Enlightenment Intensive'. After the white walls of Zen, 'Enlightenment Intensive' was to be a totally different kettle of tea.

The group was run with military precision by a young ex-

Grenadier Guard. It consisted of four days and three nights sitting opposite a partner, one saying, 'Tell me who you are,' and the other answering as best they can. Sixteen participants, equally divided between male and female, formed couples that changed every five minutes. A ten-minute lemongrass tea-break came every 40 minutes, and a 20-minute respite allowed for the two frugal, fruit-only meals. Lemongrass tea prevented bodily dehydration, but when words dried up, succour didn't flow from an old tin kettle. Long silences brought threats of expulsion from the group; words, however absurd, *had* to be found. The only escape was five hours of sleep at night, and even then, 'Who am I?' buzzed with the mosquitoes till dawn, when it was time to sit up and start all over again.

After the first 24 hours, identification with the obvious socially-induced conditioning, is seen to be false. Neither name, body, nor mind, am I. My profession isn't me either. Into the second day, the rational runs out and imagination rises in its place. 'Well, perhaps I am a butterfly. No, I'd rather be a wise old owl.' On the third day, with imagination wearing thin, exasperation defends the ego. Distraught disciples walked with their asking and sang with their answering. Answers came with laughter and with tears, but the question pounded on. 'Tell me who you are?'

On the fourth and final day, with the desire for Enlightenment far less ardent than a longing for the ordeal to end, madness arises. 'I'm just a cosmic orgasm,' some weary fairy warbled. 'Tell me who you are,' her partner persisted with all the indifference of a cracked gramophone record. Sabda too was reduced to gibberish. A French sannyasin moaned 'I'm a stomach. An *empty* stomach.' And a Texan drawled, 'Well, Ma'am, when I get outta here, I'm the guy who ain't never gonna touch another drop of lemongrass tea!'

'Enlightenment Intensive' ended with the sound of a tinkling bell, the smell of incense, soft music and a large dish of biscuits brought in by the orange guardee and his two assistants. The marathon was over. Sabda wanted to linger a while with the other ordealists, but she was leaving early the following morning and not only had to pay her debts and pack her bags, but wash her hair and get ready for her farewell *darshan* too. So she kissed her orange comrades goodbye, and on her way out heard the Texan's loud voice above all the others saying,' I may not know who I am, sir, but I sure know who I ain't.'

That evening Sabda sat before Guruji to say goodbye. He asked how she had enjoyed her stay, and whether she had any questions.

'Yes,' she replied. 'Guruji, you said not to miss any opportunity to love – that love transforms...' Guruji nodded gravely. 'You also said, harm nobody.' He nodded again. 'Well, in my situation the two are totally incompatible.'

Shri Nakshatra looked penetratingly into Sabda; he knew what she was referring to. A moment passed and then he replied, 'I still say love, Sabda. Love is perhaps the greatest of lessons and you will grow through it. Not necessarily in the way you expect, but there is a Divine Purpose behind everything in life. Don't you be worried. Nobody will be harmed.' Pausing a moment, he added. 'Remember, if the day is God's, the night is also His.' With these words echoing and re-echoing in her mind, Sabda returned to Paris wearing orange.

A gray dawn filtered through the grimy skylight over Sabda's front door as she stumbled out of the creaking antiquated lift on the top floor, fumbling for her keys. Her eye was drawn to something wrapped in cellophane at her feet – a large bowl of primroses. Picking up the bowl, she entered her apartment kicking her long-suffering holdall ahead of her. The flowers might have come from Virya who had promised to appear later that evening to collect the latest discourse tapes, but the card beneath the cellophane read, 'I love you darling,' so that exempted her.

Sabda closed her eyes. 'You will grow through it,' Guruji had said, and thoughts of Othila swirled in her mind like leaves before an autumn wind till the slamming front door returned her to reality with a shuddering bang.

Relishing the comforts of her cosy little flat, Sabda sank into a hot scented bath and mused on primroses. Half an hour later the water was cold, but she still hadn't decided whether it would be 'yes' or 'no' to Othila's next advance. 'Sleep first, decide later,' she said, getting out of the bath. Having dried herself, she found both her nightgowns in the laundry basket where they had lain for over a month, so she slipped into bed naked.

The sun had set and the apartment grown dark when, through the multiple veils of slumber, Sabda heard the doorbell. It rang again. Remembering Virya's pre-arranged visit, she grabbed her bathrobe and padded sleepily to the door.

'I don't want to intrude or disturb you.' It was Othila standing there, a shy smile countering the look of surprise on Sabda's sleep-befuddled face. 'I just wanted to be sure you got home all right.'

'What time is it?' Sabda asked, wrapping the bathrobe more firmly across her chest.

He looked at his watch. 'Six, but I can see all is well – I'll leave you to sleep.'

'You shouldn't have come,' Sabda stuttered. 'I thought we agreed we would not . . .' The sentence was cut short by the trill of the bedroom telephone. 'Well, come in while I answer it. Virya should be here any moment,' she added over her shoulder as he followed her in.

It was a 'welcome home' call from Virya, who also explained why she couldn't come round that evening as planned. Sabda reached for a comb and put some semblance of order into her hair as she talked. Then replacing the receiver, she returned to where Othila waited.

'I won't stay,' he said. 'Please forgive the intrusion.'

In spite of a sudden longing for him, Sabda was in no state to offer hospitality and accompanied him to the door. But before she could say goodbye, her hand was gently removed from the door-handle and her face firmly tilted towards his.

The embrace waltzed them backwards into the living room, where his nearness made her aware of her nakedness beneath the bathrobe: he became aware of it too. 'I've missed you more than you know,' Othila murmured, as slowly and sweetly, the inevitable began to happen.

Chapter Nineteen

When sannyasins return from the Ashman to regular employment wearing orange and a *mala*, they aren't necessarily received with open arms. Highway workers were the most fortunate as they had to wear orange anyway. But wearing unmitigated sannyasin colours in jobs where conventional decorum is expected, amounts to something of an art. Office workers usually kept their city suits to dark ochre and burgundy, and their *mala* under the tie or even deeper. Nevertheless when it becomes known that a colleague is hooked on a controversial Indian sage, it takes some living down. Sannyasins who defied convention by flaunting orange inappropriately, risked harsh criticism or worse. Some disciples flouted Nakshatra's directives altogether, making their orange a private rather than a public matter. But Guruji declared that if seekers weren't prepared to make a small adjustment in their outer appearance, what hope of transforming the inner?

Virya was indeed exceptional. She didn't tone down her garb – she toned it up. Her robes, an uncompromising sunset orange, were always ankle length and her *mala* made a bold finishing statement. She may have drawn her salary from a highly conservative organization, but not only did her colleagues admire her for daring to be different, the OUE, wanting, perhaps, to prove how broad-minded they were, had no qualms about sending her to speak at symposia and conferences all over the world.

Sabda's situation was rather different however. If she had tried to exchange an orange coat for the habitual white one, she'd have been out on her ear, and unlikely to find another nursing job giving both time and money for trips to India. From the start, she'd insisted on a white coat instead of a blouse blanche, and although both Maude and Lisette had eventually followed suit, this had been quite pushy enough. It was the new name that let the cat out of the bag, for medical unit staff used a first-name regimen, so when Anna asked to be called Sabda, she owed her colleagues some explanation.

Overall it might have been worse. When Maude and Lisette learned that their black sheep had turned orange and changed her name, they limited their reaction to a 'what did I tell you' look in their eye. What was said behind her back she didn't care about. The distant doctors pretended not to have noticed; the secretaries and lab technicians remained as charming as ever, but Dr Roch was not happy. His dignity would not allow for an immediate reaction, but when it came to Sabda's yearly performance report he took the opportunity of saying that her *mala*, emblem he called it, was not part of the uniform – though he could hardly have seen it under her white coat – and should she wish to leave his unit, he would not raise the slightest objection. Creating fear was one of his tactics, but he couldn't seriously fault Sabda's work capability, neither could he terminate her contract without offering Personnel a better reason than the one he had in mind. Sabda accepted these attitudes as all part of being a sannyasin, but she stayed on in her First Aid heaven.

Othila, on the other hand, was interested in all aspects of Sabda's guru trip. They no longer tried to stem the tide of their feelings for one another, and spent as many happy hours together as they could. The exchange was not confined only to lovemaking; they were compatible in many ways, and could merrily discuss just about every subject under the sun. Othila inspired Sabda with his plans for Africa, and she relayed her unfolding discoveries in human psychology and ancient wisdom. Often they would listen to the taped discourses that fascinated Othila just as much as they did Sabda. Time together was of course limited, and there were a thousand things they couldn't do together, but Sabda took this slow beginning to the love story of her life as just a temporary inconvenience. After all those years of waiting, Othila was at last there, and that was enough.

How marriage with a sannyasin would fit with Othila's official and international diplomatic role, was something to be sorted out later. If he decided to follow Guruji's teaching too, it would be for him and Guruji to decide how to manage a public life; but they weren't there yet. In the meantime Sabda was ready to face all the obstacles that lay ahead, and felt that Destiny, responsible for bringing her to this point, would naturally sort out the inconsistencies.

Although Othila's marriage appeared to be held together by convention and the children, it still counted. He loved his children, but of Conchita he said little. Once he showed Sabda a photo of an attractive middle-aged woman with sparkling eyes. Anna thought she would like her if ever they met, and did not forget that Conchita had borne and reared her beloved's children, seen to schools, laundry, food and supported him all the way up his professional ladder to the top. Sabda had only admiration for Conchita, which made the role of 'other woman' even worse. But Guruji had confirmed that there was Divine purpose in everything, and that nobody would be hurt.

A year passed and their affinity deepened; Othila referred to the possibility of a serious future together. Confident of his love, Sabda did not press for detailed plans; she assumed he wanted his youngest child settled in university, and an honourable understanding with his wife before he could offer her anything. In the interim there was little she could decently do, except shelve her own needs – and wait.

Another year flew by, and still the moment for an honest proposal had not ripened. The pressure of a relationship that demanded constant discretion was taking its toll. Sabda needed to move from the shallows of romantic love to something deeper and more fulfilling. Behind her habitual tact and understanding, frustration was mounting and patience wearing thin.

'What about Conchita?' Sabda said one evening, after Othila had again made guarded references to his future hopes. 'You once told me you loved her too.'

'I said I respected her,' Othila corrected, anger in his voice.

'I should jolly well hope so. She does everything for you.' Sabda snapped.

'Look, darling, I'm not going to argue, or burden you with *my* problems. Don't you trust me?'

'What do you think I've been doing all this time?'

'I know, I know.'

'I had a baby scare when you were away in Sweden last week,' Sabda said. 'Fortunately it turned out to be a false alarm, but it reminded me that I would like to have your child too. Have you ever considered that?'

The expression in Othila's eyes hardened. 'What would you have done had it not been a false alarm?'

Sabda looked askance. '*We*, you mean?'

'What I mean is, how would you feel about a child of mixed blood?' he amended lopsidedly.

Sabda didn't mean to accept the diversion, but found herself saying, 'I'm willing to face the difficulties of mixed blood, so long as my child is healthy, happy and welcomed into a secure and loving home.'

Othila nodded, but to Sabda's surprise, made no comment. Their time together that evening was too short for arguments. Forgetting that love is not only blind, but deaf, dumb and . . . barmy, Sabda postponed this vitally important subject to await a better time, at a later date.

Such a moment never came. About three months before Anna's next visit to Lonavala, a bizarre change crept into Othila's moods. It was a strange combination of elation and nervousness; he suddenly seemed to be afraid of Sabda's response, as though testing the temperature of the water before wading in. After two years of an ever-deepening bond between them Anna found this decidedly odd. But as he would not say what was going on, she put it down to stress. Othila hadn't had a holiday for over two years, during which time workload and life-strain had pushed him to the verge of a breakdown.

Sabda was forever urging him to slow down, but Conchita was able to do more. She called a doctor to the house and after an extensive medical check-up, Othila was prescribed a three-week rest by the sea, and a long series of anti-stress injections that the Organization's nurse could give him when he returned.

A rented beach-house on the island of Bermuda was decided upon for Othila's recuperation; Sabda saw it as the perfect place for him to retrieve the strength he needed to face life anew. For all she knew, Conchita, who had more than one interest and activity outside her home, might well express the need for freedom too. How else could 'nobody be harmed'? Moreover, the timing of their vacation couldn't have been better; Othila would be leaving Paris two weeks before Sabda's month in India, so the six-week separation would give him plenty of time to convalesce, gather perspective, and above all, come to a decision.

Tender farewells were said in the infirmary, Othila murmuring that this would be Sabda's last visit to Lonavala *alone*. This could mean only one thing, and it shone as a light at the end of her tunnel. One week later, Sabda stepped onto her Bombay Boeing with the lightest of hearts.

Chapter Twenty

> Want nothing. Where there is desire,
> Say nothing.
> Happiness or sorrow, whatever befalls you,
> Walk on.
> Untouched, unattached.

'Man lives in misery,' Nakshatra began,' the misery of wanting. Somewhere behind this misery he senses that his true nature belongs in bliss – that too he would grab . . . which is why you are all here! (laugher) Well, nothing here is 'up for grabs' – rather the contrary. Desire is a disease and Sosan, a naturopath. Don't fight it, he says, starve it of energy and it will leave of its own accord. Guruji's words were poignant. His words were always so. Even when Sabda missed the meaning they remained poignant, for she loved them as she loved music.

The Ashram population had tripled since Sabda's last visit, and the prevailing organization had tightened still further. A huge open-sided hall, holding more than a thousand, covered most of the garden, and was now the place for morning discourse and meditations. Darshan, however, remained on the covered patio at the back of Guruji's bungalow, but packed to capacity every evening.

Speaking with Guruji was still possible upon arrival and before departing, but now the bookings had to be made weeks before setting foot on Indian soil. Disciples truly seeking union with their Master felt his presence anyway, and often found their questions answered in indirect ways. After discourse people were frequently heard to say that their specific problems had been addressed; that had been Sabda's experience too. The Buddha field works in mysterious ways, and even the loss of plane tickets, the theft of last remaining funds, or a bout of hepatitis could lead sannyasins to vital insights and lasting changes in their lives. There were still a few familiar faces, but Tarika and Sangeet were not there.

The arrival *darshan* that Sabda had booked from Paris led, in time, to a place on the floor at Nakshatra's feet. For a long moment he looked at her without speaking. As she waited to hear what he would say, she felt no compulsion to re-open the 'Beloved file'; her relationship with Othila seemed so full of promise.

Nakshatra chuckled. 'Everything perfectly good, Sabda,' he said at last. 'But I feel you need to become a little more centred. Mm? When you are one with yourself, nothing can trouble you for long. Once you have learned the knack of being centred, peace becomes effortless, and you will be surprised how bothersome people and events go out of their way to avoid you.' Having said that, he suggested several groups, all aimed at centring.

There were diverse techniques to engender the heavenly serenity of which Guruji spoke, one of which involved eating, walking and encountering people while blindfolded. Another consisted of spontaneous intuitive questioning. During this exercise, a hefty Scot left his place in the circle and walked boldly up to Sabda. 'Eh, lass,' he said in a broad Glasgow accent. 'Have-y-got-a-mun?' After hearing Sabda's 'Yes,' he returned to the circle doubled up with laughter. He laughed so long and so infectiously that all present began laughing with him. Nobody seemed to know what the joke was, and although totally mystified, Sabda laughed too. She didn't read anything into it because absurdities were to be expected in the Ashram – it was part of the teaching.

After five weeks of awesome discourses, 'centring' groups and escapades into town, Sabda felt as balanced as she ever could be. Her holdall bulged with gloriously coloured silk, sandalwood carvings for her friends, and a brightly painted Kashmiri pen and stationery stand for Othila's office desk.

All too soon she sat before Guruji to say goodbye. On this occasion her Spiritual Master started by speaking obscurely. 'The moment before dawn, Sabda is the greatest – have you noticed? All nature holds her breath. Will the sun reappear, or not? There is a moment of profound silence, and then the first twitter of a bird. It is a signal, and out of the silent gray dawn a mighty chorus soars to meet the light. Listen for that first twitter, Sabda, listen for it.' Sabda was bewildered, but Guruji did not invite a question. With Othila never far from her thoughts, however, she could not repress an enquiring look. Guruji nodded.

'Don't you be worried, Sabda. Just remember that a Divine purpose lives in everything. I am with you. Come back soon, Mm?'

When Anna's plane touched down at Orly, Virya was there with her car. She was eager to have the latest news, and a new stock of taped discourses for her Thursday evening gatherings.

'How have things been with you?' Sabda inquired after answering a multitude of questions about the Ashram.

'Hectic as usual. Remember Konsu Mapeta – the guy with the bleeding hand? Well, he's leaving and the whole division is in an almighty flummox.'

Something inside Sabda turned a double somersault, but with amazing casualness she managed to say, 'Oh really. Was it unexpected then?'

'Oh, it's been on the cards for a good three months,'

Virya replied. 'But the call came a little sooner than we anticipated. His government contacted him while he was vacationing in Bermuda, and he accepted the post right away. I guess he knew it would come, but he's giving us precious little time to tie things up and find a replacement.'

'When is he going?' Sabda asked.

'He gave a meagre four weeks' notice, of which barely two remain. He's in Moscow at the moment.'

'Rather short,' Sabda conceded, hoping her tone still sounded unconcerned.

'Boy, you can say that again!'

'I didn't know you worked that closely with him.'

'He's my boss's boss. Quite a bit of his small stuff filters down to me.'

'Couldn't he have given more warning?' Sabda asked hoarsely, so as to keep the information flowing.

'He's supposed to give three months minimum, but in view of the importance of his future post, the DG couldn't very well make stipulations.' Virya laughed as she continued. 'There's a wailing and gnashing of teeth on the eighth floor, I can tell you; he was quite a ladies man. Sally practically went into hysterics when she heard.'

'Sally?'

'His second secretary. She used to work with us, but nagged and nagged until she was transferred to his office.'

'Do I know her? What does she look like?'

'Pretty, auburn hair, milk-white complexion. It's no secret, she's crazy about him.'

'Perhaps it's mutual?'

'Could be. But he's married with kids, you know.'

'Oh!'

'Did you get the tapes OK?' Virya asked, changing the subject.

'Yep. They're in my hand luggage.'

When the car stopped in front of Sabda's apartment

building, her luggage was extracted, and a large packet of discourse tapes handed over. 'Thanks so much for meeting me, Virya,' Sabda said. 'Don't bother to park. I'll phone you when I get sorted out.'

Sabda collected her mail from the concierge before going up to her empty flat. No flowers met her at the door, but a plain postcard was among the mail. '*Sorry no time to write as I would like – have not been working like a black, but like two of them! Will be in Moscow when you get this, but back the day after your return. Will phone. Hope your trip was rewarding. Love, Othila.*' Nothing about leaving. He undoubtedly preferred to break the happy news and explain his plans in person. *Their* plans, perhaps?

The card received an excited little kiss before being propped up on the bookshelf. Sabda then undressed, took a bath, and sank into a bed that always seemed softer and fresher after each visit to India. She undoubtedly needed sleep, but this latest development provoked a fidgety state of wakefulness, and her mind would not stop searching for reasons why Othila hadn't mentioned his foreseeable departure. She distinctly remembered his farewell promise. How could he have said such a thing if he'd known months before that he might be leaving? Unless, of course, he was sure of taking her with him. Even then, why hadn't he discussed it with her earlier? Had Conchita found another man at last?

On Monday morning Sabda walked into her infirmary glad that there were no curious colleagues asking about her month away. More than anything, she needed space to ruminate.

On Tuesday the telephone buzzed all day long, but Othila neither came nor called, which was not like him at all. Presuming he'd been delayed in Moscow, Sabda expected a call that evening; he usually phoned her when abroad – and from trickier places than Moscow. By midnight she assumed him to be in a plane on his way home, and stopped waiting. In view of the new appointment, and all the questions she would want answered, he'd rightly judged it wiser to wait till he got back to explain things. In any case, he'd need the anti-stress injections more than ever now, so she was sure to see him in the infirmary on the following day.

Speculation concerning Mapeta's departure and the nomination of a successor was the talk of town. On Wednesday afternoon somebody came down from the Director's office for an aspirin, and in the course of conversation bemoaned the 'black hole left by K's leaving us'. Yes, he'd returned from Moscow on schedule two days ago, dead beat. Sabda wondered whether she should send an innocent message reminding Mr Mapeta about his medical appointment, but confident that there would be a perfectly acceptable explanation for his apparent negligence, she decided not to stress him further.

By Thursday, three clear days and nights had passed without news; Sabda couldn't imagine what was going on, and her nerves were beginning to fray. The time for reasonable explanations was past. Othila's direct office line was out of bounds, but she dialled it anyway. For one full minute the dialling tone came loud and clear, then clicked into silence. Anna replaced the receiver.

On Friday evening, Sabda's patience snapped. The staff were starting their weekend, but Othila would probably still be at his desk. Grim-faced, she grabbed the phone and dialled his direct line again. As she did so, the waiting room door clicked and the buzzer sounded.

'About time,' she snorted, slamming down the receiver. Her blood was up. She rounded the desk and opened the door ready for battle.

Virya stepped forward, with a smile that immediately evaporated. 'Jees, Sabda! What's going on? You look terrible!'

'Take no notice.' Sabda replied pulling herself together a fraction. 'I'm in a mood swing that's all. Jet lag, probably.'

'Well,' Virya said hesitantly, 'I came to see if you'd be free this weekend. I was planning to . . .'

Sabda was not free that weekend, thanks all the same. No, she didn't want to share it. Yes, she was perfectly all right, really. No, it wasn't anything important. Yes, she'd have to work it out for herself. No, nobody could help – thanks all the same.

By Saturday evening, Othila had been back for almost a week, and still not given the slightest sign of life – or love. With pendulum-like regularity, Sabda's emotional state now oscillated from love to hate, and from trust to suspicion.

On Sunday morning, she awoke knowing exactly what Othila's silence meant and lay staring at the ceiling in disbelief. For two-and-a-half years Othila had made her believe that he loved her. She'd always accepted the possibility that he might never be able to marry her; though it did look as though Destiny was working in that direction. But in all that time, it had never entered Sabda's head that he was simply using her for as long as convenient.

She had to tell someone her thoughts or die. Throwing off the bedclothes she went to the telephone. It was early, but Marie-Claire would understand. The phone rang for a long time, and then the timid voice of Marie-Claire's seven-year-old daughter, answered. 'Daddy has taken Mummy to the hospital.' Sabda remembered that Marie-Claire had been in and out of hospital twice since the start of her third pregnancy; she thanked the little girl, said she'd call back later, and hung up.

Tears would have relieved the tension, but anger kept them dry. If she couldn't talk, she had to move, she couldn't just do nothing. The kitchen floor needed scrubbing, she'd not done it before leaving for India and it was filthy. Tackling the hated job now seemed easy, and absorbed the surplus of negative energy bubbling in her cauldron. 'Perhaps he's only avoiding me so as not to see the pain he's causing,' Sabda thought as she scraped a blob of grease off the tiles with a knife, but when the grease was gone, she'd switched to supposing his silence to be an avoidance of what her anger could do to his precious reputation. She choked on these thoughts even as she wavered on a filament of disbelief, but whatever her emotion, the tiles of the kitchen floor sparkled as never before.

Spring sunshine filled the infirmary on Monday morning, but Sabda hardly noticed it. She hadn't slept. In just one week, Othila would be gone. Virya had mentioned that these next days would be filled with his farewell parties, and went on to extol Mapeta's charisma, intelligence, straightforwardness, decency and fair play. He was *so* dedicated, and had done *such* a wonderful job, that the DG was sure to grant Mapeta's country generous funding after he had left the Organization.

'How very *nice*!' Sabda remarked, but Virya missed the sarcasm. Sabda had never wanted to slap anyone's face harder than Othila's. If it were possible, she'd leave it stinging for the rest of his life!

The impact of the farewell parties was swift to reach the infirmary. On Monday afternoon, the door crashed open to reveal a pretty auburn-haired secretary announcing that she was about to vomit. Anna hastily steered her to the lavatory, and afterwards installed her on the infirmary bed. Her name; Sally Clark.

'What brought that on?' Sabda asked, pouring the remedy that would settle her stomach.

'Well, Nurse,' the ashen-faced secretary replied. 'It's the first of my boss's leaving parties. I'm his secretary and had to do all the organizing, you see. There wasn't time for a proper lunch, and the fruit cocktail had rather a lot of rum in it.'

'I see. Well, sip this,' Sabda said, handing her the medicine glass.

'At least, I think it's that.' Sally hesitated. 'I've had bouts of nausea lately and I've been meaning to see you about them, but there's not been time. It's chaos upstairs – absolute chaos! Everything's got to be finished before he leaves.'

Remembering Virya's statement about Othila's being 'quite a ladies man', and Sally 'crazy about him', Sabda couldn't help wondering ... 'This nausea, when does it come?' she questioned,

'Oh, I know what you might be thinking, Nurse, and to tell you the truth I'm not sure myself. My periods have never been regular, you see. And, well, it would be an absolute disaster if I were pregnant now.' She began to sob.

'Hey, don't jump to conclusions,' Sabda encouraged – advice she might have taken to her own heart. 'If you bring me a pregnancy kit and an early-morning urine sample, I'll do the test for you first thing tomorrow – OK?'

'Thank you ever so much, Nurse. I really am a bit overwrought. You see, he couldn't possibly marry me – not in his position – and I've no idea what to do!'

The thought of 'mixed blood' jumped to Sabda's mind as she said, 'Don't count your chickens, Sally. It's probably just a false alarm.'

But Sally wasn't listening. Her far-away look was picturing the worst. 'And to top it all,' she burst out, 'he's leaving!'

Hearing this, the colour drained from Sabda's face; she sank onto the edge of the bed at Sally's feet. 'Now, Sally,' she said with as much authority as she could muster, 'It's probably nothing to worry about; just a matter of overwork, skipped meals and emotional upheaval.'

Two calls broke the silence in Sabda's flat that Monday evening; both made her leap into the air at the first ring – but neither came from Othila. She tried to empty her mind with meditation, but gave up and poured herself a glass of wine instead. Finally she went to bed resolving to march up to the eighth floor next day, whatever the consequences.

Where meditation had failed, the wine succeeded in calming Sabda sufficiently for sleep. Before dozing off however, she remembered the old Hindu illustration of *maya* (illusion) demonstrated by the terror of a man who thinks he sees a dangerous snake, when it's only a piece of rope. And then she recalled Guruji's words. 'You will learn from it – though not necessarily in the way you expect.' True, she hadn't expected this. But what, precisely, was she supposed to learn?

Tuesday morning marked the eighth day since Othila's silent return. Sabda approached the infirmary thinking that if there was no reply to Othila's phone, she'd storm upstairs as planned and confront him – though when she'd find time she didn't know; her first patient was standing at the infirmary door already. Drawing nearer she recognized Sally, a bulging paper bag in one hand, a bunch of roses in the other. She had more colour than the day before.

'Hello,' Sabda said, unlocking the door. 'You certainly look better today.'

'I feel a lot better, thank you, Nurse,' Sally replied, handing over the paper bag. 'The flowers are for you – you've been so understanding.'

Sabda held them to her nose appreciatively, saying Sally shouldn't have gone to so much trouble at such a busy time.

Sally laughed a little. 'No trouble at all. Anyway, we don't mind the work, you know, because he's such an exceptional person. I've worked for top brass Africans before, but Mr Mapeta is one in a million.'

'So I've heard,' Sabda replied dryly, taking the pregnancy kit and jarful of urine out of the paper bag.

'What time shall I come for the results?' Sally asked. 'You

see, he's invited all the staff and their spouses for a farewell dinner at his residence this evening, so I'll have to leave a little early to get my hair done.'

'We should know by two.' Then the $64,000 question. 'Will you be taking your boyfriend along to the dinner?'

Sally's face lit with a big smile. 'He'll be there!' she replied, but immediately looked away to hide a wave of sadness. Sabda tensed. 'It'll be our last evening together before he flies back to Abu Dhabi. He's training to be a pilot; his course is just over and he has to go home, you see?'

Potential aggression pivoted into warm compassion as Sabda realized she'd seen but a rope, not the most hideous of snakes ready to poison further the uncertainties of her path.

'How would it be if I phoned the results to you the moment they are ready?' she said sweetly.

'Oh, I'd be ever so grateful, Nurse.'

Communication with Sally created vicarious contact with the man Anna still loved but wanted to tear apart. 'By the way,' she said, making it sound like an afterthought, 'would you please remind your boss about his medical appointment?'

'No problem. But he'll not have time today, that's for sure.'

When the timer for Sally's test rang, it showed that she too had seen a rope. Sabda dialled Othila's office. Sally answered, and almost collapsed with relief when she heard that the test was negative. Sabda then asked for a quick word with the boss.

'He's in a meeting, I'm afraid, and after that he'll be going straight home to uncork the champagne. But I gave him your message,' Sally replied.

During that day, Sabda had not found a moment to storm upstairs as intended, and now it was too late. She would have to let Othila leave her like a thief in the night. 'If only,' she reflected, 'he had simply said that a life together was impossible. And if he had had the decency to mention the likely break-up when he knew that change was imminent, I'd not be feeling torn, but ready to congratulate him.'

That evening Sabda was going to have supper with Virya to meet friends from the US. She was glad of the invitation as it would take her mind off things. In order to get away on the dot of six, she had locked cupboards and drawers ahead of time. Her coat was ready on the back of her chair and she was sitting at her desk with three minutes to go, when the buzzer sounded. Smothering an oath and praying for a quick aspirin rather than an everlasting nosebleed, Sabda pressed the 'Enter' button and waited for the door to open. When it did, there stood 'the man she was destined to meet'. His features had changed radically; he'd become almost a stranger since their last meeting seven weeks before. The skin stretched tightly across his face, his jaw twitched with suppressed tension and his eyes – smaller and sharper than usual – watched keenly for an attack to counter. Sabda denied him that pleasure; the ball was in his court. She waited.

'Don't be angry with me,' he blurted. 'Sabda, I'd no idea it was all going to happen so soon.'

Sabda raised an eyebrow; this spruce little lie confirmed her darkest fears. Othila looked at the ceiling as though dealing with an obstreperous child.

'It hasn't been easy for me either, you know.'

'What hasn't been easy?' Sabda pursued. 'I don't remember you telling me your plans.'

'You know very well . . .' he said sternly, and was about to elaborate when his regard met with the roses on Sabda's desk and a flash of jealousy momentarily blocked his line of thought. 'You know very well . . . what I'm trying to say,' he stuttered.

Sabda stared at him, unmoving, as the accuracy of her conjectures became blatantly clear. He had never intended to do anything but use her. 'What *are* you trying to say, then?' she insisted.

The mouth that had often kissed her so tenderly, opened with a contradictory twist as though Sabda had no right speaking to him like that. No right to hurt him. No right to make him lost for words. 'Believe me Sabda. I . . . I had no idea it was all going to happen so fast,' he repeated.

'So you knew, and didn't warn me?'

'It wasn't like that. You must believe me . . .'

'Oh I did. Absolutely. Especially when you left me with the notion that you'd be with me on my next trip to India, and possibly for the rest of my life. Remember? Now what did you mean by that?'

'From the very beginning you knew I would return to Africa, Anna – Sabda, I mean.' He spluttered in tones of belligerent justification.

Stunned, Sabda simply stared, watching him try to forestall the kind of truculence she realized he must have experienced with other women – and from the way he spoke, it was clear what kind of women they must have been. He feared a scene – a scandal that might tarnish his precious career.

When his garbled case for the defence ended, a wall of silence rebuffed the absurdity of his arguments, returning them to sender unopened. Anna had to renounce the monumental slap he deserved; she wasn't sure now if he might report her for unprofessional conduct. His deceit was unbelievable. But then, for two and a half years Sabda had only seen him lover-side-up and never glimpsed the canny politician – a role he played with equal excellence.

Othila loomed silently opposite Sabda's desk, but from the expression on his taut face, he appeared confused. He registered the contempt of Sabda's silence, but didn't know how to react. Sabda had been deeply in love with him when she left for India, so where was the tirade? Parting was not going to be so tricky after all, and soon he'd be back in Africa and away from it all. He pushed his luck a little further.

'While I'm here,' he murmured, looking anxiously at his watch, 'perhaps I'd better have my injection.'

Othila needed his anti-stress injections to carry him through the strain of his last week in the Organization, and unless he'd have time to use the main medical unit, Sabda could expect at least three more visits before he left. Without comment, she prepared the shot.

'Who gave you the flowers?' he enquired lightly, as the needle plunged into his tense derriere. Sabda remained mute.

But after Mr. Mapeta had pulled up his trousers, tucked in his shirt, straightened his jacket, and turned to face her, she looked him squarely in the eye. 'And what is that to you *now*?' she replied.

When he had left the infirmary, Sabda called Virya and cancelled their supper together. She needed to cry, but tears wouldn't come. Neither would sleep.

In the days that followed, Othila came for his injections, hurrying in with a look at his watch, hurrying out in the same manner. Given all the warm adulation greeting him elsewhere else, the infirmary must have seemed an icy humiliating place, but this was poor revenge.

In spite of everything Sabda still hoped he would regain his senses and find a way to restore her respect for him. She wanted to believe that a living heart thumped beneath the immaculate striped shirt and, before his last injection was due, she had thought of a way to check this out. 'Could you do just one last thing for me before you go?' Sabda asked sweetly when the injection was over.

'If I possibly can,' he replied.

'I want you to . . .'

'Go on,' he said impatiently.

'It's really important to me – and perhaps even to you.'

Othila relaxed. She was speaking nicely to him again. 'Well?' he said with a charming smile. 'What is it?'

'It's just that I'd like to know what you would think of a man who treated your daughter in the way you have treated me.'

Othila's face suddenly bloated, his eyes widened and the veins in his neck stood out over the shirt collar. He backed to the door, his mouth opening and shutting several times before uttering a word, and then only one: 'Woman!'

On the morning of his departure, Othila turned up unexpectedly in the infirmary to stand in front of Sabda's desk, proffering an expensive little box on an outstretched palm. 'Just a souvenir,' he said sheepishly.

Intense pain and anger flashed from Sabda's eyes as she stared at the final pay-off. She'd have thrown it out of the window, but air conditioning prevented her opening it. 'That will not be necessary,' she said with a disdainful wave of her hand.

Shocked, Othila looked first at the unaccepted gift burning a hole in his palm, and then into Sabda's eyes. 'You'd better ask God to forgive you for this,' she said. 'Because I never will.'

Silence prevailed as Othila's trembling hand returned the gift to his pocket. No more was said, there was no need. 'Hell hath no fury like a woman scorned.'

Chapter Twenty-One

When a man is loved in secret, secret too must be the mourning of his loss. Virya and acquaintances in the Organization were never to know. Marie-Claire was herself in trouble with a difficult third pregnancy, and others would only say 'what else could you expect from a...!' As for sannyasins, they'd cry 'karma' and she had no intention of 'sharing it' with them. In any case, the whole wretched affair was just too humiliating to confide – even if consolation were possible.

Sabda carried on trying to appear as though nothing troubled her, but hopeless, useless hindsight kept creeping in the back door of her mind. Othila's strange hesitation, testing the temperature of the water before stepping in, three months before was about the time, Virya told her, that both the press, his senior colleagues, and Mapeta himself, were speculating on his glorious promotion. She could see now, that he'd been afraid that the news might have reached her, but on finding that it had not, instead allowing her time to prepare for a break-up, he had purposely left her in the dark. What more did she need to know about his 'love' for her than that? And while a woman can bear a parting where love exists, or existed, neither heart nor her pride can ever forgive being used and discarded without a backward glance.

Nevertheless she reproved her foolish self, upbraided a

cruel Destiny and railed against Guruji, who might at least have warned her in clearer terms. 'Stuff the Beloved!' she yelled at her empty love nest.

But instead of releasing tensions, Sabda's revolt only passed from mind to body. First, large breast cysts had to be removed, then a cystic thyroid needed the knife. Gallstones followed, resulting in yet another operation, and even then it took months for Sabda to see that this surgical cycle was only the price of unexpressed shock, frustration and anger.

Working with the problems of others in the infirmary helped Sabda maintain perspective. The wound was ugly, but marriage to its perpetrator would have been uglier. Yes, Sabda had supped with the Devil, enjoyed a lengthy meal, and been treated to a surprise tour round Hell afterwards. It was time to turn the page and with Christmas on the horizon, there were preparations for her annual pilgrimage to India to concentrate on.

On all previous occasions, Sabda had felt a definite pull to the Ashram. It was as though Nakshatra leaned from his boat and hauled on the ropes till the disciple was drawn to the gunwales. But this time, instead of that unmistakable lure, she was assailed by a nagging premonition that she'd not be seeing much of her Master on this occasion. In view of this, and rather than have something else to blame herself for, Sabda took greater care than usual over eliminating all perfumed substances and even adopted a vegetarian diet, for three good months before leaving Paris.

'Give my love to everyone at the Ashram,' Virya said, hugging her friend at the airport. 'And take care.'

The flight was smooth. Sabda ate the soggy microwaved macaroni cheese supper, watched the film, and then slept until the Captain's voice came through on the intercom. 'Ladies and Gentlemen. We have now begun our descent over Bombay. The temperature there is thirty-six degrees centigrade, and it is ten-fifteen pm, local time.' Smiling,

Sabda turned her head towards the window. The city sprawled beneath her like a cloud of fireflies. She could just make out the bay with its necklace of lights, and the pang of emotion that always erupted when India spread below, turned on tears. That night was spent in the Centaur Hotel and she treated herself to a taxi up to Lonavala on the following morning.

The Ashram had changed beyond all recognition. The canteen was now a fully-fledged vegetarian restaurant. There was a Bhodi Bank and a Supernatural Supermarket; but the eight-holed lavatory block, the wonder of its day, had adamantly refused to evolve, though its queue stretched to Nirvana.

More space was on everybody's mind. Newsletters fluttered on the noticeboards informing Sannyasins that a larger Ashram was being planned in Gujarat and specially chosen pioneers were already out there working on construction. The Lonavala Ashram was scheduled to transfer within 12 months and Guruji to follow as soon as his house was built.

With all this in the air, the atmosphere had lost its casual charm. Personal contact with Guruji was now restricted to the hoards of first-timers coming to take sannyas. The 'comers' and 'goers' were admitted to Darshan still, but only to watch and listen; anyone wanting to commune personally with their Spiritual Master had to do so on a higher level. Sabda looked around to see if she could find a few familiar faces to hob-nob with; just a few remembered her from the year before, but Tarika was in Gujarat designing Guruji's quarters, and Sangeet, leading groups back in Amsterdam.

'Perfume very strong!' the 'sniffers' said the following day when Sabda turned up for discourse.

'Are you sure?'

'Quite sure, Ma,' said the sniffer, barring her way.

Supposing she had picked up perfume from the Bombay bed she had slept in the night before, Sabda didn't argue but went back to her hotel and washed her hair so as not to be turned away again. But the next day, and for the fortnight that followed, it was the same story. Time was slipping by; Sabda began to remonstrate. When arguing was of no avail, she tried pleading her way into discourse, and was reluctantly allowed to sit in the back row where Guruji seemed as a sail on the horizon. But even that was not to last, two days later an uncontrollable barking cough kept her out of discourse for the remaining two weeks of her stay.

With all opportunities to see Nakshatra barred, Sabda wondered if perhaps her intuition had tried to tell her not to come at all. This was her fourth consecutive year without a restful holiday, and in view of all that had happened, recuperation in a tolerable climate would not have been amiss. Instead of signing up for groups, she went for walks along the peaceful river, and attended only one meditation a day.

'Perfume very strong,' the sniffers moaned again, when Sabda presented for her farewell *darshan* on the evening before her departure.

'Look,' came the angry response. 'I've not touched any perfumed substance including toothpaste for sixteen whole weeks. Tomorrow I leave, and it'll be a year before I can return. *So will you please let me in?*'

The sniffers remained adamant, but as they were shaking their heads, Sabda seized her *mala*, held it first to her own nostrils, and then to theirs. *That* was it! Those wooden beads had hung around her neck day and night for four years, and now all the perfumes of Arabia seemed to emanate from them. 'Oh why hadn't I thought of that sooner?' she reflected whirling the necklace over her head and dumping it in the astonished sniffer's hand. '*There's* your perfume very strong,' she said angrily.

Grudgingly, a *mala*-less Sabda was allowed through the gate. Once inside, 'Arrivals' were ushered to the right,

'Departures' to the left, and those without a *mala*, presumably taking sannyas, made to sit in the front row. Mistaken for one of the latter, Sabda found herself sitting right opposite Guruji's chair, and from this coveted position, Destiny revealed the underlying reason for her visit.

After a few minutes Nakshatra appeared, silent as a ghost in the mist. He sat with his customary grace, crossing one leg over the other, allowing the sandal to dangle in its characteristic way, but Sabda felt that something was different. She observed closely as he greeted each new aspirant, looked deeply into them, slid the *mala* over their heads, took the clipboard, wrote their new names, handed them the ivory notepaper, and then explained the meaning of the new name. Sabda heard every word, every intonation. His gestures were the same, the words typical, and his appearance as she had always known it; but his presence had changed. Silent, yes, but lacking that velvety depth she had always felt before. A subtle difference had come over Guruji that she couldn't quite identify.

It was only as he blessed the last aspirant with 'Very good, Govind, very good.' That it clicked. The voice! The timbre of Guruji's voice was slightly but definitely altered and, crazy as it may seem, it gave Sabda the impression of a man imitating himself.

After Darshan, Sabda spent an hour looking for the sniffer who had kept her *mala* and eventually retrieved it.

On the long flight home, there were hours to ponder all that had, and had not, happened during Sabda's five-week visit. Obstructions and disappointments were everyone's lot, but was it a mere coincidence that the emblem of her discipleship had to go before Guruji could be seen? Was her place directly opposite his chair a simple error? If she'd sat anywhere else, all those observations might have been missed. As for the observations themselves, whichever way she looked at them they presaged ill. Had she unwittingly proved unworthy of sannyas? Was this his way of throwing her out? Sabda returned to Paris still wearing her *mala* . . . but wondering.

An envelope from the Swami's centre was waiting in the handful of mail handed to her by the concierge on her return. It contained a printed card rimmed in black. Sudah had died. Shocked, Sabda turned the card over and read a note in the Swami's handwriting scribbled on the back. 'She collapsed with a heart attack and died in hospital three days later.' For a moment Sabda was too shaken to move, but when thoughts returned they were pleasant ones. She was grateful that her friend's passing had been swift; Sudah wouldn't have taken kindly to a hospital treatment, and was not in the least bit frightened of dying.

'Well, better there than here, Sudah dear. I'm happy for you,' Sabda murmured. But the happiness she felt for Sudah did nothing to keep her tears from falling.

Three weeks after her return to Paris, Sabda stood before Virya's front door, it was ajar. 'I'm in here,' Virya's voice echoed from her empty bedroom where she was jumping on an overloaded suitcase. 'This is *it*!' she said triumphantly when Sabda appeared. 'Man, this is it!' Without the slightest regret, Virya was off to pioneer the New Ashram – and raring to go. Sabda eyed the pyramid of possessions. 'All this going with you?'

'Yes, Ma'am.'

Virya was going to leave a great gap in Sabda's life, but she couldn't help smiling to see her fearless orange renunciant up to her eyes in belongings – sewing machine, electric typewriter, knife sharpener and silk pyjamas to boot. With so much enthusiasm in the air, however, she overlooked the presages of her *mala*-less *darshan* and wondered if one day, she too, would wind up in Gujarat. Of Sabda's last *darshan*, Virya had said, 'For heaven's sakes, Sabda, you read too much into things.' Well, hopefully she was right.

'Why don't I sit on the suitcase while you lock it?' Sabda suggested. 'Then we had better go. I've booked a table for eight at *La Vie en Rose*, for our last supper together.'

'Wow!'

'Well, it's a great occasion. I don't want you to forget oysters and *canard à l'orange*. Oh yes, and they do a wonderful *mousse au citron* too. My gourmand friend, Paul, used to take me there sometimes.'

'Well,' Vyria said giggling, 'Guruji never said a word about austerities, did he?'

'It all depends on the love and awareness you bring to it.' Sabda chaffed.

'I've never had any problem bringing love and awareness to good food, have you?

'Never!'

Two days later, Virya was gone; Sabda couldn't wangle leave to see her off, but a gang of Sannyassins went with her to the airport.

After Virya's departure, a rented dance studio on the cheap side of Levallois-Peret became the venue for the burgeoning Nakshatra Centre of Paris. It was a Sannyassin's home from home, but Sabda only turned up for the regular weekly video-discourses. She was still at loggerheads with herself over her puzzling perceptions of that last *darshan*, and the discourses arriving from Gujarat did nothing to dispel her uneasiness. Guruji's eyes had faded into ordinariness, his voice lost all majesty and his discourse no longer infused a meaning beyond the words. 'Isn't it terrible?' she'd say to her fellow Sannyassins, but they only looked back uncomprehendingly. A letter to Virya about her misgivings brought no comfort, and a note to Nakshatra received no reply.

The grind of time did nothing to relieve Sabda's dilemma. She had foreseen a life-long allegiance to her Master, his teaching and truth. She had firmly believed he would lead her to Enlightenment – 'The Beloved' – in every sense.

Nothing could ever eradicate what she had already imbibed – it was now an integral part of her. So how could he possibly be telling her to 'go'?

A year passed. Sabda made no move. The Gurjurat Ashram was attracting hoards of followers until, quite suddenly, Shri Nakshatra died.

Along with all Sannyassins everywhere, Sabda was stunned by the news. The Paris centre continued its regimen of meditations, telling participants that Guruji lived on in the hearts of those who loved him. Poster-sized photo's pinned on the walls showed Nakshatra's body carried with singing and dancing to the burning ghat down by the river. But his demise left a hiatus of uncertainty.

Rumours and gossip about the future passed from mouth to ear and back again. Nobody knew what to believe until a bulletin from Gujarat, addressing Sannyassins as 'beloved devotees' arrived, setting out certain changes. It had been Guruji's wish that his teaching be propagated and the meditations continued in Gujarat and around the world. However, orange was no longer appropriate and disciples were free to revert to any name they wished. The mala had to go too. But as a sacred thing, the mala had to be returned to the earth.

'Another chapter finished,' Anna pondered putting her teaspoon down and watching her after-lunch coffee swirl in the cup. The hubbub of the cafeteria was going on around her, and two girls from the typing pool at the next table punctuating her thoughts with snippets of their conversation. She was pondering on life and where it was taking her. 'I've come too far along the path of self-discovery for it to end in a cul-de-sac like this,' she thought. 'But it feels as though my river had flowed into a sandy desert and is about to dry up completely.' She had read that this *could* happen. 'Maybe that *has* happened! she conjectured.

'Well that's what *we* thought,' one of the typist was saying emphatically. 'But affaire wasn't over – not by a long chalk!'

This remark rang in Anna's mind as she took her lunch tray to the disposal trolley; she recognized Destiny's voice. 'This isn't the end of your spiritual adventure,' it was saying – 'No, not by a long chalk!'

Virya had plans to return to Sacramento. 'The Buddha field seems to have vanished, and the Ashram not a place I want to stay in,' she wrote. A little later, another letter said she had found gainful employment, and although nobody would ever replace Guruji, she was exploring the rich spiritual opportunities of California.

When it came to returning her mala to Nature, Anna decided it would go into the Seine from the lovely old Pont Alexandre in the centre of Paris. 'Life is a bridge, pass over it.' Nakshatra had said. 'A bridge is not a place to build your house,' and neither is a Master, Anna added. Which reminded her of another ancient Sage. 'I'm only a finger pointing to the moon,' he told his disciples. 'Don't clutch my finger, look at the moon (truth). It was only then, as she stood mid-river holding her mala over the bridge, that Anna understood what Nakshatra had been trying to say at her last *Darshan*. He'd been saying, 'My finger aches from pointing to the moon. Now for heaven's sake, Anna, *look at it!* Look at it for yourself.

The seeker of truth stood on a bridge in more ways than one, that sunny afternoon. On the bank she had left behind were memories of *The Initiate*, sunstroke, the Swami, and Sudah. There was Michel the fraud, Othila the man she'd been destined to meet and, of course, Nakshatra. They had all slipped like sand through the hourglass of her life, and now the mala must fall before she could proceed to the other shore.

'God knows where I go from here,' Anna murmured as

the 108 beads floated away to merge with the Ocean. But that night a dream, had she known how to interpret it, offered a clue.

It was one of those dreams that portend something important, but she didn't know what. She had stood alone in an empty ballroom while the music of life played heedlessly on. She wanted to leave, but the door by which she had entered was gone, and the exit a slit too narrow to pass through.

'Why?' she screamed up at the conductor on his rostrum. 'Why?'

With a perplexed frown he turned to look down at her. Evidently the lady was still most ignorant. But he condescended a reply. 'Karma, dear Anthia, Karma!'

'Anthia! Who is she?'

'Let the orchestra tell you that,' he said. And with a brisk stroke of his baton, he halted the waltz they'd been playing, and summoned the thrill of a hundred bouzoukis. A crystalline voice entered the shimmering sound. It rose in a crescendo of joy, and then sank in grandiose melancholy, tinging the music with nostalgia for glories and sorrows past.

Anna knew that melody. It echoed in her blood and in her bones. It's title, on the tip of her tongue, was the key to an undiscovered door, but she could not remember it. The bouzoukis trilled on. Caught in their rhythm, she started to dance, slowly at first, then turning, turning, turning in Othila's arms. But when the conductor faced her again, the orchestra stopped, Othila vanished. 'Do you remember now?' the mysterious conductor insisted.

'Yes, yes,' Anna replied, but then awoke the song remembered. '*Acro-po-lis, adieu.*'

Chapter Twenty-Two

'The mills of the Lord turn slowly, but they grind exceeding fine.' It was the slowness of these mills that gave Anna, grinding away her karma of 'service to fellow humans' in the medical unit, the impression that nothing of significance was happening. But this was not so.

Othila's departure was now two years behind her. It was time for a phoenix to rise from the ashes, and yet life was not blooming anew; the opposite was happening. The friends on whom Anna had always relied started moving off to the country. Marie-Claire, who had never deserted Anna – even when she became a sannyasin – now lived out at Pontoise, and promising new associations were not forthcoming.

Destiny has many a strategy for keeping a ship on course, aloneness being but one of them. Not only that, Anna's path was strewn with situations requiring patience, understanding and caring. These were the lessons pushed under her nose like the rice pudding of old when the unfortunate child was not allowed out to play until the plate was clean. With Othila's departure, Anna moved into another seven-year cycle and one where, like the Nannies of old, Destiny stood over her forbidding her out to love again, until her 'services' had been accomplished.

May had emerged from an icy winter, into the delight of a Parisian spring; it was time to think of a holiday. But with man and Master gone and friends draining away, Anna had no idea where to go, or who with. To stave off the gloom, she called the Club Mediterranean for inspiration, 'I don't care where, so long as it's sunny and soon,' she said

'No problem,' the Club Med's sales lady responded. 'We have a ten-day bargain holiday on the island of Corfu.'

'Sunny and soon?' Anna reiterated.

'*Oui, bien sure.*' the lady reassured. 'Starting next week.'

'Perfect!'

Having committed herself with a signature and a cheque, Anna could not retract. She expected a battle royal with Lisette over leave at short notice, but to her amazement, Lisette remained calm and cooperative.

Seven days later, Anna was basking on a Corfu beach.

'How about an excursion to Athens and Delphi?' somebody was asking as Anna lazed in the sun. Looking up, her eyes met with those of a Club Med hostess smiling down at her.

'Athens and Delphi?'

'Yes. A two-day excursion starting in Athens with a visit to the Acropolis, city tour, folkloric evening and so on. One night in Athens, and then on to Delphi. Like to come?'

'How much?' Anna asked.

A big smile beset the hostess's jolly face. 'Play now – pay later!' she replied gaily, delightfully unaware of how commercial the truths of the Universe can be. 'Your cabin-mate, Gloria, has signed up. It should be good fun.'

Single accommodation in that Club Med village hadn't been available, so Anna shared a bungalow with an art student from Maryland, Gloria Grant. Gloria was a lively companion, and a worshipper of Greece.

'OK. I'll go,' Anna replied.

A yellowish morning mist hovered over the port of Corfu as the weighty *Aphrodite* backed majestically away from the quay and turned to embrace a sparkling Ionian Sea. The group of bronzed Club Med excursionists in short shorts and T-shirts hung over the rails watching the harbour fade into the distance across an undulating expanse of blue and green.

When *Aphrodite* docked again, it was at a mainland port about an hour's drive from the capital. Across from the ferry, an old tour coach waited, its driver standing at the door like Noah ready to count his animals into the Ark. He was an oldish man with a ragged gray beard, but his eyes, appraising slender brown legs as they mounted the steps, seemed young indeed. When satisfied that none of his livestock were missing, he hopped aboard himself, switched on 'Zorba's Dance', and let in the clutch.

At first they jogged merrily through sun-baked boulder-strewn countryside, where goats straggled among the rocks nibbling thorny bushes. Gnarled olive trees, their trunks blackened with age, stood sporadically along shimmering inclines like old men pausing for breath, and lime-washed hamlets clustering around domed oratories, pierced the sky like white-crested waves.

With the approach of the capital, however, bucolic purity yielded to ungainly suburbs where it was difficult to tell whether the unplastered walls either side of the road were in the process of going up, or crumbling down. Soon the pug-nosed tour coach pushed into denser traffic and honked its way to the foot of the world's most resplendent landmark, the Acropolis of Athens. Here, Noah's sister took the relay with her clipboard, registering the names of each tourist as they stepped down onto hallowed ground.

Anna raised her face to the rock and beheld the stately Parthenon columns gazing agelessly across the city to the sea beyond. An earthquake-like tremor rushed up her spine – she felt slightly sick.

'Cold?' Gloria remarked. 'You're as white as a sheet.'

'It's only coach travel. I'll be fine when we get to the top.'

The group set off across the coach park to climb the steep ramp-like incline towards the pillared gatehouse of the citadel. The pages of Sylvia's guidebook fluttered in her hand. 'This must be the Sacred Way,' she said, sending a series of aftershocks through Anna's body.

Having passed the gatehouse, Anna turned to Gloria. 'You go ahead with the tour. I'll catch you up when I feel better.' Regretfully, Gloria agreed and caught up with the group, while Anna sat on the ground in the shade of a pillar, laid her head on her knees and shut her eyes.

Soon the nausea was gone, but Anna had no inclination to rejoin the tour or even open her eyes; she felt perfectly at home where she was. Without realizing it, she had slipped into the state between sleeping and waking, and believed she actually belonged to the place where she now sat.

Then came the sound of heavy wheels grinding and crackling on a rough stony road. The resonance went with a vision, dim at first, but then she began to see a horse-drawn wagon labouring uphill with a couple of happy newlyweds sitting behind the reins. 'How long do we have to put up with Roman occupation?' she heard the girl saying as she looked admiringly into her husband's eyes.

Detached yet lucid, Anna proceeded to watch all that had befallen Anthia when Athens was a province of the Great Roman Empire. It started with a mother-to-be and an old priestess. The vision then moved on to Astraeus, Phyleus and Jocastra in the Place of the Potions where she encountered the handsome Centurion. On seeing Othila in Roman uniform, a wave of attraction rose, but sank into fear when Anthia was carried into his villa. Terror seized her again as she faced the human corridor leading to the cliff's edge. Head held high, eyes focused on the sky, she could feel the contact of bare feet on the cold marble steps that descended onto paving of a different texture; every step precious. Then came the blow toppling her forward, and suddenly sky spun dizzily into sea, and the sea into rooftops; a flash from the sinking sun, then blackness, blackness, blackness. Anthia had left her body, but suddenly she could see again. The Centurion was there – riding a plough horse and wearing a hood. He looked different now – gray and fearful – but quite unmoved by the sight of Anthia's corpse lying among the boulders. Just one cursory glance and he turned away – but not for sorrow. Then Anthia, or was it she, calling angrily after him. Somebody was touching her shoulder. It wasn't him. Where was she?

'Never forgive who?' an American voice twanged in Anna's ear; her head still rested on her knees. Sitting up she saw Gloria back from the tour, and remembered where she was. 'I must have been dreaming,' she said.

'Nightmaring from the sound of it.'

'Was the tour good?'

'Far out! Anna, did you know that right there,' Gloria pointed to the eastern rampart, 'was the place they used to punish unfaithful virgins by . . . man, you do look peaky! Lunch will put you right though. Come on, our group is eating in the old part of town.'

'Thanks, but I think I'll skip lunch today.'

'That bad, eh? Does coach travel always affect you like that?'

Anna repressed a smile. 'No, this was rather exceptional. I'll be fine tomorrow.'

'I sure do hope so,' Gloria replied. 'It would be awful if you missed Delphi too.'

Chapter Twenty-Three

Anna returned from her Club Med holiday in a daze – which the sight of Maude and Lisette immediately shook out of her. They had suspended their usual afternoon routine and stood side by side like two birds on a branch, ready to relay the fateful news the moment she stepped into the infirmary for afternoon duty.

'We're losing Dr Roch!' Maude said, as though her beloved *Patron* were on the point of death. 'He's retiring, and we're getting another Colonel – Dr Chambaz.'

'OK by me,' Anna replied.

'Yes,' Maude put in, dropping her voice and her tight-lipped loyalty for once. 'But the Devil you know . . .'

'Sure to be changes,' Lisette piped up edgily.

'Modernization?'

'Of course not! But we'll all be moved,' Lisette announced, making it sound as though she were privileged with forehand knowledge. She was trying to inspire dread, but Anna didn't react. If Lisette happened to be right, however, it would be the end of civilization as Anna knew it; only later did it occur that Colonel Roch would certainly have warned Colonel Chambaz about the English nurse's unnecessarily innovative ideas, and advised him to let sleeping troublemakers lie.

Dr Roch's farewell cocktail party was a sober affair held in his cheerless consulting room enhanced with flowers out of

Maude's own pocket, and bunting out of Lisette's. Champagne and canapés, financed by the directorial entertainment allowance, were passed around and when everyone was on the way to relaxing, Dr Roch tapped a gold fountain pen against his glass and launched into a short farewell speech. Beside him stood his successor, a small, round, military man with a no-nonsense mouth, inscrutable eyes behind gold-rimmed spectacles, and a balding crown. While the devil they knew was talking, all eyes surreptitiously studied the one they didn't. What would he be like? Dr Chambaz's return oration afforded the answer when he said, that to improve on his predecessor's organization would be '*absolument impossible*!' He therefore had strictly no intention of changing the smallest detail! 'Be assured,' he reiterated. 'Everything will go on exactly as before.' Maude and Lisette exchanged glances as a wave of relief rolled over them. Ironically, Anna too, was satisfied.

Work routine, and the treadmill of everyday life, provided an uncomplicated background for the assimilation of all that Anna had learned about her past life. She now understood her unshakable belief in a man she was destined to meet. Her blinding passion for someone so totally different and devastatingly inappropriate. One by one, the similarities between lives past and present rose to consciousness like fish rising for air. She and Othila had come from radically different backgrounds in both lives. There had been a repeated lust for power on his part, and a renewed thirst for truth on hers. Union twice forbidden, twice indulged, and anger without forgiveness the residue of both, and that was the problem!

Slowly Anna accepted the inexorable workings of karma. Her karma – how Othila's would affect him, was his business. But now at least she knew that it was her unreleased resentment towards the man she had been destined to meet that was keeping her life on hold. Forgiveness for herself would be needed too, and she shrank from hauling up the past.

The years were rushing by and she didn't want to remain alone for the rest of her days – and nights.

Forgiveness was not a subject Anna had studied before; it tended to be a word people used and left at that. Life had somehow pulled her over its ruckles without her ever having to deeply forgive herself or anybody else, and now this very act had become a passport to the fulfilment of her deepest desires.

First she cast her mind over Nakshatra's teaching and couldn't pinpoint anything specific pertaining to forgiveness. He had concentrated on going beyond that very need by bringing his disciples to understand ego, its ways and its illusion. He taught detachment and acceptance, so that hurt or insult would not become the drama and the karma it had produced in Anna's life.

'Let not the sun go down on your wrath', the wise book said, but what is to prevent it rising again at dawn? 'Vengeance is mine sayeth the Lord.' 'Yes, karma,' Anna thought, with a hollow laugh. 'What sweeter vengeance than that?' greater sympathy went to, 'To understand is to forgive', but the better Anna understood Othila's motives, the more difficult it was to excuse them. And as for, 'Love the offender but not the offence', the two were so inextricably entwined, there was no way she could disentwine them now.

Anna's social vacuum persisted. Months of loneliness meandered by. The job to be faced simmered on the back burner of her mind and was about to boil dry, when an article in a woman's magazine at the hairdresser attracted her attention. 'Forgiveness is a process,' it stated. 'A process of releasing without rancour the suffering caused by a person, situation or event.' Ah! A process? That sounded more manageable than a command. 'First, look the causative trauma straight in the eye and make sure you are not enjoying it in some way.' Enjoying it? Anna shut her eyes and, with the hairdryer roaring around her ears, hauled Othila before her vision and there it was. Anger, love, attraction, repulsion and a certain semi-enjoyable self-righteousness, all fighting each other with equal tenacity, while a worm of self-pity gorged on thought and memory. It was unbearable.

She opened her eyes and read on. 'Second. Don't do anything immediately; forgiveness can't be forced. Trauma only leaves peacefully when it has been accepted in all its ugliness. Third. When feelings get hungry for revenge, feed them on anything positive that comes to hand, be it only one sunny hour. You will thank yourself – later. Fourth. If you persist in inviting it, forgiveness, or letting go, sneaks in of its own accord.' All this reminded Anna of the sempiternal advice offered by Guruji and many Masters before him. 'Be a watcher on the hills', and allow whatever is, to be. Swallow it whole and judge not.

The article appealed to Anna. She followed its suggestions for a full year, and a new perspective slowly dawned. When a movie she was watching showed a heavy-footed storekeeper running breathlessly and after a nimble-footed lad who had filched only a candy bar, she saw the analogy. 'That's me!' The changes were subtle, however, and seemed to be happening in spite of herself.

Destiny watched and waited while three more years went by. Through the highs and lows of everyday living, there were periods when Anna meditated with constancy, and others when drifting happened. The only light that never dimmed was the certainty of her voyage, however slow, towards a more refined understanding of herself and those about her. As for enlightenment, she knew that to be a stupendous, but unpredictable, gift that might come if she dropped all desiring. To keep the flame alight, however, she attended many lectures and talks on that inextinguishable subject – but Anna wasn't looking for another Guru.

Sifting the chaff from the grain of oneself becomes terribly tedious, but whenever Anna rested on the oars, she felt that her willingness to see the voyage through, became the current taking her there anyway.

Seven years had passed since Othila had left; a cycle of absorption was nearing its end, and the frivolous adolescent whose heart was set on becoming wife and mother with the man she was destined to meet, was now 37. People still remarked on her attractiveness, and yet a thick pane of unbreakable glass seemed to stand between Anna and everything she wanted to attract.

No cycle, however long, lasts forever. Bittersweet Destiny who had guided Anna along her stumbling path now glanced up at the cosmic clock, nodded to the Lords of Karma, and put its head around the infirmary door in the guise of a memorandum.

'*Please find enclosed the World Education Assembly Information Booklet and Delegate List. The First Aid Post, for which you are responsible, being the nearest medical facility to the conference arena, you will be expected to remain on duty until meetings are terminated and all delegates have left the building. Security will give you permission to leave. NB. page 3.*' The latter was ringed in red ink.

Mega-international conferences were a regular event at Anna's end of the building. The information booklet lay on her desk, and although it was home-going time on a Friday, and Anna had a train to catch, she could not resist a quick flip through it. Page 3 was headed 'Services', but revealed nothing of import; just the whereabouts and opening hours of the bank, cafeteria, post office, and of course the First Aid post, promoted to 'medical facility' for the occasion. She turned to page 4. A map of the Metro. Then flipped back to page 3. Again the word 'Services' shimmered beneath her eye. She stared dumbfounded at it as Astraeus's words came back to her. 'In some future time service will be expected of you again.'

'And to think I never realized it before!' Anna thought,

as all at once she saw why the prevailing conditions of her youth had forced her into the nursing profession. 'You will never forget the Mysteries, but find them in another place, at another time, and in another way'. Of course! Oh my God! Astraeus had looked into her future and seen 'sunstroke' Nakshatra and Othila, coming and . . . going.

When Anna came out of her stupour, she looked at the time and leapt to her feet. She was spending the weekend with Marie-Claire, Jacques and their three children at Pontoise, and had just missed her train! Having phoned Marie-Claire with abject apologies, she raced around the infirmary locking up, then sped downstairs and into a taxi that deposited her at the Gare du Nord just in time for the next one. Anna had not seen Marie-Claire for some time; this was a weekend she'd really been looking forward to. What was more, it would recharge her batteries before the conference hoards descended with their sore throats, sore heads, sore stomachs, sore feet, sore everything.

A relaxing weekend it really was – walking and swimming with the children, feeding the neighbours' pony, playing charades in the evening, and having a long, long chat about married life with Marie-Clare.

All too soon, however, Monday morning was there again. Anna unlocked her cupboards and took the 'delegate list' from the desk drawer. Of all the many conferences hosted by the WEO, the World Education Assembly was the largest and offered the greatest variety of colourful, interesting and often amusing patients. This gathering not only comprised the educators themselves, but a large supporting cast of surveyors, architects, statisticians, caterers, paediatricians etc., whose expertise formed the infrastructure that made education in the developing world possible. Browsing through the names on the list Anna looked for those she might recognize from the World Education Assembly five years previously.

The Assembly was, of course, headed by a President who had to keep an orchestra of 3,000 delegates in harmony till the two-week fantasia drew to a weary close, usually in the early hours of a Sunday morning. This assignment invariably went to an experienced international dignitary, always too busy and important to come to the infirmary, so Anna skipped page 1 and turned to see who else would be there.

Yes, the Congolese, Mr Boya, had come again. 'Would you have a little "dynamite" for constipation' he had asked last time. And so was Mrs Zia, a thin headmistress from Lahore who had requested that something be done to keep her eyes open in the day and shut at night. Ah, and that red-faced worrier from Scotland, Arthur McDonald, Department of Statistics, a fixture on this conference, tortured by heart-burn. Then Anthony Bonell, with the Department of Architecture, why did his name sound familiar? Anna was trying to put a face to this delegate, when the waiting-room buzzer interrupted her.

'Hello, Nurse! Remember me?' was the cheerful greeting of a secretary Anna hadn't seen in years. It was Sally. But now her luscious auburn hair was rolled into a chignon on the top of her head, and she appeared to be in the latter stages of pregnancy.

'Of course I do. Things seemed to have developed since your last visit though.'

Sally smoothed the flowery summer dress over her undisguisable bump. 'Oh yes. I got married five years ago and stopped working when I was expecting our first.'

'So this is to be the second, then?'

'Right.'

'Coming soon, by the look of things,' said Anna, offering a hand to help the gravid lady to her feet.

'Yep. Three weeks,' she replied, waddling into the infirmary.

'Three weeks! Should you be working?'

'Nope. But they asked me to help out for the conference, you see.'

Anna looked disapproving.

'I know I shouldn't,' Sally grinned unashamedly. 'But I just couldn't resist the chance to work for the President again.'

'And what's so wonderful about that?' Anna asked, more focused on the girl's condition than the implication of what she had just said.

'Well, I've worked for him before, and know his little ways, you see?' She still hadn't dropped her habit of adding 'you see' to every statement – but with unrevealed emotion, Anna saw!

'Who's that?' Anna inquired innocently, wondering how she would react to the sound of his name.

'Oh, didn't you know? Konsu Mapeta is President this year.'

'Of course! How could I forget?' Anna replied, a frenzy of bubbles fizzing up her spine. 'Well, I hope he won't overwork you, Sally. If you crumple, medication is not advised.'

'Yes, I know. But my doctor wants regular blood pressure checks if you wouldn't mind, Nurse.'

'No problem. Come whenever you can.'

'I'll never forget how kind you were the first time I came to see you. Gosh, that must have been all of seven years ago, just before K left. How time flies!'

A reserved little laugh escaped from the back of Anna's throat as she secured the blood-pressure cuff around Sally's fleshy arm.

'Is the pressure all right?' Sally asked anxiously; Anna's face looked strangely different.

'Just fine,' Anna replied calmly. 'Absolutely normal.'

'Oh good. Then I'll be back tomorrow, if that's all right?'

Anna agreed, and when Sally left, sat staring blankly at the wall not at all sure how she felt about what she had heard. A strange hollow occupied the space where her feelings for Othila used to be, and yet she was not indifferent to the news. Could the dried-out seeds of affection spring to life again and grow to no avail? Seeing him would tell her that. Yes, she would have to see him – if only for a second.

As the conference got under way, delegates came thick and fast. Among them one whose badge read, 'Pet Sorensen. Norway. Dept. Architecture', reminding Anna of the other name she couldn't place. After Sorensen had taken something for his allergy, Anna asked about A. Bonell, working in his department.

Yes, Sorensen had often participated in Third World projects with Tony, but Tony had never made it to the Assembly before. Perplexed, Anna shook her head. 'What does he look like?'

'Tall, mid-forties, brownish hair, brownish eyes, glasses, quiet, dry humour – British!' Again Anna shook her head; the description matched nobody she could think of. 'Look,' Sorensen said, 'why don't you come up to our office and introduce yourself?'

'Have to stay here in case there's an emergency,' Anna replied. 'Anyway, I'd feel a perfect fool if he turned out to be a total stranger. Don't say anything to him – please.'

'My lips are sealed,' assured the Norwegian mischievously as he made for the door.

'Just a moment,' Anna pursued, 'Perhaps it's his wife I'm thinking of. Do you happen to know her first name by any chance?'

Sorensen turned and thought. 'A very pretty woman, as I remember. Olivia? Or Odile was it? No – sorry! I only met her once, and Tony's been divorced for quite some time now.'

The first week of the conference raced by. Anna struggled to keep Othila out of her mind, though couldn't prevent herself from wishing that he'd come to the medical facility and transform her memory of him.

The second week of the conference raced by also, leaving Anna's wish to see *Monsieur le Président* unsatisfied. But the 'jamboree', as Greening had called it, was not yet over. An official notice stated that the conference was to continue on into Saturday, and unlikely to end before midnight.

On Saturday Anna woke earlier than usual, as she had her weekly shopping to do, and had to be on duty by ten. Her head buzzed with a garbled dream of the Acropolis and a nebulous notion of Astraeus having spoken, though she couldn't recall his words. She knew, too, that if she wanted to see Othila she'd have to find him herself.

It was a beautiful August morning. Paris chirped like a happy bird under a clear blue sky. With her usual shops all closed for the holidays, Anna made her way to the market stalls stretching along the boulevard. Everything imaginable could be bought there. Dawdling through French markets was a ritual Anna adored, but today, a quick rush through with a short shopping list was all she had time for.

Butter, cheese, bread, yogurt, potatoes, fruit and a couple of vegetables would see her through the week, but as she turned towards home, a little black shift in good-quality cotton gyrating on a hanger next to the fruit stall, caught her eye. It had the horizontal neckline that suited her so well, and the 'sack line' was 'in'. Factory rejects from market stalls were risky buys, but at 25 francs there wasn't much to lose. When she got home, Anna tried the dress on, and left it on. Black was not a colour she usually wore, but this dress had something irresistible; it enhanced the texture of her smooth translucent skin.

Nobody has time for the medical facility on the closing day of a big conference, and as for the President, he'd be closeted in private committee rooms all day, only to emerge to deliver the closing address at the plenary session. It was during the plenary that Anna planned her momentary glimpse; the idea caused an unbearable mixture of thrill and dread, but she would see him if it was the last thing she did.

Time dragged. Tension mounted. First a letter home was cast aside in favour of a detective story, but before long she turned to a pile of glossy magazines. Tim, the talkative security guard, looked in from time to time to report on how the conference was progressing. At eleven, he poked his head around the door again with the information she'd been waiting for. 'Due to end at midnight, darlin',' he said.

'Midnight! Are you sure?'

'Sure as eggs is eggs.'

'Then do me a favour, Tim,' Anna said. 'Give me a buzz when the plenary begins, would you mind?'

'*Pas de problème, Madame.*'

'Promise?'

'Irishman's word.'

At ten to twelve, Anna glanced up at the infirmary clock. Tim still hadn't phoned. Thinking he'd forgotten, she shed her white coat and was about to go down to the conference arena, when he burst merrily in, waving a bottle. 'The closing address is well under way and the conference will end on schedule,' he said. 'So we just have time for a tiny tot before it finishes.'

'Not this evening, thanks,' Anna replied.

'Relax! It's been a long day's night. A drop of this is exactly what you need!'

'No – really,' Anna repeated, thinking frantically of a way to get Tim out. As the cork popped, the long hand on the wall-clock moved to eleven fifty-three. Tim helped himself to two medicine glasses and filled them. 'Here's to us,' he said jauntily, as he perched on the edge of the desk and lit a cigarette. 'Relax, Nurse. Unbend! Nobody'll come at this hour.'

'Excuse me a moment,' Anna said, making for the door. 'I'll be right back.'

In the corridor all was deadly hush; 3,000 delegates sat in the great arena below, listening to Othila's closing speech. It was now or never. Anna closed the infirmary door and was about to make for the descending escalator, when the chief of security walked by asking if she had seen Tim O'Donnel. Anna shook her head, but backed into the infirmary again.

'Quick, Tim! Your boss has just gone down the hall and he's asking for *you*.'

Had a black adder slithered under the door, Tim could not have moved faster. In seconds, his jacket was on, his glass emptied, his cigarette extinguished, and he was gone. It was five to twelve now. Anna waited a moment so as not bump into Tim again, and then rushed towards the escalator. She hurtled down the thick steps, eyes fixed on the arena's wide exit doors giving onto the hall below, but just as reached the last step, they opened and a mass of people gushed into the hall like water from a dam. The conference had adjourned.

Desperate, Anna pushed furiously against the exiting tide. It was slow going, but she elbowed and edged until the podium came in sight, but not a single soul lingered upon it. She wanted to scream, but faces she knew kept popping up in the crowd so she slipped out through the fire exit, back into the entrance hall.

It was over. Finished! All Anna wanted now was get back to her infirmary and release the sobs aching in her throat. At the foot of the escalator three men stood in deep in conversation. A tall bald African in the middle, two shorter men on either side intent on a few last questions before *Monsieur le Président* left for Africa. Heart pounding, Anna walked towards them. The three stepped back that she might move onto the escalator, and as they did so, Anna looked up into the face of the man in the middle. No embers flared, nor love nor hate arose. Without pausing in his conversation, Othila looked back, with vacant eyes. 'Still scared of scandal?' Anna wondered coolly as the escalator moved upwards. For some reason she wanted to laugh. 'Was that all?' she asked herself, 'Was that, really, all?'

At the top she turned and looked down. Across the hall a crowd of departing delegates ballooned behind the three arched doors giving onto the street, but the men at the bottom of the escalator were gone. It was over now. Nothing to forgive. No wound to lick, but somewhere within her, the chorus of dawn had begun.

With delegates still in the building, Anna returned to her infirmary and donned her uniform, its whiteness contrasting starkly against the black 25 franc dress. 'You will again wear white,' Astraeus had said, and an eerie tingling began to creep from the soles of her feet to the roots of her hair. It was the ringing telephone that brought her back to earth.

'Chief's given you the OK to leave,' Tim said. But as he spoke, the waiting-room door clicked and the buzzer sounded.

'Thanks. But I have a last-minute patient by the sound of things.'

'Tell 'em to push off and have yourself a nice weekend, darlin',' Tim chortled.

'Same to you,' Anna replied, and calmly replacing the receiver turned to open the waiting-room door.

Standing squarely before her was a tall man in his mid-forties whose brown curly hair was lightly streaked with gray, and whose eyes behind the glasses bore a familiar glint.

'Sabda!' he exclaimed, as if he had just found something precious. 'Do you remember me?'

A smile spread slowly across Anna's face as she recalled a peaceful river, a boy fishing, a man tilling the soil, and a youthful sannyasin saying that two minuses could not make a plus. The delegate's badge read 'A. Bonell. Dept Architecture'.

But Anna replied, 'Yes, Tarika, of course I remember you.'